Salt Magic, Skin Magic

by

Lee Welch

www.leewelchwriter.com

First published in ebook format by Lee Welch 2018

Copyright © Lee Welch, 2018

ISBN: 978-0-473-44452-5

Chapter One

October, 1851

Soren, Lord Thornby, opened the rectory field gate and checked the back of his left hand for the hundredth time. He'd written the word 'leave' on his skin in black ink. His hands had trembled as he'd done it, and the 'l' had smeared against his cuff. But he could read it plainly enough.

Leave.

The gate was on the Raskelf estate, which belonged to Thornby's father, the ninth Marquess of Dalton. The hummocky field belonged to the rectory, which was a mile away in the village. A few bedraggled, black-faced sheep grazed at the far end, and Thornby knew he should shut the gate, but somehow did not quite like to. Keeping his left hand in front of him as though offering an arm to an invisible lady, he took a deep breath and stepped across the estate boundary.

As he did so, he realised he'd be late for dinner if he didn't go back to the Hall *now*. It would be unforgivably rude.

But his gaze was on his hand. *Leave.*

He stood, one pace away from the gate, breathing hard. It was mid-afternoon. The weak autumn sun was still some distance from the horizon. Dinner was always at seven. He fumbled for his watch, hand shaking so much the glass front gave fractured reflections of sky, hedgerow, and his own pale face. It was not yet three. But perhaps it would be best to go back now anyway.

As he put the watch away, he saw the writing on his hand again. *Leave.*

Yes, he must *leave*. Heart pounding, he took another step. But he was trespassing. He glanced around, shoulders hunching with guilt, a cold sweat prickling out on his back. This land belonged to the rectory. He shouldn't be here.

He tried to breathe deeply. He was leaving Raskelf. Why shouldn't he walk across a field? The rector wouldn't mind. Although Father was damnably rude to the fellow, the rector had no quarrel with Thornby.

He took a third step.

And stopped. Idiot! He'd left the lid off the inkwell. These days the staff at Raskelf was composed of the incompetent or the unreliable—those who couldn't secure a position elsewhere. Thornby could almost see the inkwell tipping under a careless duster, a black puddle engulfing the work of months. He must go back at once and put the lid on.

His arm was at an odd angle in front of him, as if he expected a bird of prey to swoop down to his wrist. Foolish; there'd been no falcons at Raskelf for years. Something black was on the back of his hand. He rubbed at it, but it wouldn't come off. It was writing, very smudged. A word written in ink.

Ink! Yes, he must hurry home and deal with the inkwell. The gate was only a couple of strides away. He shut it so the rector's sheep couldn't wander and hastened back to the Hall, the chimneys of which could just be seen, rising above the yellows and coppers of Ramparts Wood.

Raskelf Hall, the ancestral seat of the Dezombreys, was a huge mish-mash of styles and additions, punctuated by mullioned windows and so many chimneys and baroque flourishes that Thornby always felt it resembled a vast and sickly hedgehog. He approached the northern entrance, at the back of the house. A month ago, the doorway here had been graced by a fine white marble portico, but it had been sold to pay some unavoidable debt of Father's. The doorway now looked naked and a little surprised, like a man caught with his trousers down.

As Thornby grabbed the cheap new iron handrail to spring up the cheap new sandstone steps, he noticed the blurred scrawl on the back of his hand.

Leave.

Daylight seemed to fall away and the air to grow thin, as if the shadow of the Hall was set on stifling him. Nausea swept over him and his legs turned to water. He dropped to a crouch on the steps, tugging at his tight cravat.

Back at the Hall. For the thousandth time. Back to put a lid on an inkwell. The very banality of the reasoning turned his blood to ice.

Because he'd been trying to leave the estate for a year and a half. He'd tried everything. He'd tried walking across the boundary in an ordinary way. He'd tried riding across, but no matter which horse he took, the creature always refused. He'd tried crawling across in the mud, as if by abasing himself he might be let go. He'd tried flinging himself across, screaming. Sometimes he told himself he felt no more than one of the statues in the park—his heart was marble, his mind marble—he would walk and not stop. But nothing worked. Nothing. Every time he found himself turning and walking back, for some trivial

4

reason like a lidless inkwell. He was trapped as effectively as if an invisible wall surrounded the estate.

His throat was closing so tight it might choke him. A harsh sob of rage and frustration escaped, and he gritted his teeth against another. A tear fell hot on the back of his hand. He would claw his own skin off to get away. Not just from Raskelf, but from himself, from the stupid, weak self that couldn't walk across a field.

Father claimed to have the power to let him go—if he married money as Father wished. But Thornby loathed his father and trusted him less than a footpad in a dark alley. And if he swallowed his pride and did as he was told, could Father really free him? Or would Thornby merely have involved some innocent girl in his ghastly predicament?

Father hinted often enough that it was weakness of character that kept Thornby here. Father had forbidden him to leave, and deep down, so deep Thornby couldn't acknowledge it, he must want to obey and so he did. But *surely* it couldn't be that? Thornby had no trouble disobeying his father in every other aspect of his life. In fact, it gave him a grim satisfaction. He was twenty-seven; not a child to take his father's word as law.

So, why? *Why* could he not walk across a field and escape? If it wasn't weakness of character, could it be to do with magnetism? Mesmerism? He'd heard of Elliotson's remarkable experiments, making ladies tell the future or dance and sing. He couldn't remember being mesmerised, but perhaps that was part of the trick?

He knew what some of the servants and the village people thought. He'd seen the sideways looks, the fingers crossed in a sign to ward off black magic. And of course he'd heard rumours, over the years, about devil worship and magicians who summoned spirits. But surely all that was flummery, tricks to fool the credulous. Some people might believe in it, even practice it, but magic was not a real enough force to hold an educated man against his will. And in any case, Father was no magician—was he?

Yet, sometimes, in the dark hours of the night, when sleep would not come and reason grew fevered, there seemed no other explanation.

***

A year and a half ago, Thornby had been sipping Madeira in the sitting room of his Mayfair house. Between sips, he'd been reading aloud an art review in *The Times* for the edification of a recent acquaintance—an amusing fellow with a fine arse and a hungry mouth, but who was developing a distressing tendency to gaze at Thornby like a moon-calf.

Then, incredibly, Thornby's father was announced.

The ninth Marquess of Dalton shouldered into the room at the same time as the quavering announcement, for all the world like a locomotive engine, right down to the steam coming from his ears. A pair of footmen in the blue-and-gold livery of Raskelf flanked him; strapping fellows both, with thick necks, and thighs that rubbed together when they walked. Not that Thornby was looking at their thighs. He jumped up.

"My lord. Father. This *is* a surprise. How do you do? May I—"

Lord Dalton faced the windows and addressed the golden London twilight. "Well, you damned whelp. What are you trying to do? Ruin the family name?"

"You've seen *The Times*? The review of my picture?" Thornby had done a number of things that might ruin a family name, but the painting and subsequent review were the most recent. He realised he was still clutching the paper in question, and tossed it onto the chaise longue.

"'Lewd and indecent debauchery', it says. What were you thinking, boy?"

The moon-calf, who'd been watching with open mouth, now had the decency to stand and clear his throat. "Perhaps I should, er, I beg your pardon, Lord Dalton. Good day, Thornby." And he slid out between the footmen like a well-tailored eel escaping a trap.

Thornby watched the back of his father's head uncertainly. Father had barely spoken to him for almost twenty years. Was he really here after all this time to give Thornby a dressing down about a painting? The last time Thornby had seen his father had been a year ago at the man's wedding to the second Lady Dalton at a fashionable London church. Thornby had arrived at the service with a green parrot in a cage and a startling magenta waistcoat, and received nothing but a haughty glance.

"*Well?* What were you thinking?" repeated Father, still directing his words towards the windows.

"Mostly of composition, sir. In truth, I didn't intend—"

"You're not a *painter*." Father spat the word out, as a man might say "You're not a *cockroach*." "You're a gentleman, or you damn well should be!"

Thornby thought of a number of things he might say about the nobility of the muse, but it seemed wiser not to. Father's fists were clenched and brandy fumes were issuing from him in such measure one could almost see a haze above his tall hat, which he had not removed.

"I confess, sir, I only submitted the picture because I lost a wager," Thornby said.

"And that makes it better, does it? Damned impudence."

"As a gentleman, I could hardly back out."

Father wheeled, with the air of a man making up his mind to something unpleasant, and looked at his son properly for the first time. Thornby, who had been reaching towards his glass, froze. The sounds of a spring evening in London seemed suddenly louder; the rumble and clatter of a passing carriage, footsteps, and the muted roar of busier streets further afield.

Father's weather-beaten features were puce with annoyance. Probably he'd been handsome once, with straightforward, manly features, now blurred by time and extremities of emotion. He was thick-set and tall, and Thornby stood straighter in order to look him in the eye. Thornby was damned if he was going to be intimidated in his own home. Next to his father, he was skinny as a rail, and his fashionable narrow necktie and red silk smoking jacket suddenly felt as louche as a whore's paints.

Thornby was used to being stared at. Mostly, he enjoyed it. But he did not like the way Father was looking at him now. Then, even as they glared at each other, Father's expression grew unfocused, and became almost one of longing—an emotion Thornby was far more accustomed to seeing on the faces around him. Father murmured something under his breath. Could it be some sorrow, some shade of tenderness had entered his voice?

"Sir, I—" A note of genuine regret entered Thornby's tone, but his father cut him off, expression changing to a rather stagy rage that put Thornby in mind of a villain in a bad play.

"You're coming to Raskelf to cool your heels. Then you'll marry some respectable girl before it's too late."

"I shan't. I suppose I'm a bit sorry about the painting since it seems to upset you. I only did it for a lark, but I—"

"A lark? A lewd painting?" Father's voice rose. It could surely be heard throughout the house, and probably in the square too. Yet Thornby thought he detected a false note, an edge of boredom, as if Father grew tired of his role of outraged paterfamilias. "You're coming to Raskelf, and you'll stay until I give you leave."

"No, really. Awfully kind of you, but I don't think I shall." Thornby exaggerated his father's bored tone and picked up his glass.

Father hit him; a hard, calculated slap that snapped Thornby's teeth together. The glass fell to the hearth and smashed. Thornby put a hand to his mouth and it came away red. He glared at his father. No one struck Thornby and remained unscathed. At school they had learned not to, eventually, for he always hit back, even if it meant a thrashing. But even as he curled his hands into fists, something stopped him. One did not hit one's father, however much one wanted to. One could not.

"It's not a choice, boy. You're coming. Then you'll stay. Once you're married, we'll see."

Father gestured to the footmen and one of them twisted Thornby's arm behind his back and wrestled him down the stairs while Father shouted orders about trunks and carriages. Thornby had a confused impression of the horrified faces of the housekeeper and maid, peering up from the lower staircase, then the enormous Raskelf footman manhandled him out into the street without hat or coat.

Thornby's trunk arrived at the carriage just behind them. Father's louts had not given Thornby's valet much time for packing. Passers-by were staring, but the crest on the carriage door, and the glares of the liveried footmen, caused them to hurry past. Thornby was hustled inside. Father sat opposite and the carriage jolted into motion.

"I say, my hat—" Thornby began, but Father's face stopped him. His lordship looked as if he'd won the Derby, but then been handed his winnings wrapped up in the filthy handkerchief of a consumptive beggar. It was such a strange look, and so intense, that Thornby felt he would do anything to stop it.

"This carriage has seen better days," he said, fingering one of the torn and weather-stained curtains, thinking to goad his lordship into a rant about finances. It was common knowledge that Father was facing ruin. If he wasn't disowned first, Thornby could hope to inherit mainly debts.

"Now, boy." Father's voice was trembling with emotion. "Listen carefully, because I'm telling you that as of now, you and yours are *mine*."

If Father's rage had seemed stagy earlier, this seemed positively operatic. Perhaps Father had gone a little mad. Thornby hardly knew the man, after all. Thornby had left Raskelf, aged eight, for school, and seldom gone back there after his mother's death a few weeks later. But even as a child he'd heard rumours of his father's eccentricity; his wild, incontinent grief at the death of his wife, his obsession for buying useless coastal bits of Scotland and Ireland, and his hare-brained schemes to grow seaweed as a commercial crop for fertilisers. But perhaps Father's financial strife had pushed him over into something worse.

"You hear me?" Father went on. "Your possessions, your household, those ridiculous cufflinks, the shirt on your back. Everything. Mine."

Thornby, who had curled protective fingers around one of his coral and gold cufflinks, now found himself unable to hold anything at all. It was as though Father's words had paralysed him. He fought to stay upright on the swaying seat. A deep, claustrophobic chill settled over him. The very air seemed to have grown thick, and a hideous sense of invasion crept over his limbs as though something was claiming them as its own.

And then, as quickly as it had come, the fit passed. Father turned to watch the London streets go by, and Thornby laid his head against the side of the carriage, glad of a few moments to recover. The oddness of the situation—riding hatless through London with his father—was staggering. The coach turned onto Regent Street; it looked as if they were heading straight for the station.

How long would Father make him stay at Raskelf? A fortnight? A month? Raskelf Hall was in the middle of nowhere, hard by the North York moors. Thornby liked the countryside well enough for a spot of shooting in the autumn or hunting in the winter, but it was spring and the London season had begun. He was supposed to be attending a dinner party that very evening, followed by rather more fun later on, carousing with some fellows from one of his clubs.

Father had mentioned marriage. Twice, in fact, and in most threatening tones. But Thornby was only twenty-five, and certainly not inclined to marriage yet. Or, probably, ever, but he would not be telling Father *that*.

Anyway, the marriage idea would soon blow over. More importantly, no arrangements had been made about Thornby's valet. Perhaps Thornby could send a message from the station. Or perhaps Father would lend Thornby his own man. Thornby hardly liked the idea. Father looked spruce enough, but there was something repellent about borrowing his valet, who doubtless carried tales.

Thornby's head swam, only partly from the after-effects of the blow. His tongue was swelling where he'd bitten it. And yet, despite the pain, the inconvenience and the worry, the novelty of the situation—Father paying attention to him—was at least interesting. Any normal father would have taken a horse-whip to Thornby years ago, and most of society would have thought it none too soon. Perhaps Father was finally taking some paternal responsibility. The idea was mainly alarming, but still.

Thornby remembered, at school, boys getting letters or half crowns from their fathers. Sometimes boys had told of beatings, or lectures, or new ponies as well. He'd wondered then what it might feel like to be a person of interest to his father. Lord Dalton had never written, never visited, never sent a package. In the holidays, apart from one seaside trip so disastrous Thornby tried never to think of it, he had generally been sent to the house at Beck Hill, fifty miles from Raskelf and barely in the same county.

He looked at Father's profile, now a fume-reeking shadow against the darkening streets. *Well*, he thought, *when it becomes dull at Raskelf I can always leave.*

***

He realised he was still grovelling on the new sandstone steps behind Raskelf and forced himself to his feet. The Hall towered before him, a grand and crumbling cage. To make matters worse, Father was somewhere inside. He'd arrived home yesterday for the winter, followed some hours later, and in a different carriage, by the silly second Lady Dalton. Thornby was damned if he'd give either one of them the satisfaction of seeing him with reddened eyes and trembling hands.

He looked terrible these days. The months of prowling and fretting had caused him to lose weight, and there were new lines to his face that spoke of strain and anguish. He found himself muttering aloud as he paced the endless passages of Raskelf, jumping at shadows and drinking too much. No wonder the servants were afraid of him. He turned his back on the house.

Before him lay the estate with its rolling parklands and woods, its fields and becks. The park was just as much of a prison, but at least it had open skies. He headed back across the long grass to the boggy path that encircled what was left of the estate. There had been no boundary path when he'd arrived at Raskelf a year and a half ago, but his own feet had worn one bare. He'd always believed the land was entailed, but legalities notwithstanding, Father had disposed of great swathes of it. And every time a piece of land was sold, Thornby's path must change. Always he was forced to skirt along the edge of whatever land still belonged to Father. It was the strangest thing to stand on the edge of the new boundary and look at the track his own feet had once made, and to know that he could no more walk there now than walk upon the moon.

Still, the estate remained large enough that if Thornby took the long way round he'd be late for dinner, which would reliably antagonise Father. Annoying Father was now all he lived for. Thornby had no doubt the dinner table tonight would be the usual battleground. Yesterday evening had been surprisingly mellow; the presence of the mysterious Mr Blake had put everyone on best behaviour.

Blake had arrived yesterday too, just before dinner. And Thornby, who seldom saw strangers these days, had wanted to stare like a rustic at this gentleman from London. Blake had sleek black hair, dark watchful eyes, and a mouth that turned down slightly at the corners. He was handsome enough, with an air of confidence, but his mouth gave him a grim look. Not a man to trifle with. He looked to be in his early thirties, and dressed conservatively in a plain, dark waistcoat and grey coat. He looked, in fact, the picture of the well-to-do industrialist he claimed to be. But he'd come without a valet, which was mighty odd for a man of that type, and he'd brought with him an enormous trunk so heavy it had taken six men to lift it.

Blake had said he was a friend of Lady Dalton's cousin, another wealthy industrialist. And Lady Dalton, who generally flinched if one so much as looked at her, had agreed. She'd looked damn glad to see Blake, actually. How lovely if she planned to cuckold Father with him, but she probably hadn't the imagination.

Most surprisingly, at dinner, to Father's aggressive enquiry about what the devil he thought he was doing at Raskelf, Blake had said, almost dismissively, 'You've known me for years, my lord. Remember, you invited me down any time.' And Father, to Thornby's lasting astonishment, had said 'ah, yes', and gone back to his consommé, just as if he were the kind of man who gave open invitations to the type of fellow he sometimes described as 'bloody jumped-up trade'.

Thornby was disposed to like Blake, who never fawned, and who carried himself well; upright, but not stiff, and with a determined city energy that Thornby had desperately missed. And Blake's eyes, so dark they were nearly Latin, were very fine. Yes, if Thornby let himself, he could enjoy looking at Mr Blake.

Blake didn't seem to like him, though.

Over the roast beef, Blake had given Thornby a peculiar, intense look and said, 'I think you remember me from Oxford, Lord Thornby.' Thornby had almost agreed, to be pleasant, because anyone who dared to speak to Father in such an offhand manner was obviously a man of character. But since Blake was so clearly *not* an Oxford man, though he spoke well enough, Thornby had said with genuine regret, 'I'm afraid not, Mr Blake'. To his surprise, Blake had gone as white as his nice lawn shirt-front, and then looked daggers at him for the rest of the meal.

A nagging pain from his bad foot brought Thornby back to the present. With Father back, the pressure to marry would redouble. And yet, how *could* he marry? Even if he was willing to swallow his pride, how could he involve some innocent girl in all this mess? What if he married and Father trapped the lady here too? It was an impossible situation. His throat was growing tight again, hopelessness threatening to drain away every ounce of vitality. There was only week after week, month after month, until—what? Until he died, or went mad? He sighed and his breath formed a cloud in front of him.

This was no good. He must not give up. Didn't Virgil say that adversity is only overcome by endurance? So, he must endure. Father would be alert for any sign of weakness. Thornby needed to drum up some anger, some energy, to get through dinner and prove he wasn't beaten yet.

He lifted his chin and walked faster along the boundary path, feet sending up splashes of mud. He began muttering curses and kicking stray sods. He worked up to shouting at sheep and gesticulating at the occasional farmhand. Both sheep and men stared at him with the same blank, open-mouthed incredulity. He knew it did nothing for his reputation in the village, but sometimes, when despair grew so tight it would crush his very soul, there was nothing for it but to shout unreasonable things and shake his fist at hedges.

"You know what I've missed, you pastoral savages? You damned Philistine sheep? I've missed the season. Again. Do you have any idea what that means? I've missed the Academy Exhibition. I've missed Millais' Ophelia. And what's more, what's worst, what's damned *insupportable*, is that I've missed the Great Bloody Exhibition! A Crystal Palace with trees inside and every damned wonder you could ever hope to see, and I've missed—"

Someone was watching him and it was not a grubby farmhand. He lowered his arms from a particularly expressive flourish. He was now at the farthest possible distance from the Hall, in an area that bordered on open moorland, recently sold to the Howarths. And there, just off the path by a clump of heather, was Mr Blake. Blake was lying on his coat, hands behind his head, as though Thornby had woken him from sleep. Quite how Thornby could have missed him at first, he didn't know.

Thornby could feel his cheeks burning. He didn't much care if a farmhand saw him acting like a lunatic; it would give him a story to tell later over a pot of ale. But Mr Blake was a guest. A rather handsome guest.

Well, Thornby could hardly slink away. He raised his chin and kept walking.

Blake fixed him with an intense stare, dark eyes boring into Thornby like augers. If Blake had been a real gentleman, he would have looked away and given Thornby a moment to recover his composure. But Blake barely blinked, lying there like an eastern potentate while Thornby approached. Would the man not get up or acknowledge him in any way? Thornby was suddenly very conscious that his clothes were forty years out of fashion and not especially clean. And that not long ago he had been so heart-sick he had nearly wept. Did that show on his face?

He decided to give like for like and walk past without speaking, but the ridiculousness of the situation hit him almost at once. They were now only a couple of yards apart. They were staying in the same house. In a few hours, they would be dining together. Was one really going to stride past as if the man were invisible?

He stopped. Blake was still lying there, still staring. Even lying down, he had the capable look of a man used to getting things done.

Thornby gave him a nod. "Good day, Mr Blake."

Blake got to his feet, face darkening. "So, you *can* see me. How clever." He gave a sarcastic bow. "How did you manage that? Reveal charm?" His grim mouth twisted scornfully. "Well, here we are. Let's stop playing games, shall we?"

It was Thornby's turn to stare. A charm? What games? Of course he could see Blake—he was there in plain view.

"I don't know what you mean."

"I know," Blake said. "You can tell me what you're doing to Lady Dalton. Then you can tell me why. And *then* I'll decide what to do with you."

There was such menace in his voice Thornby nearly took a step backwards. What was this about Lady Dalton? He generally had as little to do with her as possible. He had, perhaps, not been especially civil to the snivelling creature, but he hardly felt it necessary to be charming. And in any case, he hadn't seen her all summer. Because *she* had been in London for the season, while *he* had been here.

Despite his confusion, the injustice stung. *He* was the wronged one. *He* was the one bloody well being kept at Raskelf by mysterious means. Lady Dalton could do what she liked. She could leave, couldn't she?

There was, too, a very private reason which made the baseless accusation sting the more for coming from Mr Blake. Lying in bed last night, Thornby had allowed himself to entertain one or two fantasies in which Mr Blake overcame his initial unfriendliness and permitted certain delicious intimacies. Clearly, that wasn't going to happen. Blake thought him a cad who was bothering a lady. Thornby looked away from his dark-browed glare, feeling a fool for having allowed the fantasies in the first place.

13

It was then he noticed a narrow tape of supple leather that lay on the grass, encircling Mr Blake and his overcoat. It had faint blue writing on it, in some angular foreign script. Inside this peculiar item, a white handkerchief was spread on the rough grass. And on top of the handkerchief lay a small heap of orange sand with a blue glass eye balanced on top.

Thornby's skin began to crawl. Protestations of innocence died on his tongue. He must get away from this madman. Quickly. He backed a step and found his voice. "I'm afraid I have no idea what you mean, sir. Good day." He bowed and walked on, fast.

Chapter Two

"You little bastard," John Blake muttered.

He pocketed the glass eye and the sand, coiled the spancel, and began to follow Lord Thornby—heir to Raskelf, sometime painter of immodest pictures of ladies, and, it now seemed clear, witch—since only another magician could have seen through the invisibility conferred by the sand, eye and spancel charm.

John had had a trying couple of days. He wasn't used to life in a country house, especially one as grand and ancient as Raskelf. And he wasn't used to being on such close terms with the aristocracy. He'd agreed to come here as a favour to a friend and he was deeply regretting it.

George Catterall, Lady Dalton's cousin and only living relative, had taken John for a very good dinner at his club, and over the brandy begged him to rescue the lady from her step-son, the evil Lord Thornby.

"She's beside herself," Catterall had said, in a low voice. "She says whenever she stays at Raskelf her things go missing, or turn up in places she never left them. Or she finds odd things in her rooms, like acorns, or pebbles in her shoes. She's certain someone's using—you know—the stuff you do. I can't ask anyone else. I don't know anyone else who uses it except Rokeby, and I wouldn't trust him with tuppence. She says it all began when Lord Thornby came home. But he won't leave and, well, to make things worse—" Catterall's broad, fair face, already pink with fine wine and brandy, flushed red and his voice dropped to a whisper. "Deuce take it, John, she's got connubial troubles. Dalton doesn't treat her like a wife anymore, and she's convinced it's some sort of spell."

"I see." John glanced around the womb-like comfort of the club dining room. The gentlemen at the adjoining table seemed half-asleep in a haze of beef and burgundy. "There are other reasons for a man to cool off. Dalton's a fair bit older, isn't he? Maybe he just can't."

"He's in his fifties, but she says it was all right until Thornby came along. God's teeth, man, she's not making it up! She's not that type of girl. Thornby's terribly peculiar. She says he dresses in some fancy old-fashioned get-up like a Regency buck. And *looks* at her sometimes in *such* a way, she says, and refuses to go to church. And you remember that fuss over a lewd painting last year? That was him." Catterall took another sip of brandy. "I can vouch for him being odd; he took a parrot to her wedding. We could all hear it screeching in the vestry. And afterwards he gave it to her as a wedding present! Now that's peculiar, you have to admit."

John sipped his brandy and sorted through this catalogue of sins and oddities to decide if there was anything in it. Possibly the strange looks meant something. Acorns, stones in the shoes, things going missing—all these could be magic, or just ordinary mischief. The parrot? Animals could be familiars, but there his experience stopped. John's area of expertise was the inanimate: iron and glass, salt and sand. It was true he was hoping to escape the factories and foundries, but this seemed a step too far.

"Thornby may be a bounder, but that doesn't mean he's using magic. In any case, I'm an industrial man. Society isn't my thing. I wouldn't know what to do with a marquess's son turned witch. Come on, man, my father was an ironmonger. I'd be horribly out of place."

"My dear fellow, you're too modest. I know what you've been doing for Paxton at the Crystal Palace; hasn't been all anti-leak charms, has it? You fought off a thousand possessed bats, if what I hear is correct. Please, John, I'm begging you. I feel responsible. I should never have let her marry Dalton, everyone knows he's facing ruin. But she would be Lady Dalton and wouldn't hear reason. After this Crystal Palace business it'll be child's play for you, eh? A breath of country air. Paxton doesn't need you at the moment. Just see if someone's using magic on her; you can tell that much, can't you?"

So, John had come to Raskelf, and found the whole set-up much worse than he'd imagined. To start with, the whole rambling, crumbling pile that was Raskelf Hall was saturated with old magic. It reeked of the stuff. It clamoured with it. The blackened wood panelling, the tarnished silver, the murky paintings and the uneven parquet floor; all murmuring and chattering with memories of magic.

And the inhabitants were worse. Lord Dalton had the charnel stink of something old and rotten, possibly a curse. Dalton's spinster sister, Lady Amelia, was an invalid who seemed to live in an old orangery in a haze of wintergreen and sickly palm trees. There was also a Mr Derwent, an elderly second cousin, who'd been a collector of antiquities until the money went. John had stood, horrified, in front of the few artefacts that were left, listening to them seethe with malice and wounded pride. He'd even caught a whiff of something rough and recent from Lady Dalton, as though she'd taken to dabbling in magic in self defence.

And, worst, to his amazement and alarm, his charms had no effect on his prime suspect, Lord Thornby. To be so impervious, the younger man must be a magician of great skill. John had set the Judas Voice sigil with great care before dinner last night, but it had not worked on Thornby. Of course, all John had had to set the charm with was an old stocking filched from Thornby's room by Lady Dalton's maid—not a token of the highest order, but it should have worked at least partially. And now Thornby had seen past the sand, eye and spancel charm; John had never known that to fail before.

Now Thornby was walking along the moorland path, calm as you please, nose in the air, apparently admiring the autumn colours in the distant oaks in the park.

"Stop, Lord Thornby! I want to talk to you."

Thornby walked faster, slight limp becoming more pronounced.

"Stop, I say!"

John felt in his pockets for his vials and pouches, then changed his mind and simply put on speed. He'd come to this remote part of the grounds in the hope of a rest. He'd not slept much last night with the walls of Raskelf muttering and whispering, and the antiquities from Egypt shrieking muffled curses from the other side of the corridor.

The thought of Thornby had kept him awake as well; so resistant to the Judas Voice— that had given John an unpleasant moment—and so unapproachable, with that aristocratic hauteur you could never breach. And so strange. Why did the man wear such peculiar clothes? Today it was tight black pantaloons and a high stock that would have been fashionable forty years ago. And over this bizarre Regency costume was a rusty black greatcoat with wide cuffs, and a tricorn hat that would have looked well in the previous century.

And, yes, Thornby was handsome—heart-stoppingly so—with arrogant grey eyes, a mane of brown hair that almost reached his collar, and a preposterous red mouth. He was tall and thin and carried himself like a fencer. There was, too, something whip-taut about him, some unbearable tension that made you feel he might lash out. Or suddenly kiss you. Thornby had looked John up and down when he was introduced, finally unbending so far as to give John a slight inclination of the head. And John's mouth had gone as dry as if Thornby had extended one of those elegant white hands and given his balls a gentle squeeze.

It was tiresome, really. It made it so much harder to concentrate. He must make sure he didn't allow his attraction to the man to cloud his judgement. Possibly Thornby was using a glamour spell. John couldn't sense one, but sometimes by their very nature they were difficult to detect.

So, he mustn't think about how good it would be to slide his fingers inside Thornby's old black pantaloons, how good it would be to taste his lovely mouth, and wipe that damned snooty expression off his face. If John had been in London, he would have gone to one of the houses that catered to men of his taste, and tried to forget about it. Here in the middle of rural Yorkshire it was far too dangerous to approach anyone, and in any case, farm lads were not his type. He'd simply leave as soon as he could tell Catterall he'd done his best.

They walked in single file for perhaps five minutes. The path smelt of rotting leaves, and a biting wind began to make its presence felt as they crossed into an open piece of moorland. Splashes of muddy water were spotting the back of Thornby's coat. John used the close proximity to feel for magic. Like last night at dinner, he could sense nothing emanating from Thornby. There was certainly no demon reek, so Thornby probably wasn't a theurgist, or if he was, he was a very fastidious one.

But then Thornby didn't feel like a materials man either, and John could generally recognise his own kind. So, how *had* Thornby broken those charms? Now John was closer, and had longer to concentrate on Thornby alone, he thought there might be *something* magical, at the very edge of his awareness, but he couldn't put his finger on it. Most magicians used demons or materials, but there were other ways, so perhaps Thornby used some unfamiliar method.

John charged his ward stone, and put it back in his pocket. He patted his bag of salt and checked his Gelomorous twine and the demon trap, just in case. Whatever spells Thornby cared to throw at him, he was ready. In fact, he was almost looking forward to a fight. It would be a pleasure to best the little sod and make him apologise to Lady Dalton.

They reached an open place a hundred yards from a small pine spinney. The dark trees were contorted sideways as if fleeing the icy wind. The sun, behind its grey pall of cloud, was beginning to set. Thornby suddenly stopped and swung around.

"Well, Mr Blake? I suppose you'd like to explain yourself?" Thornby's chin was up, beautiful mouth curved in disdain.

"Look here, your *lordship*." John infused the word with contempt. "You may have broken a couple of simple charms, but you're no match for me. I studied at the Dee Institute. I'm sure you know what that means."

"The *Dee* Institute?" Thornby looked heavenward, as if for inspiration. "That's not in Oxbridge. Some working men's establishment, I suppose?"

Even while he was being insulted, John couldn't help admiring the lovely clean lines of Thornby's profile. How he'd like to wipe the jeer from those pretty lips. How he'd like to watch those proud eyes close in surrender. How he'd like— He hunched defensively. Thornby was too attractive to be true. "A glamour? It won't work."

"A *what*?"

"What do you have against Lady Dalton?"

"I beg your pardon?"

"You heard. Are you jealous?"

"Of *her*?"

Thornby looked so astonished John felt a moment of uncertainty, but it was better to plough on. The sooner it came out, the sooner he could leave.

"She thinks you're using magic to frighten her," John said. "And I think she's right. You saw through my sand-eye charm just now, didn't you? So, you've a bit of craft at least. But it's not on. Aren't you a gentleman? Well, I'm a friend of her cousin, and I'm here on his behalf"—he advanced a pace—"to make you stop."

"Magic? Sand-eye?" Thornby backed away, shaking his head. "You've lost me, Mr Blake. Magic isn't real, is it? It's tricks and superstition. Something for low types, perhaps, but hardly something *I* should dabble in. And why, pray, should I take any notice of Lady Dalton? She was a fool to marry my father, but I should hardly—" He frowned, stared at John. "Wait. You say magic's real? You say you know about it?"

"I told you, I went to the Dee Institute."

"And I told you I've never heard of the place. And I'm certainly not doing anything to Lady Dalton. But if you know about such things, perhaps you can tell me; why can't I leave the estate? Is that magic?"

"Perhaps you'd rather stay and plague your step-mother?"

"Haven't done your crib very well, have you Mr Blake? She hasn't been here for months. Of course, it's been the season, but she didn't stay long last winter either."

"No, because she's avoiding you."

Thornby rolled his eyes. "Have you asked the servants, Mr Blake? Have you talked with Stewart, the estate manager? If you can catch him sober enough he'll tell you; I *can't leave.* If I wanted to annoy Lady Dalton, wouldn't it be more practical to follow her to London or Hertfordshire or wherever it is she goes? But I've been here. All summer. Again. I've been stuck at Raskelf for a year and a half, and I damn well wish I wasn't."

There was something convincing about Thornby's attitude. If Thornby had been of any other class, John would have thought he was telling the truth, pure and simple. But

Thornby had such a high-handed manner. Then there was the matter of the broken sand-eye charm. And what was this story about not being able to leave? John had noticed no magical boundaries when *he'd* entered or left the estate. Was Thornby trying to gammon him?

A note of strain entered Thornby's voice. "My father says it's his doing. He's quite open about it. Says if I marry as he wishes, he has the power to let me go. I don't know if that's true, and I don't know that it's magic. In fact, I thought it might be mesmerism."

John frowned. Mesmerism sounded unlikely, and when he'd first met Lord Dalton he'd received no sense of magical power from him. On the contrary, he'd felt the man to be labouring under some awful stinking burden. "But you'd leave if you could? You'd leave Lady Dalton alone?"

"You do harp on that! I'm not doing anything to her, I tell you. But you're right. I'd be delighted to leave this benighted bloody place and live my life again."

"And see Ophelia. And the Crystal Palace."

"Quite." Unexpectedly, Thornby blushed, and turned his gaze to the pine trees.

John admired the blush with a part of his mind, actually wanting to smile at the memory of Thornby haranguing the countryside. A thrill of triumph was twisting in his belly at having broken Thornby's haughty facade. He had to resist an absurd, fleeting urge to boast a little about his involvement with Paxton. *I helped to build it, you know, the Crystal Palace.* Ridiculous. He decided to call Thornby's bluff.

"All right. Why don't you leave? Now. You could walk to the nearest village. I'm sure you could commandeer a carriage to get you to a station."

"I turn back. Every time." Thornby folded his arms, trying for nonchalance, but instead looking like a boy accused of breaking a window. John was surprised to see that he was trembling.

"Perhaps this time will be different."

"Why should it? I tried earlier. I wrote on my hand. I..."

Thornby looked so distressed, John felt a moment of sympathy, quickly followed by suspicion.

"Come," John said. "If your father has a spell on you, I need to see it working to understand it. The boundary is there. Why don't I take your arm?"

John took Thornby's elbow in a vice-like grip and walked him off the well-worn path that marked the estate boundary. He could feel Thornby quivering with tension, but no spells. After only a pace or two, Thornby began to struggle. John grabbed his forearm as well.

"Come, my lord, we're walking across the moor. You can go anywhere you please."

Thornby's head was bowed as if he were walking into a storm. He was muttering something about being late for dinner.

"That doesn't matter; you'll be having dinner in York. You know, I can't detect a trace of magic being worked against you. Not one tiny jot."

"Howarth's land. Trespassing—"

"Mr Howarth won't mind. Not going to poach his grouse, are we? Don't you think it fascinating that, as far as I can tell, there's no magic? No binding, no barrier, nothing."

John took another couple of steps, forcing Thornby to stagger after him. But then Thornby began trying to escape in real earnest, twisting like a hooked fish. John clung to him, kept pulling.

"There's no magic," John said through gritted teeth. But, even as he spoke, he felt again that faint, barely detectable, *something*. Glamour? He thought not, though it was hard to concentrate with Thornby thrashing around. They took another step, and Thornby fell to his knees, groaning, doubled over as if in pain.

"Come on, man, get up."

He bent to pull Thornby to his feet and saw that the skin on Thornby's forehead was tearing open, blood running down his face. Blood was trickling from his nose; blood was all over his hand, and seeping from under his fingernails.

"What the devil!" John recoiled, letting go. Shock and shame coursed through him in equal measures. He had only meant to prove there was no magic, but instead—

He watched in horror as Thornby crawled back inside the boundary of Raskelf and collapsed.

Chapter Three

Thornby woke to yellow sunshine across his bed, dust motes dancing lazily above him. It must be late. He yawned, and winced, and the pain from his face brought yesterday's events flooding back.

He jerked upright. He was on top of the covers, still wearing yesterday's mud and blood-spattered clothes. His left hand was wrapped in a blood-soaked bandage, dried blood crusted black under his fingernails. He touched his face, feeling more bandages. His left elbow twinged; it was bruised from Blake's grip.

Blake had forced him to walk onto Howarth's land. Thornby had, at the time, half-hoped that with the forceful Mr Blake at his side, he would simply be swept away from Raskelf, across the moors to freedom.

But then, of course, he had wanted to turn back.

And Blake had not let him.

Thornby shuddered. It hadn't merely been the pain of his tearing skin. It had been that hideous sense of strength and spirit draining away, as if some unseen presence was sucking his essence, leaving him nothing but bone.

He got up, cautiously removed the blood-soaked bandages, and considered himself in the glass. Ghastly. The skin was broken open on forehead and cheekbone as if he'd been flung against a stone wall. The back of his left hand was one big graze, and his fingertips stung as if he'd been shredding nettles.

He dimly remembered Blake helping him back to the Hall, half carrying him. Thornby had been weak as a kitten, every step an eternity of weariness. He'd never taken so ill after trying to leave, but then he'd never got so far before. On his own, he'd managed three or four paces at most. With Blake, he must have taken seven or eight.

Most of the details of the long walk home had faded, but despite the circumstances, the sensation he remembered best was that of Blake's arm around his shoulders. He closed his eyes to recall better the warmth and strength of Blake's body next to his. A surprising pang of excitement twisted down through his gut to his groin.

Well, not so surprising. He hadn't bedded a man for eighteen months, and Mr Blake was quite handsome, even if he was an overbearing bastard. When they'd got back to Raskelf, Blake had taken him to a seldom-used cards room, cleaned the wounds with some smelly stuff, and dressed them. Thornby had been too exhausted to speak, but Blake had seemed to understand that Thornby didn't want anyone informed of the situation. Then, pushing Blake away, he'd staggered up to bed and been asleep before he could remove his coat.

And now, despite his torn skin—or perhaps even because of it—his stomach was knotting with something that felt a lot like hope. The wounds were proof, and they rather seemed to be proof of magic. What was more, Blake claimed to be a magician. He'd talked as if magic was as real as turnips or table-legs, as if breaking charms and casting spells were plausible, everyday things.

Did Lady Dalton really think Thornby was casting spells on her? He hardly knew her. He avoided her mostly, assuming that, since she'd accepted his father, she must be the biggest fool or the most ruthless social climber in England. She was the orphan daughter of a wealthy industrialist, and had once been fabulously wealthy. As far as Thornby knew, her money was already gone. Father had disposed of it like chaff upon the wind.

He could think of no reason why she would blame *him*, not Lord Dalton, for her troubles, but why would Blake lie? Thornby didn't feel he was a man who made mischief. For all his talk of spells and magic, he seemed intensely practical; a man who took action and expected results and had no need of falsehoods. And he had not been entirely heartless; having conducted his experiment, another man might have walked off and left Thornby bleeding in the mud. Blake had not done that.

Then he remembered Blake saying, "You're no match for me", his voice full of scorn, and the pleasant glow of having had a strong arm around him faded. Truth be told, Blake was rather terrifying. If he was a magician, what did that mean? One heard rumours of men who sold their souls in return for occult powers. Was Blake of that type? A devil-worshipper?

A memory popped into his mind; he'd once seen what appeared to be a freshly-skinned baboon galloping down the Strand, dodging carriages and pedestrians. He'd exclaimed, grabbing at his companions, but they'd seen nothing. How they missed it, he'd never understood, for the thing ran right by them, glistening red, jaws agape. Someone had suggested it had been an injured dog, and Thornby had tried to forget about it.

He stood before the looking-glass, heart racing as if the hideous baboon-thing had just careened through his chamber. Was it possible he'd truly seen a devil conjured from the pit of hell? After all, dogs didn't usually have claws like scythes, or forked tongues.

Did Blake consort with devils? What was in that big, heavy trunk? Did he have some baboon-like familiar lurking in his room? He had no valet. Did that mean he was so unspeakable no decent man would work for him?

Thornby imagined himself approaching Mr Blake and asking for help, and could barely suppress a shudder. If only he had something to offer the fellow. In the past, he'd generally bought his way out of trouble; it was amazing what a judicious sovereign could do. But these days he hadn't a penny to his name. He'd had nothing since London. Father had stopped his allowance, and he'd never been able to bring himself to beg. He hardly liked the idea of playing the supplicant now, but then he liked the idea of approaching Mr Blake empty-handed even less.

So, who to accost for a loan? The staff were no good, and Aunt Amelia had nothing. Mr Derwent likewise. Thornby would rather die than approach Lady Dalton, and the village people thought sixpence a princely sum; they were out of the question. What a vile equation this was, weighing up the easiest mark! He sighed. Perhaps the rector could be prevailed upon? Thornby began to change his clothes.

***

John spent the morning roaming around Raskelf, talking to the servants and looking for recent spells or traces of demons in the more public parts of the house. He kept turning corners and finding yet another long corridor with doors letting onto dust-sheeted rooms, another gloomy gallery, another cold marble staircase, another infestation of black beetles.

His fingertips were dry and grey from touching dusty surfaces. Cobwebs trailed over his cuffs. He was tired of the sound of his own footsteps and the murmurs of the house, and he could not shake the feeling of being watched. But he found no traces of recent magic.

He'd started the morning with two aims: to interview Lord Dalton and to avoid Lord Thornby.

Speaking to Lord Dalton would help him to assess the truth of Thornby's claim that his father was keeping him at Raskelf, possibly by magical means. It would also let John get a better look at the curse that was following Dalton around like a swarm of flies on a night-soil cart. John felt sure the two things must be connected. But Lord Dalton had left early to visit his neighbours, the Howarths, and was not expected back for lunch. John learned this from Warren, Lord Dalton's valet, who was fussing endlessly in his lordship's rooms.

At least John had been successful in avoiding Lord Thornby. Possibly this had been made easier by the fact that Thornby seemed to be avoiding him too. Thornby did not appear all morning. If he had breakfasted at all, he had done so in his room, and he had certainly not joined his step-mother and aunt at church. Apparently, he never went, much to the scullery maid's horror. But then, if he couldn't leave the estate, of course he couldn't go.

Thornby seemed like an innocent man. Ever since John had watched his face tear open on Howarth's land, a horrible suspicion had been growing in him that he had behaved like a bully and a boor. The thought that he might have to apologise was enough to make him curse under his breath. He could almost *see* the supercilious triumph, almost *hear* the condescending tone. Being wrong was bad enough, but being wrong in front of a superior little prick like Thornby—*damnation*!

But. If Thornby was innocent, why did good charms not work on him? What on earth *had* gone on yesterday on Howarth's land? John had detected no magic even while Thornby's face tore open in front of his eyes. So, to be absolutely sure that Thornby was as innocent of witchcraft as he claimed, John had to get into his rooms.

Magicians couldn't help leaving traces of their art in the places they lived. Raskelf Hall taken as a residence was far too big, but Thornby's own rooms would leave John in no doubt. No one could talk to inanimate things as well as John; he was the best the Institute had seen. Even the theurgists admitted it, much as it galled them to be beaten at anything by a materials man.

Of course, he felt a natural disinclination to go nosing around in another man's rooms, but if he hoped to escape the factories and mills one day, this was probably the kind of thing he'd have to get used to.

Eventually, just before lunch, John looked for the hundredth time out of one of the warped and bubbly old windows on the first floor, and this time caught a glimpse of Thornby heading towards the village on an old black horse. He had a purposeful air, and John would have given much to know where he was going. But now was the perfect chance. One of the housemaids had pointed out the door to Lord Thornby's room. John went there and tapped on it, heart beating rather fast. There was no answer, but the door came off the latch and opened an inch.

Thornby's bed-chamber was as shabby as the rest of Raskelf. Faded red silk damask adorned the walls, and faded red brocade hung from an old four-poster. A shaft of sunlight lay across the bed, and the room had the same sense of potential, of energy only momentarily absent, as an empty stage. An ancient-looking clothes press, as big as a small cottage, contained a few of Thornby's old-fashioned clothes. There was a small room off to one side—perhaps an old powder room, to judge from the collection of empty wig stands—and on the other side, a small study.

John put a hand on the door-frame between study and bed-chamber and closed his eyes. As his mind cleared, the magical susurration that filled Raskelf and disturbed his sleep came into focus. He was beginning to get used to it and to feel that this was nothing out of the usual for the old place. He was used to more modern buildings—mills, factories, foundries, or his own rooms in London—but Raskelf had a long history. Traces of magic from past centuries were held here.

He let the old wood tell its secrets. It had seen a werelight; white spangles conjured from a posy of flowers, but that was a hundred years ago. It remembered blood and screaming, and the carrion-sweet stink of a demon, but that was older still. And, in the distant past, some fertility magic to do with corn, so faint it was barely a whisper.

There was nothing else.

He went into the study. An easel displayed a half-finished water-colour of Raskelf Hall at dawn. It was rather fine, not that he was any judge. Thornby seemed to have only one brush and one very small, nearly-empty box of paints. John looked through the books: Ovid, Virgil, Herodotus, Shakespeare—all old and bound in blue leather, probably from Raskelf's cavernous library. No books of magic.

A floorboard creaked in the bedroom and his heart leapt into his mouth. But it was just the old house, talking to itself in an ordinary way.

He opened the drawers in the desk and rifled through the papers. There were a lot of ink and pencil sketches of plants and woodland animals. Also, a few drawings of Lady Amelia, a sketch of Stewart, the drunken estate manager, looking surprisingly noble, and a couple of self portraits. Thornby had a lively and expressive style, but no magic emanated from the drawings.

John put everything back, reserving one of the self-portraits, which he put in his pocketbook. A good likeness of a person, drawn by that same person, could be a useful ingredient for a charm if he needed it later on. Not that magic had seemed to work on Thornby yet, but it would certainly be better than an old stocking.

He had been half avoiding the bed, with all its associations, but the place a person slept was a powerful touch-point. He went back into the bedroom and put his hand on the once-rich red brocade hangings. They had faded on the side closest to the window to a dirty beige. The brocade remembered a love charm from fifty years ago, and a slightly older spell to get a woman pregnant with a boy. But neither of these were related to Thornby. John breathed deeper and stroked the brocade, beguiling it, his magic running up and down its threads. It wanted to please him, but had nothing more to tell.

As he drew his fingers away, it offered him a flash of Thornby; head flung back, long throat exposed, nightshirt bunched around his chest, one hand wrapped around his erect cock, his slender body gilded by firelight.

The image went straight to John's groin and he cursed under his breath. As if he needed any more distractions of that kind. But he could hardly blame the brocade. Sex wasn't magic, of course, but inanimate objects would sometimes mistake it for such, and offer it up to a magician. His entire body was quivering with tension and he took a deep breath, trying to relax.

So, there was no recent magic, not one tiny thing.

Which meant he had indeed accused an innocent man and bullied him into a course of action that had left him injured. His heart sank. So, now he would have to do it. He would have to face up to Thornby and apologise. And try not to think of Thornby frigging himself as he did it. Marvellous. That would make it a *whole* lot easier. His head throbbed, in tandem with his groin. *Damnation.* Where was all this leading? What was he doing here? Why wasn't he in Manchester checking the spells on the looms? Or in London making sure no-one had another go at the Crystal Palace?

The gong for luncheon made him jump again. Truly, this sneaking around in another man's rooms was repellent. And yet, even at the Institute they'd never counselled against intelligence gathering, if the cause was just or for the good of the Empire. *Discretion. Restraint. Independence. Sometimes the ends justify the means.* True, those lectures had been aimed at the theurgists who were going into politics, the military or the church, but he supposed the theory held true in more personal situations.

Lord Thornby, thank goodness, was not present in the dining room.

John and Lady Dalton made polite conversation while they ate watery pea soup and over-cooked trout. John tried several times to engage Lady Amelia and the elderly cousin, Mr Derwent, in the conversation, but his sallies went nowhere. Mr Derwent had a Ming seal in his pocket; John could hear it hissing affrontedly.

On his first night here, dining by candlelight, he'd thought Lady Dalton had looked nervous, and thinner than he remembered her. Now, by daylight, he was shocked at the change in her. He had met her once at Catterall's place in London before her marriage. She had not been beautiful even then, but her kindness, vivacity, and youth had lent her considerable charm. He remembered that evening in London he had been tired and silent, absorbed in some trouble from the foundry. And although she had been an heiress engaged to marry a marquess, she had taken a great deal of trouble to draw him out and introduce him to her friends.

Now her once fresh complexion was marred with blemishes which echoed the plum colour of her dress. The charm she was wearing reeked of rancid milk and cough pastilles. Her eyes, of a very pale blue, were sunken, and she gasped when Mr Derwent dropped his spoon against his bowl. She was trying to put a brave face on it, but she was miserably afraid. A spark of anger lit inside John, ruining his appetite.

After lunch, when he offered her his arm and a turn about the garden, she grabbed him like a drowning woman and pulled him onto the urn-lined terrace at the front of the house.

"Mr Blake, where have you been? Where were you yesterday? I was afraid you had left! Have you spoken to Lord Thornby? Have you told him he must stop it?"

"I have spoken to him. But he knows nothing of magic, I promise. He's not doing anything to you."

The house loomed over them, spires and baroque ornaments bristling. On the other side of the terrace, beyond the stone urns, an over-grown yew hedge rose nearly as tall as the house. It was oppressive, like walking in a tunnel. He steered her along to where the hedge stopped, giving a view onto a very green field. They were outside the empty west wing now. He kept walking, trying to shake the feeling that curtains were twitching as they passed.

"But he is!" She lowered her voice. "Or someone is. There was a hedgehog under my bed last night. I could hear it scratching about before I knew what it was. And it seems— uncanny, somehow. How could it have got in, unless someone put it there? And who could it be but him? Does it—does it *mean* something?"

Up close, the charm she was wearing had a practiced feel; rough, but put together with confidence. It was mostly to do with sex and fertility, but there was a ward in there too, to protect from evil. She hadn't made it, yet it had a female feel. She'd probably bought it from a country wise-woman. Bizarrely, the thing kept reminding him of cattle, until he realised that whoever had put it together was more used to making charms for cows. Probably without meaning to, she'd given Lady Dalton a charm that might make a bull think her fair game. It was terribly dangerous. He must get it off her, and give her something better.

"A hedgehog?" he said.

"I told my maid to put it in a hat box in case you'd like to look at it. It's in an empty stall in the stables." She blushed and ducked her head. "It's nothing, is it? I'm being silly."

"It's not silly," he said seriously. "It is an odd place to find a hedgehog. Let's go and look at it."

The hedgehog froze when he lifted the lid of the hat box. He put a finger on its spines, hoping it would keep its fleas to itself. Its nose started whiffling, its boot-button eyes peering up at him anxiously. He could feel the life fizzing around inside it. God, give him an honest iron beam any day! He tried to concentrate, and to ignore Lady Dalton who stood wringing her hands by the stable door. The creature carried no charms. It was not cursed. It had not been summoned. It was not a construct. It had not been dosed with any kind of potion. There were no wards on it. There were no traces of magic at all.

And yet, as he knelt over it, there came again that faint, strange *something* he had noticed when he was forcing Thornby to leave the estate. The moment he noticed it, it was gone and he felt he'd imagined it. Could this creature somehow be related? But how? It was certainly not anybody's familiar, and yet—

"I think it's just a hedgehog." He had no wish to alarm Lady Dalton with vague suspicions. He stood, brushing straw from his knees. "But, may I keep it in your hat box a little longer, my lady?"

She stopped wringing her hands and clasped them as if in prayer. "Please tell me the truth. Do you think there's something odd about it or not?"

He could see his answer mattered a great deal. It was tempting to shield her, but she was caught in the middle of this. He owed her the truth, surely.

"Yes, there's something odd. I think I'm imagining it, but—" He gestured helplessly.

"Yes! That's it! One knows there's something wrong. But one can't..." She trailed off, then burst out, "Mr Blake, I'm *so* glad you've come! I'm so glad my cousin persuaded you. Don't you feel there's something terribly uncanny here at Raskelf? I've no proof, so I feel such a fool, but I can't help it."

He looked at her closely. Could it be she had some unladylike sensitivity to magic, including this mysterious maybe-magic he had yet to pinpoint?

"I feel it too," he said. "It's like nothing I've ever come across before. But I feel it."

She closed her eyes. 'Thank God," she whispered. "You've no idea what it's been like. And everyone thinking me a silly girl."

"I don't think that."

"No. I can see you don't." She managed a watery smile.

"Let's get this creature a drink and a bite to eat, shall we? But first you'd better give me that charm you're wearing. I'm afraid it's not quite the thing, you know."

She blushed. "Oh! How did you—oh, but of course you know. I was desperate. She said it would keep me safe."

He refrained from saying, *It might if you were a cow,* and held out his hand. Still blushing, she pulled a cord from around her neck and handed him a small leather bag that had been hidden inside her dress. It was linked to her, and the smell stopped the moment it left her hand.

"Will I be safe without it?"

"I'll give you something better. You know, I'm certain Lord Thornby is not working magic on you, but he thinks his father is doing something to him. What do you know about this story that Lord Dalton won't let Lord Thornby leave the estate until he marries?"

"He does want Thornby to get married. And he did put his foot down about some goings on in London. A painting of a—a lady from Greek mythology. I expect you heard about it; it was in all the papers. Lord Thornby has to stay here until he makes a respectable marriage."

"But why?"

"It's the family name, Mr Blake! Lord Thornby is very unwise, sometimes. The Marquess wants him to settle down. Surely any father would want that?"

"But is it true Lord Thornby can't leave the estate?"

"Dalton has stopped his allowance. I suppose that's what Lord Thornby means if he says he can't leave. He hasn't any income."

"What if I told you he really can't leave; that there's something keeping him here."

"Magic?"

John sighed. "If it is, I can't detect it, but I don't see how it could be anything else. Do you suspect anyone else around here of using magic?"

"No." She looked down at some shreds of mucky straw that had stuck to her plum-coloured boot. "I bought my charm in Pickering; that's miles away. It couldn't be Mr Derwent could it? He seems so vague and old, but he does have some odd curios, doesn't he?"

"He does," John agreed. "But, I beg your pardon, what about Lord Dalton? Lord Thornby says his father admits it openly, and has told him that once he marries, he can leave. His father claims to have that power."

There was a long pause. She bunched her hands in a fold of her dress. So, this was the possibility she didn't want to consider: that her own husband was doing these things to her. He had already frittered away all of her money. Now, as well as his coldness towards her, was he also secretly terrorising her?

"I don't know," she said eventually, her voice faint.

"Has Lord Dalton ever behaved oddly, would you say?"

"Not especially. He's always buying little rocky islands, 'skerries' I think they're called. I did think it was an odd enthusiasm when I first met him, but he believes in seaweed as a fertiliser, and, well, to me, gentlemen often seem odd in their interests. I once met a viscount who talked about the benefits of martingales for over an hour. An hour, Mr Blake! Through seven courses!"

She smiled, timidly, as if half expecting him to launch into a lecture about martingales himself. He smiled back.

Emboldened, she went on. "When I met Lord Dalton, he was different. He was courteous. He was never unkind. Perhaps he wasn't as conventional as most of the men I'd met, but I liked that about him. He never seemed to care what people thought. My parents had cared so much! To meet someone who didn't—" She paused, searching for the right word. "It was *liberating*, Mr Blake. I suppose I married him for one of the worst possible reasons, but I really thought..."

Her voice, which had become almost a whisper, trailed off.

"You wouldn't be the first young lady to have her head turned by a nobleman," John said kindly.

She looked at him blankly. "That's what people think, isn't it? I wanted the title. Lady Dalton. That's what George believes."

"That's not the case?"

"Of course I understand why people assume that."

Her voice was resigned. She was used to not being believed. He waited silently for the truth.

"He begged me. Begged me on his knees. None of the others did that. But the real reason…" She broke off again, and John averted his eyes to spare her embarrassment, expecting a tale of passion or seduction, but she surprised him again.

"I was sorry for him," she said. "I know that's the worst reason to marry someone. I was such a fool! But I'm still sorry for him, even now. I know he neglects his duties and there's no money, and he and Thornby argue terribly. But there's something driving him to it. I don't mean to say it's magic. It's more—his first wife dying. And he loved her so much. I thought—if we were married—and it did seem to work at first. Sometimes he would be so kind! When we first came to Raskelf he would bring me flowers. Not big bouquets from the gardens, but daisies or violets. He picked them himself. Or he said he did. Maybe it was the gardener's boy all along. But it all stopped when he brought Lord Thornby home."

She stood there by the stable door, a strand of dirty straw held forgotten in her hand, eyes unfocused, remembering.

John could think of another, meaner, reason why Lord Dalton might bring her wildflowers rather than bouquets, but he didn't voice it. The idea of the aggressive, grizzled marquess picking violets sat uncomfortably with his idea of the man, but then most men did sometimes behave strangely where women were concerned, especially if those women were wealthy heiresses.

So, she'd married Lord Dalton because she was sorry for him. It was, truly, a terrible reason to marry someone, but perhaps love might have grown if her husband had continued to treat her kindly. He wondered again if she had some sensitivity to magic, if perhaps she could sense the curse, and pity the man under it without knowing why. If she'd been a boy, she'd have been tested. She might have gone to the Institute or had an apprenticeship somewhere.

John made his excuses, went upstairs and began to put a ward charm on a handkerchief she'd given him. He made wards all the time, but his usual customers were factory workers or their bosses, and he usually warded from fire, from crushing or slicing injuries, from cotton fibre in the lungs, or from mistakes brought on by exhaustion and hunger. This was a different sort of job entirely; warding from the unknown, from general malice. He took his time over it. He even went back to his books at one point. Wards for ladies tended to contain a soporific, to calm and reassure. But he weighed the bag of Hochmel beads in his hand and put them to one side. He never used them for the mill girls; they needed their wits about them. If Lady Dalton indeed had some sensitivity to hidden magic, it seemed wrong to dull her senses to it while she was caught in the middle of it all.

He put the charmed handkerchief in his pocket, to give to her, and his fingers caught the edge of the sketch he had put in his pocket-book.

He took out the portrait of Lord Thornby and examined it. At first, all he could see was his own desire. There was something in Thornby's face that surpassed the classical by falling short of it. Perhaps his nose was too narrow, his mouth too wide, and his cheeks too hollow, but these imperfections let John know he was flesh, not marble, and the knowledge made his heart pound.

But after a while, he began to see in a different way. Thornby had drawn himself at a slight angle, chin thrust out to the viewer, eyes hooded. When John had first glanced at it, he'd thought it an arrogant pose. But now he looked closer and saw that it was not. In fact, he'd seen the attitude before, in people terribly bereaved; the eyes full of despair, the mouth tense. It was the face of a man held together with pride, because that was all he had left.

John sighed and put the portrait back in his pocket. He'd done as Catterall had asked; he'd come to Raskelf, he'd looked for magic. He'd proven Lord Thornby's innocence. But Lady Dalton was still in trouble. The Marquess was cursed, but by whom? And Thornby, the strangest, most beautiful, and most disconcerting man he'd ever met, was somehow trapped at the heart of it.

He could not walk away.

***

Thornby got back to the house empty-handed. Trying to borrow money from the rector had gone spectacularly badly. Thornby, hadn't, of course, been able to actually call upon the man, because he couldn't walk to the village any more, but he'd hovered at the gates to the estate until he'd been able to persuade a passer-by to fetch the fellow for him. The rector had listened, purse-mouthed, to Thornby's plea for money, then read him a little lecture about gambling debts and prodigal sons and wished him good day. Thornby, hot-faced with embarrassment and fury, had simply had to watch him go.

Hoping to remain undetected, he went up by the servant's staircase and through the gloomy Drake Gallery. He was nearly at his room when he realised Mr Blake was standing on the first floor landing, looking at a bust of Cato. Thornby stopped, hiding in the shadows behind the gallery door. Blake was standing with his arms crossed, glaring at the bust as if it had just insulted his mother. His dark, sober suiting was as immaculate as his dark, sober hair. He looked clever; not one to suffer fools. Was he really a magician? With a ghastly bloody baboon thing slavering in his room? Possibly. Yet he looked more like a business man; the type that knows the price of everything.

How could he ask Blake to help when he had nothing to give in return? Thornby could imagine himself squirming under Blake's withering stare with such clarity that he found himself tiptoeing away. At one time it had never crossed his mind that confidence was partly to do with means. Now he knew better.

Begging from the rector had depleted him. His soul felt raw with the failure and the shame. Perhaps he'd feel like tackling Blake after dinner. Thornby went back outside, to the east side of the house and down into the sunken garden. It was grey and miserable this afternoon except for some bright red rosehips just visible in the gathering dusk. He sat on the wooden seat against the west wall, completely hidden from the house.

Mother had shown him this place when he was a child. He imagined the place as it had been the day she'd shown it to him—a riot of greenery, bright with flowers, alive with bees and butterflies. They had run here hand-in-hand, laughing, breathless, hiding from Nanny. They had curled up on this very seat, and Mother had whispered in his ear that, when he was just a tiny bit older, she would show him a big and marvellous secret. He had begged her to tell him *now*, and she had smiled and said she would tell him a little secret, to see if he could keep it. And if he could keep it for a whole month, *then* she would tell him the big one. He'd agreed, and she'd pointed to the nasturtiums that grew beside the seat and shown him the beads of dew that gleamed in the centres of the round leaves. She'd told him they were fairy jewels but that he mustn't tell a soul or the fairies would be angry. He had believed her, and had come most days to the sunken garden after that, hoping to see a fairy.

Then he had turned eight and been sent away to school. And Mother had died and he had never seen her again.

He realised it had grown dark and he had grown cold and stiff with waiting. But for what was he waiting? Nothing would turn up. He was utterly friendless. He had nothing to give Mr Blake to persuade him to help, and no way of getting anything.

And now he must go in and change for dinner with his father, the bastard who was responsible for it all.

Chapter Four

Five people sat down to dinner that evening; John himself, Lord Dalton, Lady Dalton, Lady Amelia and the elderly Mr Derwent. There was an empty place setting to John's right. Lord Dalton glared at it briefly and waved an irritable hand at the butler to begin serving.

They had started the carrot soup when Thornby stalked in. John tried not to stare, and failed.

Thornby had dressed for dinner in tight black silk breeches, waistcoat and coat, black silk stockings, and a black cravat that swathed his throat. He wore on his lapel a sprig of rose-hips that glowed like tiny red lanterns. John had seen such old-fashioned clothes before, but only on elderly gentlemen who, for reasons of habit or thrift, still wore the fashions of their youth. To see such an outfit on a man as young and as handsome as Thornby was striking, to say the least. The wounds on Thornby's face and hand had scabbed over and did little to mar his elegance. If anything, they heightened the effect of the Regency rake, recently come from an uncommonly dirty duel.

John stood, and bowed, and received a glacial look.

"Good evening," Thornby said. "Forgive my lateness. Really, the days pass so quickly this time of year." He sat down, affecting a bored expression as the butler filled his glass. But his eyes were wary. He tossed back the hock as if it were water and motioned impatiently for a refill.

John had hoped to apologise to him without an audience, but thought he might as well get it over with. He'd opened his mouth to do so when he realised Lord Dalton, who sat at the head of the table, had fixed his son with an unpleasant smile.

"Well, Soren, have you come off your horse, boy?" Dalton said.

"How observant you are, Father. That's exactly what happened." Thornby flashed a glance at John, as if daring him to tell the truth.

"It's that old nag you ride. Sinbad, isn't it? I'll have Stewart take him for dog's meat," said Lord Dalton.

"Father, you can't mean to destroy the horse that threw me!" He glanced at John again. "Father's almost too fond, don't you think, Mr Blake? It was hardly the animal's fault, but then, that's Father; always blaming the innocent. You may feel a little less fond, Father, when I confess I took Pendragon without your permission and it was he who threw me. And now you've said you'll make dog food of your own horse. What a shame!"

"Full of lies, as usual. I know what happened." Lord Dalton's voice was cold, almost bored. He took a spoonful of soup. "It's the first time you've got that far, isn't it? Taken you long enough; you've always been a weakling and a dammed little coward."

John froze with his spoon half-way to his mouth, unsure which shocked him more; the public insults—in front of ladies, too—or the open allusion to whatever kept Thornby here. Lord Dalton seemed to be admitting very freely, if not his guilt, then his power over his son. At the opposite end of the table to her husband, Lady Dalton put down her spoon and bowed her head as if trying to remove herself from the scene. Lady Amelia's head had gone up at the scent of battle, mouth pursed in disapproval, but she did not speak. Only old Mr Derwent kept spooning soup, mainly into his mouth, partly over his dinner jacket.

Thornby smiled at the shadowy ceiling. The table held plenty of candles but the light seemed to cower low, unable to pierce the gloom.

"You're so right, father. A weakling. A coward." Thornby sighed theatrically. "I'd make a terrible husband. I'd better never marry. How I'd like to! One of those lovely rich ladies I'm sure you have lined up for me. But it wouldn't be fair on her." He glanced at Lady Dalton. "Would it, ma'am? Think of the terrible whelps I'd sire; like father, like son, as they say."

Lady Dalton glanced nervously at her husband, then at Thornby, then back to her husband. The men did not look at her. Dalton stared with loathing at his son, while his son affected an expression of martyred nobility.

John decided things had gone far enough. "How do you think Lord Thornby hurt himself, my lord?" he said to Dalton.

Dalton looked at him and frowned. "Blake, isn't it? Yes, I invited you." His frown deepened. "Can't think why."

"I have very valuable contacts, my lord," John said firmly. With the Judas Voice charm, it was important to sound confident. "But you have a theory about how Lord Thornby came by his injuries?" He turned to Thornby. "Injuries I sincerely regret, my lord."

Thornby gave him another of those cool, bored looks, but then a speculative expression crept into his eyes. It was almost a question, though not one John felt able to answer in public. He turned back to Lord Dalton.

"Well, my lord? You have a theory?"

"Haven't you heard the local gossip, Blake? The boy's weak in the wits, so perhaps he's been banging his own head against a wall. Or maybe he's a damned degenerate, and the years of unclean living are making their mark. It depends who you ask."

"Village gossip." John shook his head dismissively. "But you have a theory of your own? It wasn't a fall from a horse, you say? So, what was it?"

"I'm not sure I like your tone, Blake." Dalton glared at him, blue eyes rather bloodshot, mouth menacing.

"I beg your pardon, my lord. I meant no offence." John took a mouthful of soup, wondering if he'd be thrown out, Judas Voice or no.

"Father doesn't have any tone himself, you see, and so resents it in others," put in Thornby. Was he drawing fire deliberately? It was impossible to say. "But in any case, Mr Blake, it's very decent of you to care so much for my complexion. I expect Father's about to announce an autumn ball or some such awfulness some time soon, and it would be a shame if I didn't look my best for the ladies, wouldn't it? Though of course now I've vowed never to marry, perhaps it doesn't matter so much?"

"You'll pick one this time," Dalton said, voice ominous. "Or I'll pick one for you. My patience is running out."

Thornby shook his head. "No, Father. Your *money* is running out. Patience and money are two quite different things. You should look them up in the dictionary. Perhaps the marchioness could help. She could look up 'misalliance', couldn't she?"

"Leave her out of it," John said, quietly but firmly to Thornby. Out of the corner of his eye he could see Thornby's raised eyebrow, but the younger man said nothing more.

"Is there to be a ball, my lord?" John said neutrally to Lord Dalton.

There was a long pause, while Dalton glared at his family, as if daring any of them to interject. Mr Derwent finished his soup and looked around, bewildered, at the others' full bowls. Lord Dalton's weathered face relaxed slightly.

"A small party. Spot of shooting. The Greys and the Lazenbys are coming." He raised his voice to Thornby. "Miss Grey and Miss Lazenby, boy. You'll make yourself pleasant."

Thornby sighed again, like a kind schoolmaster with a slow pupil. But his knuckles were white on the stem of his glass, and John realised that, for all his show, Thornby was furious. His voice, when he spoke, was even more precise than usual.

"I wish you'd understand, Father, that nothing's changed since last winter when you paraded some ladies around in front of me. I shan't be pleasant to someone I despise, and I shan't lie to someone I like. Not that I'll make one, you understand, but my proposal would go thus: 'Marry me, please. Of course when you do, your money comes to me, and I'm at my father's mercy. So, he'll take the money somehow and trot off to Scotland, leaving you with nothing but a husband who doesn't love you and who can't leave the estate.' Doesn't it sound jolly? Any girl would leap at the chance."

"You think staying here's the worst I can do to you?" Lord Dalton spat out. "Look at you, prancing around like a bloody popinjay. I shall have to arrange a little demonstration for you, boy. You might suddenly find Miss Grey a more attractive prospect."

The open threat clearly touched a nerve. Thornby made a slight, jerky movement forward, as if he might leap across the table and brain his father with the gilt epergne. His face was like thunder, boredom vanished like the illusion it had been. John found he'd risen a fraction in his own seat, readying himself to hold Thornby back. He could hardly believe what was happening. What must the ladies be thinking? And in front of the servants! He'd been to some unpleasant dinner parties, but this was the first where he'd felt two of the party might actually have at each other amongst the condiments.

"Leave the boy alone," Lady Amelia said suddenly to her brother, cutting across the tension. She wore an evening gown in emerald green. Along with her snowy-white hair, it gave her an unearthly look, like an avenging goddess in a play. "You come back here, Dalton; you've been gone all summer again! The Ramparts cottages are falling down. The chapel's got dry rot. The place is falling apart. There's no money in seaweed. Can't you see that if you came home—What do you want with Scotland anyway? What do you want with Ireland? You could save things here, if you just came home and acted as you should." She sat back in her chair, face grey, a gleam of sweat dampening her forehead, though it was not warm in the room.

Lord Dalton shot her a dismissive look. "Stupid woman. Not a clue," he said, almost to himself. He stood and motioned to the butler. "I'll dine in the study."

Thornby stood as well. His chair fell backwards with a clatter. His eyes glittered in the candlelight and two spots of colour had come into his cheeks.

"How dare you call her stupid? You're the fool here! You think staying here is a punishment for me? You couldn't be more wrong. You know what you've done? You've given Mother back to me. I'd forgotten her; did you know that? You never let me come home afterwards, did you? And I forgot her. But now, I remember her every day. The sunken garden where she liked to sit. Her favourite ride, up to Jennie's Pot. Remember? The way she laughed at that picture there." He stabbed a finger towards a dim portrait of some grim Tudor Dezombrey who glared down at the table. "It scared me, and she said 'No, Soren, he has a stomach ache, that's all' and laughed. Remember? Well, I do. And I remember she loved me. And she loved me more than you." His voice shook on the final sentence and he wiped one eye quickly with the back of his hand. "You evil old bastard. Sometimes I wonder if you killed her."

A hush descended, laden with the excruciating awkwardness of the English during a scene. John tried to keep his face absolutely blank. He could hear Thornby's breathing, harsh as if he'd been running. Thornby's fists were on the table; his trembling made the cutlery shake.

"Soren—" Lady Amelia began, but Lord Dalton cut her off.

"Love? You don't know anything about *love*, you degenerate little whelp. I loved her truly. You understand? *Truly*. More than anything. You've never had a woman in your life, have you? You damned little mary-ann! My whole life has been for love. My *whole life*. You're all fools." He turned and walked away from the table, regal and calm.

John sat perfectly still. Whatever he'd been expecting Lord Dalton to say to his son's outburst, it was not that. As Dalton left the room, Lady Dalton burst into tears.

"Well! Family dinners. Good cheer and happy banter. We *are* treating you to some lovely Yorkshire hospitality, aren't we, Mr Blake?" Thornby had been aiming for a careless tone, but his voice shook again. He turned and walked out by the opposite door to that taken by his father.

John left the weeping Lady Dalton with Lady Amelia and followed Thornby. Of course, it was not really his place, but there had been a note of desperation in the younger man's voice that worried him. And besides, he had things to tell him.

He didn't have to look far. Thornby was slumped in a window seat in the blue saloon, only a couple of rooms away. The saloon was dimly lit by half a dozen cheap candles that were filling the air with smoke. As John approached, Thornby jerked to his feet and slammed a decanter of brandy down on a small table.

"Well? What the devil do you want?" Thornby said in tones of open hostility.

"To apologise properly for my behaviour yesterday."

"All right, you've done the decent thing. Now you can fuck off."

"You said you knew nothing of magic. So, I—" John took a deep breath. "I went to your rooms and looked about. And you were telling the truth. I'm sorry for doubting you, but the thing is—"

"*What*?! You 'went to my rooms'? You 'looked about'? You damned swine!" Thornby lunged for him. John dodged, but Thornby caught him a glancing blow on the jaw. Thornby pulled back for another swing, but this time John caught his fist and held it.

"Stop it, will you? I'm sorry. You think I *enjoyed* sneaking around? I had to be sure." He dropped Thornby's fist. "Hell, I'm not cut out for this sort of thing. Go on then, have a free hit if you like. I suppose I'd want to, if anyone went through my things."

Thornby glared at him, nursing his knuckles. "So, I'm not casting hexes at her ladyship? Such a relief to hear you say so. You can bugger off then, can't you? And tell her cousin the lady's been making up Banbury stories. Because she'd rather believe those than that her husband's a vile old bastard who only married her for her money."

"But I'm not—"

"Because you could *never* say a lady's been a social-climbing fool, and certainly not to the lady's own cousin." Suddenly the fight seemed to go out of him, and he leant against the wall in a pose of utter defeat. "Tell him whatever you like, then, but leave me alone."

"I wish you'd hear me out. It wouldn't be right to go back to London, because there's something damned odd happening. To her, yes, and to your father, but mainly to *you*."

"Yes, I'm a degenerate coward who can't leave the estate." Thornby spoke to the faded old carpet.

John winced. "It's true you can't leave. But also, my magic doesn't work on you— that's never happened to me before."

"Professional challenge, am I?" Thornby said sullenly. He reached for the brandy and took a swig straight from the decanter.

"But surely you can see the two things must be related? And to compound it all, well, you know that feeling when you see something out of the corner of your eye, but when you look, there's nothing there?"

"Maybe." Thornby said. Then he seemed to consider, and added, in a more civil tone, "Yes, actually. I have it all the time." He gave John a long look. Interest was beginning to kindle in his expression.

"Do you? Well, that's how I feel around you. There's—something. There's something about you that I can't quite—" John broke off, casting about for a way to express the fleeting strangeness he sometimes felt around Thornby. The English language did not have words for it. "There's just something about you."

To John's surprise, Thornby's mouth twitched, and curved into a slow smile. "Something about me, is there? A certain *je ne sais quoi*?"

John found himself gazing at Thornby's smile. His pulse, which had just started to slow down after that blow to the jaw, now sped back up. Damn, of course that had sounded—

He cleared his throat and forced himself to answer honestly.

"I keep nearly sensing it, then it goes. I don't know if it's magic, though I don't see how it could be anything else. But in any case, it's not like anything I've ever come across before."

"You're sure it's not my winning ways and ever-present charm?" Thornby held the decanter out to him. "Sorry for hitting you."

John put one hand to his jaw and took the decanter in the other. "It's all right. I'd have hit me, too." He took a swig. It was French brandy. Smooth as silk. Whatever economies Dalton might be making, they weren't with his wine merchant. He could feel Thornby's eyes on him, considering.

"You're quite a singular individual yourself, Mr Blake, if I may say so. It's not everyone who claims to know about magic, is it? That's very unusual. Forgive me, did that sound offensive? Perhaps that's the wrong word. Maybe I mean—remarkable."

John shrugged. "You needn't to be so polite about it, my lord. I've had a lot worse than 'unusual'. I've had un-Christian, unnatural, un-English." He took another mouthful of brandy and passed it back. "'Unusual' is really very civil."

"Unnatural, eh? And are you *really* unnatural, Mr Blake?" Thornby's eyes glittered. He was still half smiling.

John narrowed his eyes, heart in his mouth again. "Some call it that. What do you think?"

"I can't quite tell. I hope I'm going to find out." Thornby leant closer.

"What do you mean?" John could barely get the words out. Thornby's eyes had a wicked look. His lips were parted; those lips that were made for kissing. Was Thornby going to kiss him now?

"Well, you *tell* me you can do magic. You *tell* me you can detect it, or its absence. I've seen you with that peculiar glass eye and your pile of sand. I've seen you *apparently* fooling Father into letting you stay. But I haven't actually seen any proof."

"I see." John swallowed hard. He realised he'd leant forward too, just a little. He straightened his back. He was sweating all over. God, for a moment he had really thought—

Lord Dalton's comments were making him look at Thornby in a whole new light. Dalton had called Thornby a mary-ann, had said 'you've never had a woman in your life'. Random insults? Or the truth? Thornby had not denied it, and he certainly appeared to be flirting now. Or was he? The problem was that Thornby was so damned attractive, it was impossible to be objective. Why couldn't Thornby have had a hare lip, or a squint, or a few pockmarks? It would have made things so much simpler. It would have been easier to look away.

"You could be telling me tales, couldn't you?" said Thornby. "It seems a little bit too convenient that your magic doesn't work on me for some mysterious reason. I would like to believe you. I am even *inclined* to believe you. You seem as if you're a truthful sort of fellow, mostly. But you do see my problem?"

"You want to see some magic. All right. What?"

Thornby looked at him wide-eyed. "What can you do?"

"I work with materials. I could ask that decanter its history, if you like, especially what it knows of magic."

"You could make that up. How would I know? What about that glass eye thing—you thought it would make you invisible, didn't you? I want you to do that to someone else. I want to stand right next to you and ask them if they see you. Fair enough?"

"If you like."

"Now? Do you have it on you?"

For answer, John took out the items for the charm; the glass eye, the sand in its oilskin bag, and the spancel, coiled like a sleeping snake. "Where do you want me to do it?"

"Here, near the candles, where the light's best. Once you're set up, I shall lure someone in. One of the servants probably, so I hope it'll work or you'll develop a reputation for oddity to surpass mine."

"It'll work."

John put the charm together, laying the spancel in a circle on the carpet, setting the sand, nestling the glass eye on top, and sending magic through them. He straightened to find Thornby watching him, half smiling. It felt bizarre to stand within a charm he knew to be sound, and for it to have no effect. More than bizarre; positively unsettling.

"It works with everyone else," John said defensively, but a sudden doubt crossed his mind. If Thornby could see him—and he clearly could—was the charm losing efficacy?

"Even if you're gulling me, it's worth it to see you standing there," said Thornby, smiling. "You look like an obscure mediaeval saint with his attributes; St Blake who was martyred by a grain of sand in the eye."

John crossed his arms. No one had ever teased him about magic before. They had feared him, or hated him, or respected him. But no one had ever made a joke of it. He wasn't sure he liked it.

"Get away with you. I'm not standing here all night," he said.

"Only your eyes give you away, Mr Blake. They're not saintly at all sometimes, are they?"

And before John could say anything else, Thornby had vanished down the dark passage. John stood, arms crossed over his chest, that last remark ringing uncomfortably in his ears. Had he given himself away so obviously? Did it matter? He wasn't sure how he'd come to be here—why did he have to prove anything to Thornby? And yet, somehow, he did. The wounds on Thornby's face were a reminder of why.

He could feel the magic flowing around the items on the ground. It blocked out the whisperings of Raskelf, giving him a few moments of peace, until he heard Thornby's voice again.

"Let's go into the Blue Room. It's more private."

And Lady Amelia replying, "If you like."

Thornby let his aunt precede him into the room. He looked at John, then at his aunt.

"By the by, you haven't seen Mr Blake anywhere, Aunt Amelia?"

"That peculiar fellow? No, I haven't."

"Are you sure? You don't think he might be in this room?"

Lady Amelia glanced around the room, her gaze going straight through John. "Of course not. Why? Do you think he's one of your father's spies?"

Thornby stared at John open-mouthed, then glanced back at his aunt and back to John. John frowned and nodded his head meaningfully at Lady Amelia. Thornby blinked at him, shaking his head in wonder, then realised he must keep up his end of the conversation.

"Uh, no," Thornby said. "He seemed all right."

"I think he's peculiar," Lady Amelia said firmly.

"You think everyone's peculiar." Thornby grinned at her, then gave John a delighted sideways smile.

Lady Amelia gave an unladylike snort. "Of course you're all peculiar. Anyone who chooses to live on Porridge Island must be mad. Tcha! England! Suet puddings and rain."

Thornby and his aunt smirked at each other. This was clearly an on-going conversation between them. For the first time, John could see a family resemblance. Thornby looked nothing like his father, but he and his aunt had the same willowy build, and her hair sprang from her brow in a similar manner.

"Now, Soren—" she began.

"A moment, Aunt Amelia, I want to stand over here."

To John's alarm, Thornby walked over to him, turned, and got inside the spancel with him. John had to step hastily backwards to make room, trying desperately to keep heels and elbows inside the spancel and off the sand.

"What the devil are you doing?" he hissed in Thornby's ear. Thornby's silk-clad buttocks were pushing lightly against his groin in a way that was very distracting.

Lady Amelia advanced. "Why do you want to stand there? Are you quite all right, Soren?"

"Yes, I'm all right, Aunt. I just wanted to apologise. For making a scene."

"Oh, there's no need to apologise, boy. We both know what he is; he deserves all he gets. I—I'm glad you remember your mother. I wish I'd met her. She was the most beautiful woman alive, you know, when you were a child. Everyone said so. Not that *he* ever wrote, but I had contacts in Cairo at the time and they told me. And I saw the society pages in *The Times*."

"Yes, I know. But I must stop rising to the bait at the dinner table, mustn't I? Or we shall all be thin as rakes by Christmas."

She laughed. "Come, walk me to my room. I've sent that silly girl to bed, so we can sit and have a nightcap."

"All right, if you think you're up to it." Thornby took her arm, then half-turned, looking John in the eye. "A quick one. I'll look for Mr Blake in his room afterwards."

John nodded.

"If you like, dear," Aunt Amelia said. "But what you want with such a dull fellow I don't know. At luncheon he went on and on about foundries and glazing. I can't think *why* he thought we'd be interested. These modern types—all they care about is making money. Not that I wouldn't like a little myself, but it's so tedious to talk about, isn't it?"

Thornby shot John one last look over his shoulder as they left the room. "Very dull," he agreed, with a glint in his eye.

Chapter Five

John paced in his room, waiting for Thornby. He could not stop thinking of the moment Thornby had smiled and said, "Your eyes give you away." He hadn't seemed disgusted or offended. Was he—oh God—could he be *interested*? John found he'd groaned aloud.

Had that light contact between them in the spancel been a tease, or just chance? Thornby had certainly kept his presence of mind. By stepping into the spancel he'd managed to prove for himself that the magic worked on John but not on him.

But how many drinks was he going to have with his aunt? John wiped the palms of his hands on his trousers. This was ludicrous; he was fretting for a man who probably only wanted his professional skills. No wonder Thornby seemed interested. He must be desperate to get away, and John must be his first real hope in over a year.

John caught sight of the hatbox, half pushed under the bed. He would use the time before Thornby arrived to take another look at that hedgehog. In the stables, he'd worked with touch alone and found nothing. Now he would bring his materials into play. If he could pinpoint whatever was odd about the creature, maybe he'd discover something about the spell—or whatever it was—that bound Thornby to the estate.

He lit a branch of candles and took the lid off the hatbox. The hedgehog froze, then began trying to climb out, feet scrabbling on the sides of the box, nose snuffing. John refreshed its saucer of water and felt in his pocket for the crust of bread and walnuts he'd got from the kitchen. The hedgehog fell upon these hungrily and John quested towards it with magic. As before, there seemed to be nothing to find. And yet, there came again that faint hint of something unseen.

The staff had strict instructions not to enter his room unless he rang, and it didn't matter if Thornby saw him at it. He rolled back the carpet, opened his trunk and took out powdered lapis and the Osiris amulet. He charged the amulet and sprinkled a pinch of lapis on the hedgehog. Nothing.

Perhaps a more rustic approach. Moly might work. Montpelier moly seemed best, given the time of year. He opened the tin and allowed the pungent smell to waft towards the hedgehog. Nothing. He put a pinch of the dried herb in front of the creature. It sniffed it, sneezed, and went back to its walnut.

Maybe something stronger. He began to lay the salt in a reveal sigil—the Peacock's Tail—yet as he did so, he felt the salt trying to tell him something. It happened occasionally. It was a side-effect of working with materials. Most men, even materials men, didn't notice the silent things, the inanimate things, trying to talk to them. But, for John, it had always been a distraction. To have one's salt babbling something could cause one's focus to slip and the magic to lose efficacy.

His masters at the Institute had told him to discard his salt and other basic materials more often. Other men swept their salt into the fire when they'd finished with it, or kicked out the sigil and left the mess for the maid. But John, the son of a shopkeeper who straightened bent nails for re-sale, and a mother who washed and reused the bloody string from butcher's parcels, still found himself quite unable to do that.

So, although he felt a fool every time he swept up his salt—sometimes gathering it, grain by grain, with the tip of his finger—he did it anyway. By now, he'd worked with this salt for years. And while he knew it was merely the fancy of a man who worked alone and lived alone, he sometimes felt that it liked him and the magic he sent through it. He felt the same about some of his other materials. They almost had personalities.

This evening, the salt was putting the Woden's Eye sigil into his mind, which was strange because he never used it. It was obsolete. The only reason he recognised it was because it was used in teaching as an example of how the power of a once-strong and certain sigil could fade over the centuries. Yet he knew the looping, rambling lines well enough.

His hand wobbled as he made the Peacock's Tail and he had to sweep up his mistake and do it again.

"Concentrate," he muttered, unsure whether he was addressing the salt or himself.

He finished the Peacock's Tail and ran magic through it. The hedgehog drank some water and started another walnut. Nothing.

John sat back on his heels, stumped. Thornby would be here any moment and find him crouched on the floor with a puzzled look on his face. Thornby, with his tight breeches and that cool, cut-glass voice that could as easily humiliate as set your blood on fire.

More to keep busy than anything, John began to arrange the salt into the loops and curves of the Woden's Eye. It called for the devil's toenails—seven of them. He added those and set all humming with magic. The hedgehog finished crunching pieces of walnut, and started on the crust. But, did it look a little larger? No, it was a trick of the light.

Wasn't it?

John turned back to the trunk for a handful of large iron pins. They looked rather like ladies' hat pins, but made for Valkyries twelve feet tall and impatient of furbelows. He used the pins often and they had become convenient power-sinks, enabling him to focus elsewhere while maintaining his original flow of magic. The iron, like the salt, seemed to welcome him, glad of the heat and life of magic. He set them around the Woden's Eye where they balanced, quivering impossibly on their points, and sent a ward through them. Now everything was contained under a glowing orange-red dome of power, the hedgehog and sigil on the inside, himself on the outside. Nothing could get past the pins.

The hedgehog dropped the crust and looked at him, cocking its head like a curious dog. Then, there it was again—that sensation so fleeting that it was barely there. It came again, and again, and resolved itself as a strain of music; a silvery piping, a tinkle of bells. The hedgehog had grown unmistakably larger and was still growing. It reared up and stood on its two hind legs in the hatbox.

John waited, every sense alert, for a flood of magic to spill from the creature—not affecting him, but telling its tale; what it was doing, how it was doing it, and a bit about the person who had done it. But he felt nothing—or almost nothing. It was like the time with Thornby on Howarth's moorland: magical effect without magical cause. Which was impossible. His heart was pounding. He hastily strengthened the ward connection between the pins.

Yet the hedgehog, now the size of a small child, with spines as long as his hand, and teeth like a terrier, was still just itself. There was no magic on it, apparently. It stepped out of the hatbox and stretched its forelegs in a remarkably human gesture. Its face had changed too, to some hybrid of hedgehog and human. It had an insouciant air, which reminded him distantly of Thornby. Could this somehow be Thornby's creature? Had Thornby just played him for the biggest fool in the world? Was Thornby a magical genius who'd discovered a way to conjure undetectable spells?

The hedgehog sidled to the edge of the sigil and began to walk into the wards. John scrambled to his feet, cold with horror and disbelief. It shouldn't have been able to touch them. He'd once seen a man caught in a sheet of flame in a foundry accident, and it had looked just like this; the dark figure plunging through the living fire. But this fire was orange-red magic, and the hedgehog did not fall, but kept walking, dragging the magic with it across the room towards the far wall. Now the dome of magic was stretched, the way a glass-blower stretches molten glass, with the creature at one end and the sigil at the other. Christ, what if it broke? He needed to strengthen it, now.

He lunged for more pins, but before he could reach them, the ward exploded in a spray of red sparks and discordant musical notes. He was knocked off his feet, but somehow did not land on the floorboards. Torn shreds of the ward were whirling around and he was whirling with them, helpless as an autumn leaf. The silvery music grew louder. Now it was like being in the midst of a symphony orchestra playing full tilt. But it was playing no tune he could follow. And it *hurt*. He clapped his hands to his ears, but it made no difference. The music was inside his head. It was in his bones, in his blood. He was breathing it in. Christ, what to do? This was what came of listening to materials. He twisted in the air and managed to grab the open lid of the trunk. It was too late for pins. He pulled his personal ward stone from his pocket, flinging power into it until its golden glow lit up his fist and cocooned him as he hung in the air above his trunk.

The hedgehog creature turned to look at him. It was silhouetted against a new white glow of magic that seemed to be coming from the wall. Then, a host of creatures came streaming out of the whiteness towards him. Not people, not demons, but something else: women with the faces of owls, a stag with wings. There were green-eyed girls with leaves for hair, a pair of thin naked boys with bright blue skin, a hag with blackthorn fingers, and a huge shaggy dog, red with white spots like a toadstool. They were reaching for him, grabbing him with hands and claws and jaws. And their power was a musical storm, a magical lightning strike. They had him, and his magic was nothing to them.

He tried to knock them away, but there were too many. They were also grabbing at the golden streams of light from the ward stone, tearing the magic and pulling it like ropes to get a better purchase on him. Then an overwhelming pulse of music—or was it magic?—surged over him, and he was embedded in the strangeness like a fly in amber, the tatters of the ward stone in his hand getting dimmer and dimmer, until he knew no more.

***

Thornby took another shaky mouthful of brandy, perched on a cushion in Aunt Amelia's sitting room. In her youth, she'd travelled extensively in the Middle East, and she disapproved of chairs on principle.

His heart was pounding, his hands trembling, mind racing. Blake had done it! By God, he had done it! Magic was real. And not a demon to be seen! And Blake had said he would stay and help. He was curious; he was interested. He was bloody marvellous!

Whatever Father was doing, Thornby had a possible ally. The weight of months of anguish and self-doubt had fallen away. All of Father's snide hints about lack of character, all of his own fears about secretly wishing to obey—all gone, all fallen to dust when Blake stood inside that peculiar measuring tape and Aunt Amelia looked right through him.

So, he, Thornby, was still stuck here, so Blake's magic did not work on him for some mysterious reason. These things seemed, not insignificant, but surmountable. Blake would help him. Maybe Blake could tell Father, "Let your son leave," in some magic voice and Father would have to do it. Why, Thornby might be able to get away this very night!

And when he went, perhaps Blake might go with him? That look in Blake's eyes—as if he'd tear Thornby's breeches off and fuck him right there on the old Savonnerie carpet in the blue room. *Christ!* He shifted uncomfortably on the cushion. These damned tight breeches hid nothing. Did magicians do it like ordinary men? What tricks might a man like Blake have up his sleeve? Surely Thornby hadn't been imagining it? He could barely drink; his hand kept chinking the glass against his teeth. Aunt Amelia thought he was terribly upset and hiding it. She kept asking him to stay, to have another brandy.

But he excused himself and made his way on quivering legs to Blake's room. He knocked and waited. No answer. He knocked again, more impatiently. Damn it, where was the man? Thornby had made it clear he would come here. He knocked a third time, opened the door a crack and said, "Mr Blake?" round the side. Still no answer. He opened the door and stood transfixed on the threshold. If Blake's invisibility trick had impressed him, this turned his already shaking knees to jelly.

Blake's room was lit with a green-white light that emanated from a woodland path. The path, lined by tall trees, started in the middle of the room and seemed to wend its way through several walls and neighbouring rooms. Thornby thought he could see Blake in the distance, apparently standing in a sunlit glade a hundred yards away. He couldn't be sure; it was a figure, certainly, and who else could it be but Blake? Yet the figure's stance was slumped, not an attitude he associated with the upright Mr Blake.

Thornby closed the door behind him and took a step closer.

It really was utterly marvellous the way moss and huge forest oaks seemed to be growing straight out of the dusty floorboards. Was it an illusion? He reached out—would it hurt to touch it? Would it ruin it?—and touched the bark of the nearest tree. It was cold as ice, but it was definitely there. The path was slightly concave, as if it was often travelled, and the moss looked cool and soft.

He backed away, looking around the shabby spare room. Everything else seemed quite as normal, except for a large travelling trunk with the lid thrown open. Inside it was all manner of jars, bottles, pouches, boxes, vials, and objects so peculiar it was impossible to guess what they were for. There were some strange pale shapes that might be ceramic replicas of a human heart, human lungs, a human brain. There was a jar full of tentacles, and several painted wooden butterflies that could almost be children's toys.

He looked back down the woodland path. Was he supposed to walk down it, to find Blake? They had arranged to meet here, after all. Had Blake conjured this up to prove twice over what he could do? Or maybe this was it; the way out of Raskelf! Maybe if he took this path he'd find London at the end of it, Father notwithstanding.

He approached the path again. The light coming through the leaves now looked warmer, less green-white, more gold. How good it would feel to remove shoes and stockings and bury his sore foot in the cool moss of the pathway. He could hear faint, silvery music. It was beautiful, and he should walk down there to meet whatever was coming next.

Maybe this was Blake's idea of flirting? Maybe this was how magicians impressed one, before the clothes came off? It was certainly more novel than the bottle of hock and bit of Byron that had started Thornby's last affaire. He almost stepped onto the path again.

At the very edge of his hearing he could hear someone shouting. Was it Blake? It was the very thing Blake had complained of; there was *something* he couldn't put his finger on, like an itch somewhere deep inside. But surely whatever happened would be better than staying at Raskelf. He took a deep breath and stepped onto the path. He thought again that he heard shouting, but that silvery music swelled up from somewhere and he took another step, and another.

What had seemed like a long path suddenly shrank to nothing and the dark figure of Blake was now only a few yards away.

"Get out, Thornby, it's a trap!"

Blake's voice was oddly husky. Thornby whirled, to look back along the path, but it had vanished, and he now stood in a clearing in a dense wood. The walls of Raskelf were nowhere to be seen. Next to him Blake appeared to be imprisoned in a thorn-bush, only the thorns were made of something hard and clear as glass and so bright they dazzled. Blake looked different too. It took Thornby a moment to realise Blake's chin was covered in dark stubble, and yet when they'd parted in the blue room barely twenty minutes ago, Blake had been clean-shaven. And Blake looked exhausted, with lines of strain around his eyes and mouth. His lips were cracked and dry.

"Run!" Blake said urgently, pointing. "That way. Go. *Now!*"

***

John had watched in horror as Thornby opened the door to his room and gaped at the woodland pathway. It was clear to him then that Thornby hadn't hoodwinked him in any way. No one could fake the look on Thornby's face, he was certain of it. But he could see that Thornby was thinking of walking down the path, and although the creatures that had put John here appeared to have gone, he was sure they were hiding, waiting. He shouted warnings, but his voice died the moment it left his mouth. It was like shouting into a gale.

Thornby made his decision and stepped onto the path. And the path vanished, and he was suddenly right next to Blake in the enchanted woodland clearing.

"What's happened? Did Father do this?" Thornby said.

"No. Go! Find the path. It might appear if you get close."

For answer, Thornby put his hands on the glistening thorns and pulled at them.

"Leave it. I've tried. Go and look for the path before they come back."

"Who?" Thornby looked around hastily. "What is this place?"

"You've never been here before?"

"What?" Thornby almost laughed, though his gaze kept darting to the woods, and John could see him trembling. "Yes, I come here all the time, you idiot. Nothing I like better than a stroll in the woods in a spare bedroom. Christ, what is this place? What should we do?"

"Don't mention Christ, for one thing. If I'm guessing right, the people here aren't—well, they're not human. And they're easily offended, so be polite if you see anything living, whether it looks like a person or not. Now, will you go!"

Thornby bit his lip but didn't move. "This is bad, isn't it? You weren't expecting this."

"I wasn't. But this is what I could sense; that strange feeling I told you about. This is the heart of it. My magic doesn't work here."

"Why not?"

"I think my magic only works in the human world. This is a different place. You'll have to be brave, Thornby, but I think—" John broke off, wondering how many of his suspicions to tell him.

John had woken hours ago to find himself trapped. The thorn-bush looked brittle as ice, but it was impossible to break, either by brute force or by magic. He'd tried every release sigil he could think of, every counter-spell, every kind of ward. Nothing had worked. It was like a nightmare. No magic. No power. The horror of it had nearly panicked him one point, the fear and the helplessness rising up, paralysing his mind. He'd crouched on the grass in his spiky prison, eyes tight shut, forcing himself to breathe. But after a while, when the creatures did not come back, he'd found himself able to think more clearly. Perhaps he had no magic, but he still had his wits. He could still reason. He could still bargain, if it came to it. And so he had begun to plan and to think. And after a while he had found himself thinking of Thornby.

He couldn't help staring at Thornby now. He could tell that only minutes had passed for Thornby since they'd talked in the blue saloon. He could smell the brandy on Thornby's breath. Oh, what he'd give for a slug of brandy himself right now! Or better, a drink of water.

So, how much to tell Thornby?

How do you tell a man you think he may not be quite human?

Thornby looked human enough, yet the facts were suggestive. That same fleeting oddness John had noticed about Thornby and the hedgehog—and now John had been caught in the epicentre of that oddness for the last twelve hours.

As a child, John had listened to fairy stories on his mother's knee in the stuffy little kitchen behind the shop. As a slightly older boy, he'd read Tam Lin, and begged stories from the Irish washer-woman on washing day, and she'd told him of Fionn MacCoull and the Fianna and their adventures in the many-coloured land. And then he'd gone away to the Institute, trained as a magician, grown up, and completely forgotten everything he ever knew about this other world. Because fairies weren't real and neither was fairy-land.

And yet, here he was. And here too was Thornby. A man who was impervious to John's magic, as the beings here seemed impervious. A man who was bound in some mysterious way to the estate, not with human magic, but with some power John couldn't detect beyond that faint, vague strangeness.

So how *do* you tell a fellow you suspect he isn't human? John didn't know how to begin. They had bigger worries at the moment.

"Thornby, I think you might get out, even if I can't. Go and look for the path, and if you find it, don't leave it. Will you tell Lady Dalton to get her cousin to tell Rokeby what happened. Got it? Tell Rokeby I used the Woden's Eye sigil in salt, and to bring anyone he can."

"I'm not leaving you here."

"Go *on*. I don't want your bloody noblesse oblige."

"It's not that. If you're stuck here, I can't get away from Raskelf. I'm not—"

"Will you bloody well leave? Damn, *look*!"

Thornby spun around to face the procession of creatures that was coming out of the woods. John saw him wobble and cut his hand on one of the thorns as he grabbed it for support. The procession formed into a rough semi-circle about them and a woman stepped forward from the crowd. She wore a golden diadem which seemed to grow directly from her skin, and long copper-red hair. Her breasts were bare, and great folds of green satin grew out of her slender waist and fell to the moss. Her face was narrow and marvellously beautiful, marked with a pattern of blue lines and dots on forehead and cheeks. Her eyes were black as sloes and had no whites to them.

"My lady." Thornby's voice was a croak. His bow was jerky. Yet John felt a sudden leap of hope. *Be polite*, he'd said, and it seemed Thornby had listened.

The lady clapped her hands and smiled at Thornby. Her teeth were sharp as a cat's. "Oh, you're a pretty one!" Her voice was melodious as a stream. She had a strange accent, so 'pretty' sounded like 'praty'. She reached out a white hand. "What has it done to its face?" She stepped forward, and a goat's hoof peeped from under her skirts. John could see Thornby steeling himself not to flinch as she touched him.

"Poor little sweetling." She stroked Thornby's face. "It isn't whole."

"It's broken," growled the huge red dog. "Let's put it out of its misery. I'll bite its throat out."

"No!" John said loudly, before he could stop himself.

Thornby took a step backwards and bowed again, more gracefully this time. "I'm not miserable, I assure you, sir. I—er—how could I be unhappy when such beauty is before me?"

The lady smiled again, a terrifying sight, her cat's teeth gleaming white. "See, Pooka! Oh, he's pretty! Let's keep him!"

The dog sniffed at Thornby's silk stockings. Its feet were the size of dinner plates. "They're never nice for long," it growled. "Let's have it now, while it's fresh."

"Does it hurt, beautiful one?" the queen crooned to Thornby. She was again stroking his face. His back was rigid with tension. Sweat had sprung out on his brow, but he was schooling his face, wearing a social smile.

She began to hum a lilting melody, as if she were alone, stroking a pet. "And such a long way from home! What are you doing here? Did you come to look for me?"

"I, we, got here by mistake—er— Since you're here, my lady, will you let my friend out?" said Thornby. "If it pleases you. I think he's finding it tiresome in there."

"Friend?" The lady frowned. "*Friend?*"

"Well, perhaps *friend*'s a bit strong. But he is our guest. And it's bad form to let a guest get lost in the woods in his own bedroom, don't you know?"

The queen hissed. Possibly she was laughing. She gave John a sideways glare. "He prickles. And smells. He is full of gramarye, that one." She smiled again at Thornby. "You don't want *him*, do you? You could come dancing with *me*!"

She raised her arms above her head and took a few steps across the moss, so graceful she seemed hardly to touch the ground. When her skirts moved, John heard silvery music. While her attention was diverted, he tried again to make his ward stone work, throwing every ounce of power he had into it. It sat in his hand, lifeless as the pebble it had once been.

The queen held her hand out to Thornby, an inviting expression on her face. He bowed again. "My lady, compared to you, I dance like a donkey. I couldn't do you justice. Really, shouldn't we be going? We've taken up so much of your time already."

She lowered her hand, smile fading. "You won't dance? You won't stay?" She shrugged. "Well, then, what will you give me if I let you leave? A gift? A kiss?"

"I—" Thornby shot a look at John, who shook his head, as obviously as he dared. He hated to think what 'gift' might be asked of Thornby, or what a kiss might mean.

"What about a game?" said the red dog, licking its chops. "I like games better."

"All right, a game," said the queen. She walked in a circle around Thornby, forcing him to turn to keep facing her. "Perhaps you'll have a wager with me? How about this? Answer three questions truly, and you can have the guest."

"Don't," John said in a low voice. He suspected a trick, but didn't dare to say so, with her standing right there.

"Three questions?" Thornby put his head to one side and appeared to consider. "I don't think he's worth three. Perhaps one? An easy one?"

"One, is it?" The queen snarled. "So brave, my little fighting cock!" She broke off into peals of hissing laughter and the others joined her. The dog laughed so hard it seemed to dislocate its jaw.

Thornby shot John a look that said *What the hell do I do?* as clearly as if he'd spoken aloud. John said quietly, "Be careful. She'll cheat if she can."

The queen stopped laughing, abruptly. "All right. I'll give you a chance because I like your pretty face. Answer one truly and I'll let you leave. If you want him to leave with you, but somewhat *changed*, you must answer two. If you want to recognise him when you get back, it stands at three."

"I can't quite see it at the moment, but you know we're standing in my house, don't you?" said Thornby carefully. "I think I can leave when I like. So perhaps if I answer two?"

The queen tilted her head as if listening, sloe eyes not leaving Thornby. She smiled, slyly. "But it *isn't* your house. It's your father's. And you can't leave. Can you?"

She laughed again, and the court joined in, a cacophony of jeers and whinnies. Thornby glanced at John again, perhaps in order to see another human face. John tried to inject some reassurance into his expression, but he had none to give.

Thornby drew himself up. "Very well, I accept. Three questions. What's your first?"

"*My diamonds and pearls, in a box they are hid, with the sun for the satin and the sky for a lid.*" Her voice was mocking. "Where are they, sweetling, where do I keep my jewels?"

A look of disbelief crossed Thornby's face, and John almost groaned aloud. The question was impossible. How could anyone answer that? And yet, suddenly, Thornby's eyes glittered and he almost laughed.

"On the nasturtium leaves of course," he said. "In the sunken garden."

The uproar from the court was so violent that John thought the answer must be wrong and they planned to tear Thornby limb from limb without regard for the rules of the game. Thornby clearly thought so too, from the look of horror that crossed his face and the way he hunched defensively. Then the queen was snarling at them to shut up.

"Clever, isn't he?" she said, when at last the place was silent. Her voice was vicious. "But how about this? *The place is old, the house is new, the goose is red, the hound is blue; yet neither one is truly meet, which sign should grace Dezombrey's seat?* Which sign, little one? What's the real emblem of Raskelf?"

There was a long pause. Thornby turned to John, face appalled. "I don't know. It's been a red goose and a blue hound for centuries. How could it be anything else?"

"Think harder. You got the first one right."

"That was chance."

"You might know more than you think."

"All right." Thornby put a hand to his forehead. "Um, they found a mosaic of a bull when they moved the stables. Could it be that? A bull? I—"

Out of the corner of his eye, John saw something coming. One of the creatures from the watching crowd was advancing. He swung around to face it, trying again to charge the ward stone, though he knew in his heart it was pointless.

"Wait!" A note of panic entered Thornby's voice. "Give me a chance!"

But the creature came closer. John recognised it now, a small creature, half-hedgehog, half-human. It ignored Thornby entirely.

"Got any more o' them walnuts?" it said to John.

He stared at it open-mouthed for a moment. He could feel the eyes of the watching semi-circle of creatures, intent on his every move. Walnuts? At a time like this? But he pushed a hand into his pocket and found a few pieces of broken walnut mixed with fluff and breadcrumbs. He tipped them through the glass thorns into the creature's small clawed hand.

"Really, Tig!" said the queen, wrinkling her beautiful nose. "He stinks of gramarye! How can you?"

"I bean't fussy. Walnuts is me favourites." The creature put its other hand on the glass thorns and glanced at Thornby, beady eyes unreadable. "All right, poppet?" it said. Then it turned and went back into the crowd, crunching walnuts with its mouth open.

"Oh," Thornby said faintly.

"What?" John turned to him.

"The answer. But it can't be. It's just a stupid joke I have with myself."

"Say it. Don't second-guess. You got the first one right."

"All right." Thornby addressed the queen and the host of waiting figures. "It's a hedgehog. I've always thought the Hall resembles one, because of all the chimneys and turrets."

Again, uproar. Worse than before.

"So clever, so clever, so answer me this: Why can't you leave the estate?" The queen's eyes glittered—with malice, or with laughter, or perhaps with both?

Thornby's shoulders sagged. "That's not fair." John heard him mutter. Then Thornby stood straight again, and said loudly, "I tell you truly, I don't know."

"That's not an answer."

"I've told you truly. It's as true an answer as the first two. Now we'll go. Good day. So lovely meeting you."

Thornby pulled at the thorns again, and this time a huge branch broke off where the hedgehog had touched it. John kicked another and was free. The creatures were in uproar, jostling and shrieking, but at the same time hanging back, as though unsure whether the game had been won or not.

Then the red and white-spotted dog began to slink towards them, low on its belly, teeth bared. The others fell silent, and began to inch forward as well, creeping past the queen like a dark wave. She stood still, seeming to have lost interest. Did that mean they'd won? Or that she'd let the dog and the others take them? She was humming her lilting melody again, admiring a few strands of her coppery hair. John looked over his shoulder and saw the pathway open again, his room in the distance, a beam of sunlight streaming onto the wooden floorboards and the faint salt lines of the Woden's Eye sigil.

Thornby was standing, unmoving, facing the host of advancing creatures. John grabbed him roughly by the arm and pulled. They ran. Then the creatures found their voices, and they were running from squeals and gibbers, from reaching hands and flailing claws. John felt teeth at his heels, snapping like a guillotine.

They tore out of the trees into dusty midday sunshine in the guest room. John obliterated the sigil's lines with his boots, scattering salt, the devil's toenails flying to the corners of the room, his iron pins likewise. And the path closed with a screaming gurgle like water going down a narrow drain. A clawed hand reached for a moment out of empty air, and then that was gone, too.

Thornby stood bent over in the centre of the room, hands on his thighs, face white, breathing hard. Their eyes met and a sudden wild ecstasy filled John. They'd escaped! They were alive. And Thornby had done it. What mettle he'd shown.

John had used a lot of magic in that crystal thorn bush, trying to get out. He didn't stop to consider any other consequences. He took Thornby by the shoulders and pulled him upright. They were of a height. Thornby's eyes were the glowing grey of the sun behind cloud and his lips—

Thornby gave him an intense look which rapidly turned glassy, and sank to his knees, face grazing John's crotch as he did so, breath warm.

Then he threw up on John's boots.

Chapter Six

Thornby sat on the end of Blake's bed, trying to control the impulse to keep looking over his shoulder. He felt that, at any moment, something might claw its way out of the walls. His hands were shaking and he laced his fingers together and hooked them over his knee to still them.

Blake was kneeling on the floorboards beside an odd pattern of salt he'd laid out. He was rubbing bright blue powder onto an ordinary-looking key, which was absorbing the powder in a most unlikely way. Every so often, Blake touched the key to the salt. And although all this was hardly normal behaviour, Blake did it with such calm assurance that eventually Thornby's knotted muscles began to relax.

After Thornby had thrown up, Blake had taken charge. He'd brought water for them both to drink, and tidied up as efficiently as any servant. He'd offered Thornby brandy, which he hadn't been able to face. Then Blake had gone downstairs briefly, returning with bread and cheese. Not that Thornby had been able to face that either.

"What are you doing?" Thornby finally managed to say.

Blake gave him an appraising glance. "Making a chimera key. Today's Monday, so we've missed a night's sleep and breakfast. I think time works differently in that other place. Your father just sat down to lunch, so while he's out of the way, I'll go to his rooms, use this key to get in, and look around."

"You think he's got something in there that's holding me here?"

"Yes, a spell of some kind. His rooms, and your mother's old rooms, are the only places in the house I haven't looked. I'd have sworn he wasn't using magic; he just doesn't seem to have that kind of power. But where you're concerned, magic doesn't work the way I expect, so maybe I can't sense it because it's all aimed at you. Raskelf's a dashed difficult place to work. There's old magic everywhere. You've no idea how confusing it is. So, I need to get in there. I can tell a lot by touch once I'm in. I might find out a bit about this curse he seems to have on him, too."

"But can't you just tell him to let me leave? In that magic voice?"

"It wouldn't work. It has to be something at least vaguely acceptable to the person. And in any case, I've told him he invited me here. I can't tell him anything else until that wears off. Sorry, Thornby. Not that simple."

"I see." His heart sank, but only a little. Perhaps he hadn't really expected it to be that simple either. "Tell me, what's gramarye? Those creatures mentioned it."

"It's another word for magic. I think, for them, it means my kind of magic, human magic. Didn't think much of it, did they?" Blake held the key up and looked at it critically, head cocked to one side. "This'll be ready in a minute. You should get to a boundary. If I can break the spell, you'll be free. But don't let anyone see your face or you might have some explaining to do. She healed you; did you realise?"

Thornby put a hand to his cheekbone. The skin was as smooth as if he'd never been hurt. He looked at the back of his left hand; that too was whole. "Just like that, eh? Imagine what she could do in a hospital."

"Mmm, or she'd turn everyone into toads just for the fun of it."

"But she let us go, didn't she? In the end."

"Only because you answered the questions."

"That hedgehog thing helped us." He noticed the rose hips drooping from his lapel, tugged them off and crushed them in his fist.

"Thank goodness I gave it walnuts." Blake bent over his key intently. "You know, Thornby—that place—you could have stayed. She wanted you to. Would you rather have stayed than come back and dealt with all this? Because I could probably get you back there. If you wanted."

"Stay there? In that place? With those things? I hope you're joking. Didn't you see her feet? She had goat's hooves! And a dress that grew out of her middle!"

"Just because things are different doesn't mean we should fear them." Blake looked up from his key, blue powder all over his fingertips, his expression earnest. "I know most people wouldn't want to live there, but maybe you could belong. It'd be an escape of a kind, wouldn't it? She liked you. I think, in their way, they're decent enough to their lovers. I know it would be an unusual way to live, but—"

"Mr Blake, I can tell you categorically that fairy queens are not my type. Good Lord! Going back to her? I can't think of anything worse. I do *not* belong there. I'm certain of that."

"All right. Sorry. Just checking."

Blake put the key down, dusted his fingertips, and began sweeping the salt together with the side of his hand. A few grains got caught in a crack and he flicked them out with a small brush. He took an oilskin bag and began pouring handfuls of salt into it.

Thornby noticed for the first time that Blake had a nasty-looking gash on the back of his hand, presumably from that magical thornbush. Blake might well have mysterious powers, but he was clearly not omnipotent, or impervious to hurt. If they hadn't escaped, what would have happened to Blake? Part of him wanted to ignore the issue, as Blake seemed to be doing, but if something else happened, did he really want Blake's blood on his conscience?

"Mr Blake, it's not safe for you here, is it? If Raskelf's concealing some world where your magic doesn't work, well—what if they catch you again?" *Go on, say it.* "Shouldn't you leave?" *Christ, please don't leave. Please stay and help me.*

Blake was pressing his fingertips to the floorboards to pick up the last few grains of salt. He shrugged.

"I don't think it's peculiar to Raskelf. I think there are probably gateways all over the place. I didn't get in by chance. I know what I did." He glanced up, eyes amused. "Don't worry, I won't do it again."

Thornby wasn't sure the argument was entirely sound, but relief was warming him more thoroughly than Father's fine cognac ever had. Blake pocketed his bag of salt and stood up with the key. "If you hadn't come and answered those riddles, I'd still be there. Or dead by now. My thanks, Lord Thornby. You have a cool head under fire."

"Not that cool. I beg your pardon for the—unpleasantness." Thornby gestured towards the spot where he'd thrown up, feeling a fool for his loss of control.

Blake smiled. He had a trick of not smiling with his mouth; it was all in his eyes. They lit up, even as his mouth turned down at the corners.

"Being sick was quite dignified, considering. When I saw my first demon, I pissed myself. I was only ten, but still. Shows your breeding, doesn't it?"

Thornby gaped at him. "Demons? But, but—they weren't demons, were they?"

"No, no. Fairies. Demons are very different. But it's a similar feeling, I imagine."

"There are demons? Evil things with horns and fangs and so on?"

"Yes, of course. Most magicians get their power that way. They call up a demon and it does the magic for them. Theurgy, it's called."

"Then I saw one once," Thornby said slowly. "Running down the Strand in broad daylight. Like a hideous baboon, oozing red as if it had been skinned alive. No one else saw it, though." He could not suppress a shudder. A demon on the Strand. Barrelling past children, rustling ladies' crinolines and dodging through horses' legs.

Blake regarded him thoughtfully. "It was probably using an invisibility spell that didn't work on you. They don't usually let them run around like that. It had no skin, you say? Was this in '47?"

"Sounds about right."

"I remember the case. It killed its master and escaped. They tracked it down, of course, somewhere in Saffron Hill. And you saw it. Good heavens."

"What a horrible way to make magic."

"Yes, well, that's why they keep it so quiet. But theurgy is regarded as the better way. The 'Royal Road' they call it. My methods are considered rather common."

"Common," Thornby repeated faintly. Then he rallied. "Yes, but of course I knew that about you." When Blake was smiling, he really looked quite approachable. Thornby took a deep breath and said, deliberately, "Luckily, I like a bit of rough."

It was a bit of a risk. In fact, he was surprised at how hard his heart began pounding. But Blake didn't frown or turn away. He stood there, half smiling, accepting the tease. His dark eyes were remarkably expressive. He looked as if he'd like to stop talking and get down to business. Right now.

Thornby's mouth had gone dry. His pulse was roaring so loud in his ears that surely Blake would be able to hear it. So. Not a mistake, in the blue room. Mr Blake liked men, or at least, liked him. Now that was very, very interesting. He'd thought he had nothing to offer Blake, but obviously there was something that Mr Blake wanted. And he looked as though he wanted it very much indeed.

Which was damned exciting, too. Blake had a nice mouth. Nice broad shoulders. What else nice did he have tucked away beneath that very respectable tailoring?

Thornby looked away with an effort. After all, now was hardly the time. Not when escape from Raskelf might be just a few minutes away. He found himself gazing at the interior of Blake's huge trunk with its hundreds of bottles and boxes and mysterious shapes. "Anyway, it's a relief to know you haven't got any demons in that peculiar trunk of yours," he said.

Blake looked at the trunk as if remembering something. "Well. But, anyway, it's very small and well-contained. Not dangerous. You know, you're rather pale. You should have a mouthful of that brandy before you go."

"No, I shall come with you." Thornby stood, an urge to move sweeping through him.

"Why? You should get to the boundary. If I break this spell you should get as far away as possible. That reminds me." Blake reached into a pocket again. He seemed to have dozens; his tailor must make them for him specially. This time he pulled out a wallet, from which he took a five pound note. He held it out. "You'll get a long way on that if you're careful. I wouldn't stay in England because he'll probably come after you. That curse is driving him. I will try to stop it, though."

Thornby found himself staring at more of the needful than he'd seen in months. "I'm not taking your money. Good Lord, I should be paying you! I'm coming with you."

"But why? The whole point is to get you away from Raskelf."

"But it's not only about me, is it? What if some sprite pops out and asks you where it keeps its cuff-links? I've no idea how I managed to answer those questions. I suppose it was luck, but I was born here, after all. And I'm heir to this crumbling monstrosity, and maybe that gives me an edge. So, of course I'm coming. And then we'll both leave."

"What if someone sees your face?" But Blake was putting the money away. He seemed to have accepted that Thornby wasn't just going to run for it.

Thornby waved a dismissive hand. "I'll say I met a way-faring fellow with a miraculous liniment. No one believes anything I say anyway. Even Aunt Amelia doesn't really believe I can't leave the estate."

Blake considered him for a long moment. Thornby found himself unable to look away. The expression on Blake's face was difficult to identify—it was a searching look, as if he was trying to see something in Thornby that nobody had ever looked for before.

Or perhaps he was just wondering if Thornby was likely to throw up on him again.

Then Blake smiled. Not just with his eyes this time. It was an oddly vulnerable smile that made him look a lot younger. "Come on, then. Let's see what your father has hidden away."

"You'd better tell me what we're looking for. Salt lines, is it? Piles of sand?"

"Not necessarily. Look for anything you can't explain. Think of your most conservative friend; if it's not the kind of thing he'd have in his rooms, point it out to me."

Father's apartments had always been locked, as had mother's old rooms which connected to them. Even Mrs Diggins, the housekeeper, did not have keys, although Warren, Father's valet and chief henchman, did. Apart from some dim childhood memories, Thornby's mental map of the house had, for the last year and a half, had this blank space at its heart.

Watching Blake put the key in the lock of father's chamber and open the door was, well, *magical*.

***

John went into Lord Dalton's large, blue and gold bed-chamber. He started by asking the walls if they knew any secrets, trying to stay alert for the faintest trace of magic, however formless. He was very conscious of Thornby at his side, opening cabinet drawers and peering under the bed.

At his side.

With him.

During his time at the Crystal Palace, John had fought off several attacks: the possessed bats, the insinuations of Barchiel, the pathetic shatter spell those Tory architects turned out to have paid a fortune for. The bats had nearly been the death of him. But Paxton had been relying on him, and him alone. John hadn't expected anyone's help. It hadn't occurred to Paxton to offer it, nor him to ask for it. At the Institute they'd always taught independence. It was one of the pillars of discretion.

So, when Thornby had said *Of course I'm coming*, it was like being given a marvellous gift, even if it was one he shouldn't have accepted. For once, not to be alone. Being trapped in that crystal thorn-bush had frightened him more than he cared to remember. He was lucky to be alive. That was the last bloody time he would take magical advice from a pound of salt! To have someone along now who might be utterly ignorant of magical methods, but who might nonetheless be able to help if something happened—

It was such a buoyant, *happy* feeling. Happiness, in the middle of this bizarre mystery! He kept trying to put it aside, and it kept bubbling up. A gift.

His strong suspicion that Thornby was connected to that other place had not abated, but it was impossible to think of him as anything other than a man, and a brave one at that. John had to avoid glancing at him though; if he looked for a moment, he wouldn't want to look away. And then he'd forget himself again. Although, perhaps Thornby would like that? The knowledge that Thornby might truly be interested in him was making it well nigh impossible to think of anything else. He'd been at a stand ever since Thornby had said, "I like a bit of rough," with that plummy accent and those wanton eyes. Thornby would probably fuck like an officer about to go back to a posting. He had that edgy look about him, all nerves and desperation.

He would probably do absolutely anything.

John closed his eyes for a moment. Must concentrate. He was here to do a job. It wouldn't do for Lord Dalton or his valet to come up and find them here.

There were a couple of rooms off Lord Dalton's bedroom. One was a dressing room; John rifled through tweed suits and town suits and shirts and under-things, sticks and shoes and hats. The most well-worn of Dalton's outfits seemed to be a nautical looking cap, and a couple of thick jerseys of the type usually worn by sailors. Odd. But perhaps the Marquess preferred to be incognito when he was about his business at the coast. The jerseys had the faintest whiff of the curse about them—a suggestion of shit, spite, and rotting fish—but it was no more than a suggestion. The jerseys seemed to hold no clue. Probably they had just absorbed a bit of the reek from their owner from being worn so much.

In the sitting-room-cum-study next door John found a number of deeds for properties in the west of Scotland. To judge from some of the other letters and paperwork, Dalton was in the process of buying more. There were some nautical charts, and a couple of ledgers with records of payments to ships' captains. He supposed all this was to do with Dalton's commercial seaweed-growing scheme.

He searched the coal scuttle, the mantelpiece, checked behind the pictures and under the rug. There was nothing that looked remotely like the makings of a spell, let alone one powerful enough to keep a man trapped in one place for over a year.

He crossed back through the bed-chamber, where Thornby was still searching, and opened the connecting door to the first Lady Dalton's room with the chimera key. He went in and drew back a curtain a few inches, sending clouds of dust cascading down. Daylight showed what had once been an elegant lady's boudoir furnished in sky blue, gold and white—the feminine equivalent to the gentleman's room he'd just left. Now it was festooned with cobwebs, and grey with dust. Sensing Thornby at his shoulder, John re-locked the inter-connecting door.

"Mother's room. It hasn't changed a bit," Thornby said. He sounded like a man in a dream. "There's the picture with the lion. And the seashell; she used to hold it to my ear. It's dusty. She wouldn't have liked that."

"Let's look around," said John.

"He wouldn't hide a spell in here, would he?"

John knew what he meant; the room had a holy feel, a shrine to the dead woman. He put his hand to the wall. "It does feel empty. Of magic, anyway."

Thornby had opened a small writing desk. He froze, staring at a couple of tin soldiers standing at the front. "Those were mine," he said slowly, half to himself. "They were my favourites. I left them here to look after her because I had to go to school." He picked one up. "They were supposed to be enemies. One blue, you see, and one red. But they were friends. They had all kinds of adventures."

There were not many papers in the desk. Perhaps the first Lady Dalton had not been much of a correspondent. John picked up a couple of loose sheets. The first seemed to be menu ideas, the second some instructions to a dressmaker. The letters wandered about the page, large and looping. The spelling was rudimentary, at best. It was not the hand of a well-educated lady. "Is that her writing?"

"She never cared about it. She used to say I must write her letters for her. She laughed about it. I say, look over there—there are tracks in the carpet where the dust is worn away. Father must come in here sometimes. They come from his room."

Sure enough, a darker path across the dusty carpet led from the door to Lord Dalton's room to a set of blue velvet drapes on an inside wall. John followed the path across the room and pulled the cord of the drapes.

They parted to show a life-size portrait of the most beautiful woman imaginable. She was so lovely, it was difficult to look away. Her dark hair was dressed in a bun, but several tendrils curled around her fine-boned face. Her mouth was well-modelled and sensuous, and her grey eyes so beautiful one could have gazed into them forever. They were large as a doe's, tumultuous as the sea on a stormy day, and ever so slightly slanted. Around her neck was a string of pearls the exact shade of her milky bosom. She was shown half standing, caught forever in the act of rising to her feet. She wore a gauzy white dress in the fashion of the twenties, and was surrounded by huge pink and white roses and a marble column. A wolfhound with a blue collar lay at her feet, gazing at her adoringly.

There was such life in the picture you felt she would step out of it and whirl you round the room. And yet, there was something sad about her too, a subtle tension in her jaw, longing in her beautiful eyes. She was joy and sorrow and beauty and pain. John, who had never desired a woman in his life, felt that even he could have fallen in love with her.

A beautiful woman. Yet the more he looked, the more he was sure she was not a human woman at all. Her eyes. The way her mouth curled at the corners. The whole damned feel of her. She was beautiful all right. She was perilously fair. Because she wasn't human.

She was from that other place. Earlier, he had merely suspected that Thornby somehow had links to that place. Now he knew exactly who the link was.

No wonder Lord Dalton seemed half mad. This was what he had lost.

And no wonder John hadn't been able to sense the source of the curse. If she had done it using fair folk magic, it would be as difficult to detect as everything else about that place.

"Your mother," John said. It wasn't a question; there was such a strong resemblance. And yet he needed to hear Thornby confirm it.

Thornby nodded, looking a bit choked up. "It's by Lawrence," he said eventually. "It wasn't finished when I went off to school. God, she's just as I remember her."

John looked at the portrait again. He couldn't help thinking of his own mother as she'd been when he was a child—her coarse, black hair and pock-marked skin, her kind, tired eyes, her hands red and roughened with work. And Thornby had had that fantastic creature as his mother—all light and softness and gaiety and fire. What must it have been like? John could not imagine.

He must tell Thornby what he'd realised. Now.

God, what an awkward thing to have to tell a man. But Thornby had just been in that other place—perhaps even now he saw the resemblance between the fairy queen and his mother. Perhaps even now he was beginning to guess what that made him.

The silence was broken by the muffled sound of a door opening and closing.

"Father's room," Thornby said under his breath, eyes widening. "*Father.*"

John closed the drapes over the picture. Thornby shut the desk and the curtains. Then they heard a key in the lock of the inter-connecting door. Perhaps the Marquess had a fancy to gaze at his first wife's portrait and torment himself again with what he'd lost. Or perhaps he'd heard some small noise.

They fled through the passage door and John locked it silently behind them with the chimera key. They had turned their backs to walk down the passage when they heard a key in *that* door too. Had they disturbed the dust? Had the Marquess noticed?

Thornby muttered something under his breath and pulled John through the next door along. It opened onto one of Raskelf's many dust-sheeted guest rooms; black beetles scuttled off into the empty fire grate as they entered. John locked the door, listening intently. When it seemed certain they weren't being pursued, he turned and leaned on it, closing his eyes in relief. It would be much, much better if Lord Dalton remained ignorant of their search.

When he opened his eyes, Thornby was standing directly in front of him, so close they were almost touching. And there was no mistaking his expression.

"Well, Mr Blake?" Thornby said.

***

As Thornby leant forward to kiss him, Blake caught his jaw and held it. Maybe Blake didn't kiss. A pity, but some men didn't. Thornby put his hand on Blake's crotch, feeling him hardening through the wool of his trousers; a nice, thick cock from the feel of it. Thornby was about to undo the fly, when Blake grabbed his wrist as well and held that too, firmly. Was Blake grabbing it to stop him, or to make him stay? Thornby raised an eyebrow.

"No?"

Blake squeezed his wrist a little tighter, immobilising him.

"Wait," Blake said, through clenched teeth, his voice strained.

Oh Lord, had Thornby misread the situation? Surely not. The way Blake had been looking at him earlier had seemed unmistakable. Thornby had played his cards openly enough. And Blake had smiled at that nonsense about liking a bit of rough. But now—they were still standing here, unmoving, with Blake holding his jaw and wrist in a smarting grasp.

So, what the devil was going on? Was Blake wrestling with his conscience? Was he afraid of being found? Or was standing stock-still and holding his partner in a vice-like grip simply some unusual sexual predilection? Blake had his eyes closed now. His mouth was moving slightly, as though in prayer. Thornby tried to move away a little, to give Blake room, if that was what he needed.

"Are you all right?" Thornby asked. "We don't have to, you know."

Blake said, in strangled tones, "I want to. *Wait*."

Well, that was clear enough, and, actually, Blake's grip was quite—exciting. The back of Blake's hand, crushed between them, was pushing against Thornby's cock. He pressed against it a little harder. He tried to free his wrist again, to touch Blake, or to move away, and could not. He was hard himself now, achingly so.

Blake smelt heavenly—of fresh sweat and maleness and faintly of some spicy herb. He was warm too; heat seemed to radiate from him, almost visible in the cold air of the spare room. Thornby pushed against him, and ran his fingertips over the inch or two of Blake's cock that seemed to be all he was allowed to touch. God, it was fucking torment! It had been over a year and a half since anything even half as exciting had happened. He'd probably spend in his drawers if Blake let him. He realised he was holding his breath and let it out. It came out in a whimper; of lust or of anguish, he wasn't sure. Maybe both.

Then, so suddenly it made him gasp, Blake let go of his wrist and jaw, grabbed the back of his head and pulled him forward into a kiss, rough and frantic. Blake's stubble grazed Thornby's lips. So, Blake had made up his mind. Thank God.

Blake pulled away and began tearing at the front of Thornby's breeches with both hands. He was having trouble with the old-fashioned placket. Perhaps he'd never encountered one before. He almost snarled at it, dark eyes narrowed as if he'd hex it for not coming undone at his touch. Thornby pushed him away for a moment, undid it himself, and unbuttoned Blake's fly at the same time.

The moment he'd done it, Blake pulled him back into that open-mouthed kiss, hand now working Thornby's cock. Blake must have licked his hand, because it was slick. He did it just right, not too hard, not too fast; practiced. Clearly, Mr Blake was not nearly as respectable as Thornby had once supposed. Thornby moaned into his mouth, grabbing at him. And—God—for several long sweet moments, all his problems fell away. There was only the sensation of Blake's hand on his cock, and the delight of having Blake's thick cock in his own grip.

He realised his own hand was dry—it mustn't feel that good. He swept his thumb over the head of Blake's cock, feeling silky liquid spread as he did so, but that wouldn't be enough. He was about to sink to his knees to remedy the problem when Blake groaned into his mouth, grabbed him tightly, and spent. Thornby glanced down to see the pearly stuff spattering all over his own black silk waistcoat.

Blake leaned in again and bit Thornby's neck through his cravat, at the same time subtly altering his grip on Thornby's cock. Lovely, long, firm strokes, then shorter, faster ones. Thornby could feel the climax building from the soles of his feet. Blake's teeth were at his neck. Thornby came with his head thrown back, cry choked, trying to be silent.

They stood for a moment, breathing hard. Blake was resting against the door, face pressed against Thornby's neck. He sighed deeply, breath coming cold through Thornby's cravat where it was wet from his mouth.

What now? Now was a time to be careful. Thornby had run into trouble more than once in the afterglow. The moment they'd finished with a man, some men started regretting it. Some liked to take it out on the one who'd made it happen. Blake hadn't struck him as the type, but his odd behaviour beforehand might mean he'd just acted against his better judgement.

Then Blake took his hand away from Thornby's softening cock and put both arms around him, pulling him close. He did it so sweetly, so naturally, running an affectionate hand up Thornby's back, that Thornby relaxed into him, eyes closing. What bliss to stand in a man's arms, to feel his solid warmth, and to know that he would not turn nasty, but was on one's side. He let his head rest on Blake's shoulder. Blake shifted a little and Thornby wanted to plead, *Don't go. Stay with me.*

Their breathing had slowed to normal, when there came the unmistakable sound of someone turning the handle of the door they were leaning on. There was a surprised female exclamation, followed by the jangling of keys.

"Can you believe it?" Thornby said under his breath, half frowning, half laughing. "That's old Diggins. They'll be getting the rooms ready for the Greys. Come on, there's a connecting door here, too."

Thornby did up his breeches, rubbing ineffectually at the wet blotches on his waistcoat. Blake grabbed the chimera key from where it had fallen, and they slipped through the connecting door into another spare room. Blake hovered at the door to the passage for a moment, judging when it would be empty, then let them out.

They walked along the empty passage to the top of the stairs, where Blake stopped. Thornby raised an eyebrow at him. He felt, for a moment, like what he had once been; a young and careless gentleman about town. "Well, that was exciting. We didn't find anything, did we? Yet somehow I don't feel disappointed, I can't think why. What now? Want to find somewhere private? We could—"

He broke off. Blake's expression was not encouraging.

"I'm afraid I need to tell you something," Blake said.

"I see," Thornby said. Something bad, obviously. He lifted his chin. "Come then, Mr Blake. I'll show you the very fine terrace at the front of the house. It was built by the fifth Marquess in 1730 and they say it gives the best view in any of the Ridings. Mainly of overgrown hedges these days, but perhaps we can cultivate a liking for those?" He walked past Blake and down the stairs to the great front door.

Once on the terrace, however, Blake seemed not to know how to start. He looked gloomy and uncomfortable. Thornby longed to say, *For goodness sake, whatever you've got to tell me, wouldn't it go better in bed?* The happiness he'd felt a few moments ago had evaporated. So many horrible things had happened and now something else was coming. Couldn't Blake have waited a bit, and let them enjoy themselves first? The bad news wouldn't get any worse, surely? He felt a little annoyed with Blake, and knew it wasn't fair, which made him more annoyed. Damn Diggins and her hordes, too.

Finally, Blake said, "Tell me, Thornby, what do you know of your mother?"

"Mother? What's she got to do with anything? She's dead."

"Yes, but what do you know about her?"

"I wasn't here when it happened. I was eight. I'd been sent off to school."

They had called him out of class to tell him. The master's desk had glowed in the sun like a bay horse, like Periwinkle, who was Mother's blood mare. "I'm very sorry to inform you, Thornby, that your mother has died."

He had stared at the man dry-eyed, cold with disbelief. It was not true. It was some new torment that went with school, like the way the bigger boys tripped you on the stairs, or made you do things to them in the dormitories.

"You may be excused lessons for the rest of the day, if you wish. You may go to the infirmary."

No, it was a trap; if you missed divs, you got the cane. He looked again at the gleaming desk. If he touched it, it would be as warm and firm and silky as Periwinkle's flank. Mother went for a ride every morning. She would be out on Periwinkle now. It was impossible she was dead. How could she be like the maggoty starling he had poked a stick at the other day?

"I'll go back to lessons, sir," he'd said, and noted with relief the approval in the master's face.

"Very good, Thornby. You show your quality, boy, if I may say so."

So, he had gone back to his lesson. But he had waited for another letter from Mother, for another parcel. And none had ever come.

He realised Blake was looking at him, and said airily, "She drowned, you know. She went boating at midnight." He pointed west. "There used to be an ornamental lake over there, with an island in the middle. Father had it drained, afterwards. Looks nice and green, doesn't it? But the whole area is a bog. It's ruined many a good pair of shoes I can tell you."

"I'm awfully sorry, Thornby."

Thornby shrugged. "It's made the local cobbler rich as Croesus. You should appreciate that, being a working man yourself."

"What you said at dinner—do you really suspect your father of foul play?"

Thornby made an impatient gesture. "It would be convenient, wouldn't it, if I could hate him for that too? In fact, I merely said the worst thing I could think of. Much as it galls me, I think he loved her, as he said."

"Do you think it could have been suicide?"

"Why should you think that? She loved adventures; she was always getting into scrapes like some mad boy. You should have seen the hedges she put her horse at!" He thought a little more, and averted his face. "Mind you, they argued terribly sometimes. I don't know why. She would plead and rage. He was like a damned stone wall. She wept for days when he decided I was to go away to school. So, I don't know. She was volatile. Perhaps it was suicide. We'll never know. Father's word is law up here; if he says it was an accident, no one's going to argue."

"What else do you remember about her?"

"Nothing." His voice was sharp. "I don't like this way of going on. Surely even you know it's damned bad form to talk about somebody's mother?"

"I think it may be important to your predicament."

"How could it possibly be related?"

"Well, where was she from?"

Thornby sighed, with the air of one humouring a fool. "Do you think they named me Soren on a whim? She was Danish. Her name was Rosa. You saw the portrait; she was a famous beauty in the twenties and half of London was in love with her. There were all kinds of duels and poems and ridiculous wagers to bring her bouquets. Dozens of lovesick men wanting to call Father out and marry her themselves." He smiled, looking at Blake under his lashes. "I'm *very* like her, apparently. They say she drove men mad with longing."

Blake looked, for a moment, like an awkward boy. Thornby grinned. "Mr Blake, are you blushing?"

"I wish you'd take this seriously. Where did your father meet her? Here, I suppose?"

"I don't think so. I believe he brought her to England, but he'd already married her. In Denmark, I always supposed. What's this all about? Why don't you just tell me what you're getting at?"

"Have you met any of her side of the family? Any aunts or uncles or whatever?"

"I can't say that I have. But then Denmark's a dashed long way."

"They didn't come for the funeral?"

"I don't know. I didn't go myself. I was at school, remember? I suppose they thought it would upset me."

"Thornby, I—"

"I hope you're not going to say you're sorry again. Really, it's none of your business how I feel."

Blake looked suddenly very bleak, staring at the impossibly green field where Mother had died and Father had revenged himself on the lake that had taken her. "No, I suppose not."

He sounded defeated and Thornby felt suddenly odious, like the impertinent little whelp his father thought him.

"Mr Blake, I—I beg your pardon. That was damned rude. It's very decent of you to worry about upsetting me."

"Lord Thornby, I'm afraid I have a theory. Actually, it's more than a theory. I'm certain. But I don't think you're going to like it very much."

"No? Out with it, then." He put on his best social face and fixed his eyes on a particularly baroque flourish on the roof. He would not show how he felt, no matter what came. He would look at that damned ugly curlicue and get through this.

"Well, there are certain similarities, between you and the fairies. You must have noticed: my magic doesn't work on you, and it doesn't work on them. And the way you knew the answers to the queen's questions—I don't think an ordinary man would have known. And then—your mother. Seeing that portrait just now—my God, Thornby, you saw it! She had a look of that place, didn't she? She and the queen especially. You must have noticed. And her writing; it wasn't a lady's writing, was it?

"I'm afraid I don't think she was Danish at all. I think your father got her from that other place. I think he had to teach her to read and write and act the lady. I expect he said she was Danish to explain away the oddities of her accent and behaviour. I don't know how he kept her here. Maybe she really loved him, but I think it's more likely he had the same hold over her that he has over you. And, I—well, that's what I think."

Thornby felt as if Blake had punched him in the stomach. Mother not human? Which made him—what? If anyone had dared to suggest such a thing a couple of years ago, he'd have laughed in their face. Now, after all the months of gnawing self-doubt and mystery, after the horror of being trapped in that place, and the chase—

He turned, very slowly, so he didn't fall over, to look at Blake.

"Have you finished?" He'd been aiming for the tone he'd use on an impudent servant, but it came out wobbly. It occurred to him that this might be why Blake had hesitated in the spare room. This might be why he hadn't wanted to touch him at first. Because Blake thought he was some half-breed *creature*. Not human. The idea that Blake might be revolted by him, and had only managed to master his revulsion long enough for a bit of a tug—

"I'm sorry, Thornby. It's what I think."

"You're sorry a lot lately, aren't you? So, my mother was an inhuman freak, was she? And I'm one too. And even my Christian name is some sort of—of—red herring?"

He clenched his fists, shock giving way to anger. The sheer nerve of the fellow, to suggest such a thing! He wasn't sure why he was so furious, since it was clearly ludicrous. He felt strangely shivery, the way one did with a fever. He thought, for a horrible moment, he might throw up again, and swallowed hard.

Blake's apologetic expression wasn't helping. Oh God, what if Blake was sorry for him? Had he acted out of pity in the spare room?

"But it's the clue we need, isn't it? Don't you see that it narrows the search?" Blake said.

"But it doesn't!" He spat it out. "We still haven't the faintest idea what we're looking for! Christ, you call yourself a magician, but you're bloody useless, aren't you? If you were any real sort of magician you could *make* Father let me go. But for some reason you haven't offered. You could frighten him into it, probably. Or threaten him. But you haven't. All you've done is get yourself into trouble. Why the hell should I believe your theory? What is the Dee Institute anyway? For all I know it's where they send the hopeless cases who'll never amount to anything!"

"Is that what you want me to do; frighten your father for you?"

"Yes! Why not? Force him to let me go! Make him do it!"

"That's witchcraft."

"So, sneaking around and using that voice on people, and looking through other men's things is all right, is it? But thrashing a damned bully would be wrong?"

"It's witchcraft, Thornby. I won't do it. For the same reason you haven't broken into his room and attacked him in his sleep."

"I'm not asking you to murder him, for God's sake! Just to force him—I don't know. Scare him. Whatever you feel isn't beneath you."

"He's cursed. Did you remember that? Whether your mother did it, or whether it's just happened due to the circumstances, I don't know, but—"

"And that excuses him, does it? He can ruin the family and run the place into the ground and do whatever the hell he likes to all of us because he's cursed?"

"It's driving him. It makes him dangerous and unpredictable. If I did as you ask, if I frightened him—say I told his bedroom furniture to fly about the room next time he's in it—and then I went in and said I'd only stop it if he let you go—do you think he'd do it? Do you really think so? I wouldn't like to bet on it myself. I think he'd lash out. Probably at you. We don't know how he's doing what he's doing. Can't you see it's too dangerous?"

"So, you're scared of him," Thornby said, contemptuously, and had the satisfaction of seeing a spark of anger light up in Blake's dark eyes.

"Don't mistake me for some street entertainer because all you've seen so far are a few tricks. But there's a curse involved that comes from that other place. And in any case, as I've said, frightening people with magic into doing what you want is witchcraft."

"So, stop short of hurting him. But there must be—"

"Would you like me to trap him somewhere, maybe? To keep him somewhere until he does as I wish? Is that what you want me to do, to be like him?"

Blake's turned-down mouth had gone beyond grim to decidedly forbidding. He shifted his stance, as if leaning into the argument. Thornby drew himself up too, welcoming the rage that was washing over him. His fists were itching to hit something. To finally have someone to lash out at. To banish helplessness with a punch and see the result bleeding in front of him. Father had a way of making himself impregnable, of retreating behind his title and his mysterious power until it was impossible to do anything.

But Blake—

One could touch a man like Blake. One could hit him. One could hurt him.

"It sounds like justice to me," Thornby said scornfully. "Would you be brave enough to do it, if I ordered it?"

"It's not a question of bravery. I damned well won't do it," Blake snapped. "I know you're used to people doing as you say, but you can't order me around, so you can stop trying."

They glared at each other. Thornby was one trembling breath from hitting him, when Blake's expression suddenly softened. He took a step back and relaxed his shoulders, raising his hands in a conciliatory gesture.

"Thornby, let's not quarrel. It won't help. Look, at the moment he suspects nothing, so we've got free rein to look about. It's better to be subtle, isn't it?"

So, he wouldn't fight. He wouldn't give the satisfaction. But there was something in his voice, some tenderness, some question, that left him wide open. The urge to hurt him shifted focus. But at the same time Thornby remembered how the argument had started. Mother, not human. And the world seemed again to lurch beneath his feet. Every certainty, every belief, every idea he'd ever had about himself seemed to be crumbling away like ash.

"So, my mother was a fairy, was she? That's what you're saying, you know. Do you know what a fool you sound?" His voice was thin, but it was perfectly under control.

"I know how it sounds. Until last night I wouldn't have believed it myself."

"And what does that make me? You're a lunatic. I don't know why I thought you could help me. You may as well go back to London. Although I quite like your idea about attacking him in his sleep. Perhaps you'll leave your marvellous key behind when you go? Good day, Mr Blake. Since you're not interested, I've got cowslips to suck."

He turned on his heel and walked away. He had no idea where he was going, but wherever it was, it was as far as possible from the ridiculous Mr Blake and his preposterous ideas.

Chapter Seven

Dinner was nearly over.

"Where's Lord Thornby this evening?" John kept his voice pleasant and even.

"Bad form. Late for dinner," Mr Derwent mumbled. "Wouldn't be the first time."

"He does enjoy long walks," Lady Amelia remarked.

"Youth must have its day," said Lord Dalton, each word dripping with scorn. "So easy to lose track of time, eh?"

John nodded politely, but his stomach was tying itself in knots. After Thornby had left him on the terrace, he'd dragged himself upstairs. He'd been so tired even Raskelf's incessant whispering hadn't stopped him sleeping for an hour or two. When he woke, he'd spent the rest of the day looking for Thornby, but he'd not found him.

Was Thornby avoiding him? He hadn't taken John's news very well. It was a bloody difficult thing to take. She'd been his *mother*. To learn she hadn't been human; it would shake a man to his core.

God, why did Raskelf have to be so big? The place was a labyrinth—one could wander it endlessly and never find the person one was looking for. But was Thornby avoiding him, or had something happened to him? Thornby had stalked away in high dudgeon and there were culverts aplenty on the estate where a distracted man could twist an ankle. The hole they called Jennie's Pot had a cliff over twenty yards high. Of course, Thornby must know the estate the way John knew his iron pins, but it had turned foggy, which could have confused him.

Or he could have fallen foul of poachers. Some of the locals John had spoken to seemed to have great affection for Lord Thornby; his eccentricities impressed them. They expected the nobility to be different, and if Thornby was 'touched' and known to shout epithets at hedges and go shooting in court clothes, he was touched in such an odd and lordly way that it gave the local people bragging rights. But not everybody felt like that. Some of them were plain afraid of him, some with fear so deep, John felt it bordered on hate. What if Thornby met someone like that in the depths of the park?

Or what if John had broken the news too bluntly? What if Thornby simply couldn't take it, on top of everything else? What if Thornby had decided he couldn't go on? Was he even now lying dead in some ditch with his brains blown out—beautiful eyes glazed and dull, flawless skin growing cold?

John felt sick. He stopped pushing his venison about with his fork.

"Surely Lord Thornby should be at dinner by now? Shall I go and look for him?" He half got to his feet.

"Sit down, man. He'll come in his own good time," Lord Dalton said. "Farrell, more wine."

"My lord." John sat.

The Judas Voice had worked well on Dalton, but it would not stand up if he antagonised the man. He ate a bite of something without tasting it. Perhaps Thornby simply didn't want to see him. Perhaps he was regretting what had happened in the spare room. Or perhaps he was indifferent to it. John himself generally walked away from such encounters without a second thought. Just because he was aching to see Thornby again—to hold him, to kiss him, to breathe him in—it didn't mean Thornby felt the same.

"Mr Blake, will you take another glass of claret?" Lord Dalton waved a hand as if offering the entire contents of his cellar.

"Thank you." He felt it would choke him, but it seemed polite to accept.

Did Dalton seem in a more expansive mood than usual? There was something almost gleeful about him, like a boy with a secret.

John felt as if ice-water had been poured down his spine. Dalton had done something to Thornby. He knew it. *He'll come in his own good time*—there had been a subtle smugness to that comment. Dalton knew it wasn't true.

The moment he could escape from dinner, John checked every room he could think of that locked, but found no sign of Thornby. And there was no point setting any seeking charms; Thornby would be as impervious to those as he was to everything else.

John slumped down onto a cold marble step, careless of his evening clothes. The temptation to go and confront Lord Dalton was strong, but he didn't dare to play his hand so openly just yet. He still had no idea what to do about the curse. He'd once seen a cursed woman who washed her hands until the fingers were bloody stumps. What would Lord Dalton's curse drive him to do?

He must *think*. He must think like Dalton. If Thornby was correct, then Dalton wanted the money that a wife for Thornby would bring. Dalton had tried a waiting game; isolating Thornby, not even allowing him his valet, using loneliness and boredom and mystery as weapons. But Thornby's resolve had held. And now Dalton's patience had run out. So, Dalton would up the stakes—to force Thornby to obey him. The other night at dinner the

Marquess had threatened Thornby with 'a demonstration'. A demonstration that meant Thornby had missed dinner and was nowhere in the house...

God, what a fool John had been, searching the Hall! It was obvious. He ran down the stairs, grabbing his overcoat on the way out. The worst thing Dalton could do to Thornby was to take him off the estate and hold him there. The magic that bound Thornby to the estate would do the rest; it would be torture. Would he find Thornby flayed raw? Bled to death? Or with his mind gone, from being kept away too long?

No. Dalton needed Thornby relatively whole and sane if Miss Grey or Miss Lazenby were to marry him. So Thornby would be somewhere near the boundary. Probably merely trapped in some way.

Outside, the fog had lifted, but grey wraiths still swirled around, moved by a cold wind from the north. John ran west along the driveway towards the village, feeling in his pockets for the rowan twig and vial of sulphur. He dipped the twig, sending power to both until they kindled and burnt with a cold, blue, un-consuming fire. Now he had a light, he easily found the path along the estate boundary.

But which way to go? He looked one way, then the other. If he turned the wrong way, he might search all night and Dalton would get back to Thornby first. John could not allow that to happen. He forced himself to breathe, to think.

Dalton would need to keep Thornby hidden, perhaps in a wood or a lonely barn. To the west was the village, with people always coming and going. To the north, the Howarths had several game-keepers who patrolled the moors, and besides, the moorland was too open. So, perhaps to the south? Or the east?

John turned left, heading south-east along the path Thornby's feet had worn smooth over the months. He held the rowan twig high, hoping Thornby might see it and call out. He called himself, pausing often to listen. Every rustle of the wind in the trees, every bark of a fox or hoot of an owl sounded like Thornby's voice calling in answer. Occasionally John would range off the path to investigate a clump of trees, a hay-stack, or a curve in a stone wall.

Then, in a patch of woodland south of the house, he heard Thornby's voice. It was hoarse, as if he'd been calling for a long time. John ducked behind a thick growth of holly, feet slipping in mud and wet leaves. In the rowan twig's cold blue light he could see Thornby writhing on the ground under a tree, hands outstretched to the estate boundary, about a foot out of his reach.

John wasn't sure if Thornby recognised him. The younger man's face was dead white and set in a rictus of agony and desperation. He was still trying to get back to the estate, but his ankle was manacled to a huge oak with an iron chain. The strange otherness John had sensed that day on the moor was now an unbearable, relentless keening, a magical whine of panic and pain.

"Thornby! It's all right. I'll set you free." John forced the chimera key into the lock on the fetter. The charm was wearing off and the key jerked and stuck. Thornby's stocking was in tatters, his ankle raw and swollen; he must have been fighting the chain for hours. John sent a brutal surge of power into the key and the lock opened.

Thornby tore John's hands away from the fetter and forced it apart. Then Thornby was up, stumbling across the estate boundary, tearing past the holly. Once over the boundary he managed another twenty yards, crashing through low hazel and underbrush. John ran after him, calling his name, branches whipping back into his face, hoping Thornby wouldn't run all the way to the Hall. Luckily, Thornby came to a small clearing, then a particularly dense part of the thicket that wouldn't let him through. Thornby grappled with the branches for a moment, then sank to his knees, panting.

John knelt beside him and put an arm around his shoulders. "Thornby, it's all right now. It's over."

"Must get home. I'm late for...I must get home."

"You *are* home. You're on the estate."

"I have to go home." Thornby lurched to his feet and blundered into the thicket again.

"Stop it! You'll hurt yourself. You'll put an eye out. You're home. You're on the estate. You can *feel* it, can't you?"

"The estate. Yes." Thornby sounded dazed, but no longer desperate. His knees crumpled again and they knelt on the damp leaves, hazel twigs poking at their hair and faces.

"Blake?"

"Yes, it's me. I'm sorry I didn't come sooner. I didn't know where you were."

"Oh, God, I—I thought you'd gone back to London." Thornby gave a kind of gasp, and began to sob like a beaten child, face in his hands.

John dropped the rowan twig to burn coldly on the dead leaves. He put both arms around Thornby. Thornby resisted at first, then leaned into him. John could still feel a faint echo of that terrible magical desperation; that overwhelming drive to return to the estate. However Dalton was holding Thornby here, it was horribly strong. It felt primal, like blood magic, though it was too alien to be that. The mere memory of it set John's teeth on edge. And Thornby had endured it for hours.

After a while, Thornby made the gulping sounds of a man trying to pull himself together. His shoulders stopped heaving and he let out several long shaky breaths.

"Blake, Christ, I'm sorry for what I said. Please don't go back to London. I didn't mean it." He had his voice nearly under control. It only shook once or twice.

"Of course I'm not going while you're stuck here."

Thornby nodded, and waved a hand, indicating his state. "I—I beg your pardon. For being—I'm not accustomed—"

"Shh. There's no need to apologise. How long were you there?"

"Don't know. Hours." Suddenly Thornby tensed. "Oh, God, what you said about Mother—it's true, isn't it? I'm one of them. I'm not human."

"You're not 'one of them'. Your father's human."

Thornby gave a deep sigh. His voice, when he spoke, was more normal. "Father? Human? You think so?" He put a hand to his disordered cravat. "God, my throat hurts. What if I sprout horns or turn blue or something?"

"That won't happen."

"But you don't know, do you? You're in the dark about all this yourself."

"I think, if you were going to grow horns, it would have happened by now."

John could feel Thornby breathing; shaky gulps of air. John kissed his cheek and slid a hand inside Thornby's shirt, which was hanging out of his breeches, and stroked his cold and clammy back.

"I'll never get away, will I? If I'm not fully human, who knows what he can do to me?"

"Of course you'll get away." John pulled out his flask of rain-water. He kept it for magical purposes, but could easily get more. "Here, drink this. In a moment I'll put some wards up so we know if someone's coming. Did he say when he'd come back for you?"

"He wasn't there. Prout and Abbott, the footmen, did the dirty work, with his regards. They said they'd be back in the morning."

John considered. If they went back to the house and someone saw them, Dalton would probably find out. And if Dalton felt his demonstration had failed, perhaps he'd repeat it. It would be better to avoid the house. Better to lie low and let Dalton think everything had gone according to plan.

"All right. So, we'll get comfortable here until morning. Your clothes are soaking. Here." John picked up the rowan twig and brought it closer to Thornby.

Thornby jumped as if something had bitten him. "What the devil?" he yelped, grabbing at his chest.

"Sorry, sorry. That was me. I was trying to dry your clothes."

"Christ! It felt like you set my shirt on fire."

"Sorry. You'd better get everything off then, or you'll freeze. I can dry them fairly fast, but perhaps not with you in them. You throw all my magic awry, don't you? You can have my coat while you wait, but don't go poking around in the pockets. There are all kinds of things in there that are better left alone."

Thornby started trying to undo his waistcoat buttons, but his hands were shaking too much. John did it for him, then peeled off Thornby's wet coat and waistcoat and started on the buttons of his shirt. He was about half-way down when he realised Thornby was looking at him with a ghost of a smile on his drawn face. John stopped, fingers on the buttons.

"I must say this isn't how I imagined it," Thornby said, glancing at the bare branches of the thicket that hemmed them in.

John found himself smiling back. "Nor me."

"But you did imagine it?"

"Are you joking? It's been impossible to think of anything else. Even with a cursed marquess and a fairy hedgehog running around the place."

Thornby looked away for a moment. "I wondered if you weren't really interested. You know, because of earlier. In the spare room."

"You mean the spare room where I spent all over you? And you did the same to me?"

"Well—I meant the part where you thought about it for five minutes beforehand. Not that I mind, if that's what you like to do. Actually, it was quite exciting, being made to wait. But people don't usually deliberate about it for quite so long if they really want to."

"No, no. That's just—it's to do with magic. It affects how I have sex. Look, can I tell you later? I want to get you warmed up and set some wards. I want to know about it, if anyone comes near."

"Yes, of course."

John helped him get the rest of his wet clothes off, wrapped him in his coat, helped him lie down, and tied a clean handkerchief lightly around his bleeding ankle. Then John bent over him to get some things out of his coat pockets. "I've got walnuts, but no other food. I'll go back to the house for some if you like."

"I couldn't eat anyway. I'm nearly asleep now."

"All right. I'll be back soon. And listen, Thornby; next time I take off your clothes you'll have no doubt about whether I want you. Understand?"

"Yes."

"Good." He bent closer, putting his lips to Thornby's ear. "And if you like being made to wait, then I will make you wait. Until you beg. Got it? Now go to sleep."

"After a comment like that?" Thornby muttered, but he closed his eyes and was asleep before John had even straightened his back.

***

Thornby woke with a start; something was digging into his cheek. He thrashed at it and found himself with a handful of hazel twigs. Then Blake was there, crouching over him with a hand on his arm. The uncanny blue light Blake had brought with him was still burning, lighting up the coppice.

"All right?" Blake said.

"What time is it?"

"Nearly five."

"I've a head like a stuck pig. Is there any more water?"

Blake passed him a flask, which he drained. He was struck by how relaxed Blake looked, considering they were sleeping out on an October night in Yorkshire. Thornby was not, now he thought of it, especially cold himself; Blake's coat was wonderfully warm. The dead leaves underneath him felt crisp and dry. Surely, they'd been wet earlier. Was that magic?

"My clothes?" Thornby asked.

"Here." Blake passed him a pile of clothes, neatly folded, and perfectly dry, though still caked in mud and dried leaves.

"How did you do that?"

"I asked the water nicely to come out."

Thornby opened his mouth to protest, then wondered if in fact he'd just been told the literal truth. He tried to stand to get dressed and nearly fell over. His ankle, where the fetter had chafed it, throbbed as if flayed. Dried blood was caked all over Blake's handkerchief.

Blake helped him get dressed. It was a little like having a valet again, although Blake was not entirely businesslike. Some of the things he did would have seen him out on the street without a recommendation. Or arrested. Or treasured as the best valet a man ever had. Perhaps it depended on whether one liked a valet with smouldering eyes, who occasionally grazed his fingertips along one's bare skin.

"No one came?" Thornby asked, a little breathlessly.

"No people. I saw several hedgehogs, which I gave walnuts. I slept a bit too. The wards'll tell me about ten minutes before anyone comes."

"All right." Thornby swallowed. He could guess what was coming. Better to say it himself, so Blake didn't have to. "I have to go back, don't I? To the chain. So Prout and Abbott can find me there."

"If you can bear it, it really would be best." Blake took his hand and rubbed it. His hands were warm, very comforting. "I've changed one or two things about the chain, and about the ground underneath. I've got earth from the estate and I'll put it where you have to lie. The ground's so churned up they'll never notice. I think you might find it isn't so bad. It's worth trying, anyway."

Thornby blinked at him. He'd never thought of that. Over a year and a half of trying to escape and it had never crossed his mind. But then, trying to get away was like that. He was stupid about it.

"Could I get all the way to London like that?" he said, only half joking.

"I doubt it. Soil on someone else's land becomes theirs, doesn't it? But you only have to lie there for a few minutes and they'll let you go. I think the effect might last long enough to help."

"What have you done to the chain?"

"Stretched it. You'll be partly over the boundary."

"Won't they notice? You stretched it? I suppose you asked it nicely?"

"No, iron prefers orders. I told it, very firmly indeed. And no, I don't think they'll notice. Even if they do, Lord Dalton knows magic's involved here. I'm hoping he'll put it down to that. Not to someone helping you."

"That's quite clever, Mr Blake. I'm impressed."

"Tell me that again if it works. You know, you can call me John, if you like. Now we've spent the night together."

"All right. John."

84

Thornby found himself looking down at the crisp dead leaves, feeling uncharacteristically shy. But then it was uncharacteristic to have wept all over the man. Did John think less of him? He didn't appear to; he'd been absolutely decent and kind throughout. He might be trade—of a sort—but he was more of a gentleman than most of the fellows Thornby had known at Oxford. Thornby realised he was still gazing bashfully at the ground. This wouldn't do. He looked up to find John watching him with a slightly surprised, almost puzzled, expression.

"I don't think you should call me Soren. You might become familiar, and then where should we be? Good heavens, you might lay a hand on me!"

John cocked his head, smiling.

"Come then, *my lord*. Let's get closer to the boundary. I don't know when your father's men will be along. 'Morning' could mean anything. When a ward tells me they're near, you'll have to let me push you over. Think you can do it? You can't fight me. It'll slow us down."

Thornby swallowed hard, all the fun of teasing and being teased draining out of him.

"I...I don't know. I won't mean to fight you. But I can't promise." His voice wobbled. Christ, the idea of going back, of having to lie there again. His heart was pounding just thinking about it. Objectively, it was lying under a tree with a bit of iron round his ankle. But it felt like a nightmare—it was an animal state of pain and desperation. And he had to go back to it. He bit his lip. He would not cry in front of John again. He would *not*.

"Come here," John said, and put his arms around him. God, he was good to hold. John kissed the side of his face and ran his fingers in Thornby's hair. How nice it would be to get that suit off him and see what was underneath. But this embrace wasn't lustful. John was trying to give him courage. And maybe it worked, because after a while, Thornby drew away from him.

"Come then," he said. "Let's go."

***

It was, John thought, one of the bravest things he'd seen anyone do in cold blood. The moment the ward alerted him to people coming, he'd nodded at Thornby and pulled him over the boundary. And Thornby had gritted his teeth and gone. Thornby had struggled, plainly he hadn't been able to help himself, but he'd kept himself in check. He let John force the fetter round his raw and bleeding ankle. Only when John had left him, and concealed himself in the thicket, had Thornby convulsed in the mud and begun, once more, reaching for the boundary.

His hands touched it now. John hoped that was some comfort. He hoped the weak struggle Thornby was putting up was partly for show.

This time, Lord Dalton had come himself. Prout and Abbott were there too. Prout, who looked like a prize-fighter gone to seed, undid the fetter. Thornby staggered across the boundary in his muddy clothes, limping, falling, getting up again. His father watched, expressionless, sitting his restless horse like a statue. Prout and Abbott exchanged glances, but there was no sympathy in their faces. Abbott, who wore a permanent expression of baffled rage, looked as if he'd like to do worse to the lordling who was staggering out of sight into the thicket.

Lord Dalton didn't even look at the chain, now a foot longer than it had been. Prout didn't either. He simply looped it over his shoulder and the grim little party followed the rudimentary path Thornby had broken through the bushes.

John watched them go, fists balled in his pockets, until the temptation to run after them became so strong he felt it would choke him. Then he turned away. He longed to knock Dalton off his horse with a well-aimed rock and follow it up with some charmed salt to really make it sting. He'd maim Prout and Abbott, perhaps with iron pins to the feet. And then help Thornby home—put him to bed and get in beside him.

But he couldn't. He clenched his teeth. He must play a long game. And, moreover, he must play it on two fronts; the curse on Dalton, and the spell on Thornby.

So far, he'd found nothing to help him with the spell. Next, he would try tackling the curse. And that meant a tête-à-tête with Lord Dalton. John had said he had 'valuable contacts'. Maybe he could exploit Dalton's greed—for money, for success in business, for whatever it was Dalton wanted, to find out more about the curse. And then, well, he had no idea beyond a vague theory that had come to him in the thicket.

The salt had given him the tip about the Woden's Eye sigil. It had nearly ended in disaster, and at the time, he'd thought he'd never take advice from his materials again. But he'd wanted the hedgehog to reveal itself, and by God, it had done so. The salt's advice had been effective. Perhaps some sigils were not really obsolete. Perhaps they just seemed so, because their true purposes had been forgotten. As people had migrated to the towns, and built new cities, the need for magic that could affect the fair folk must have abated. He himself, a city boy, had never come across it before, nor been taught anything of it at the Institute.

So, what other sigils might the salt suggest if he asked it? What might the pins suggest, or the sand or the spancel? If he made a list of all the obsolete sigils and charms he and his materials could remember, perhaps one of them might prove useful in dealing with this other kind of magic. And then he might free Thornby and break the curse on Lord Dalton.

If he didn't somehow manage to kill himself in the process.

He began walking back the way he'd come, so he could appear to be returning to the house from the village. He had no wish to watch Thornby limping back to the house in front of him. It would be too much to bear.

Last night he'd watched Thornby sleep and wondered why it felt as if his heart was exploding in a burst of tattered magic. It was true they'd been through a lot together. Thornby had saved his life. But the sweet ache of love? After a couple of days' acquaintance and one brief mutual tug?

But was it love, or something else? John had been in love before, but this felt different. Stronger. Better. Worse. What if this was the beginning of some kind of mania? Dalton seemed half mad after losing his fairy bride. If John allowed himself to fall in love with Thornby, and Thornby did not return the sentiment, would John become like Dalton? Obsessed forever with the one person he could no longer have?

'Allow himself to fall in love'? Who was he trying to fool? There was no 'allowing himself' here. This was no sensible decision that the fellow could be a pleasant companion. There was no decision at all, no choice. Thornby made his knees weak and his balls ache. John wanted him the way a starving man wants bread.

He had always preferred well-born young men; the higher in the instep, the better. There was something about the accent and the air of privilege that made him long to fuck them senseless. To make them lose their poise and lose control; to make them writhe and moan and rut and forget themselves. Thornby was no exception.

Except, of course, he *was* the exception.

Because although he had the looks, the pretty manners and the grace of a thoroughbred, he was not actually an arrogant little bastard. Perhaps he had been once; all these months at Raskelf, in this unenviable position, had probably changed him. Now, there was something sweet about him. Once or twice he had seemed a little shy. When he wasn't being defensive, he treated John as an equal. His habit of poking fun at their different stations was disarming.

John generally lost interest in the other young gentlemen he fucked, as soon as the fucking was done. He might see them a few times, but they grated on him, even as he desired them. Thornby did not grate. By not demanding John's respect, he had won it. The way he teased was—fun.

John stopped in his tracks at that. Fun. He had not had much in his life. Life was work. It was serious. And he took his pleasures seriously too; you had to, or you got caught. Thornby made his heart lift.

And Thornby didn't seem to mind the magic. He didn't seem afraid of it, or afraid of John. John's last affaire with a non-magician had ended in disaster, when the fellow had asked him for the hundredth time what it was he actually *did* for Mr Paxton. John had told him, and the man had laughed, then scoffed. So, John had let him watch as he made a sigil to stop the Crystal Palace roof from leaking. He had thought an architect would appreciate such a charm, but no. It was dangerous, ungodly. It was wrong. It was cheating nature. And John had seen then, that the man was already ashamed of the things they'd done together, frightened of the way John made him feel, and that the magic was final damning proof. Not of something wonderful, but of something degenerate and evil. *Stay away from me.*

He started walking again, hazel twigs catching at his shoulders. Since meeting Thornby he'd scarcely thought of anyone else. He'd even forgotten his primary purpose in being here; to help Lady Dalton. The curse was the thing. If he could somehow unravel that, everyone would be a lot better off.

When he got back to the house he saw Lord Dalton going into the breakfast room. John took a moment to tidy the leaves out of his hair, then followed him in. Lord Dalton was devouring devilled kidneys. John bowed.

"Lord Dalton. A moment of your time, please."

Dalton grunted, and gestured impatiently to the chair opposite.

John sat. "I've been thinking, sir—"

"Damn it, let me eat, man. We'll talk when I've done."

John clamped his lips together and tried not to think about what the man across the table had just done to Thornby. The curse surged around Dalton as he chewed. One-to-one, the stench of it was overpowering. It mixed with the scent of the kidneys, turning John's stomach. He found himself watching Dalton's hands, hard and calloused as a working-man's. They surely never got that way from holding a polished stick and a well-oiled pair of reins.

Dalton's face was seamed and weather-beaten, as coarse as his hands. But his eyes were bright blue chinks, sharp as spite.

Finally, Dalton wiped his mouth, and let his gaze rest over John's left shoulder. "Well?"

"Well, my lord."

"Damn it, what do you want?"

"I'm here at your invitation, sir. I believe the proper question is; what do *you* want from me?"

Dalton made a grumbling noise in his throat. "Blake, isn't it?"

"Yes, John Blake."

"All right, Blake. And whose man are you?"

John bowed his head obsequiously, to give himself time to think, then said; "Currently, sir, I have connections to His Grace the Duke of Devonshire. As you may know, he has an interest in the Crystal Palace. I have been working with his man, Mr Paxton, to ensure everything at that great edifice has run as it should. Which it has."

Well, it was true enough if the Marquess decided to check any of it. And John had met the Duke a couple of times.

"Devonshire, eh?" Dalton snorted. "Damned Whig."

But, still, it seemed to have been the right thing to say. Dalton looked John straight in the eye. "So, you've contacts?"

"I hope so, my lord."

"And? What are they?"

"What contacts do you need?"

"No, Blake, it doesn't work that way. You tell me what you've got, and I tell you if I need it."

Damn. "Just so." John bowed again. "I have contacts in theurgy."

Dalton made a small noise of scorn. "They're no good to me. Bloody load of charlatans. What else?"

John frowned. "I assure you, sir, my contacts are of the finest—"

"I'm not interested, damn you. I've tried them all. Tried them years ago. Useless, the lot of them. What else?"

Interesting. So, Dalton had tried magicians and found them wanting. Was that because he'd tried to get them to remove the fairy curse?

"Marine botanists," John said. It was a stab in the dark, but maybe the seaweed business link would be a way in.

"Botanists, eh?"

"Yes, specialising in maritime flora."

"Mph. Don't need a botanist."

"Medical gentlemen."

"Doctors? What do I need with doctors?"

"I don't know, my lord. If you would only tell me your requirements, I could perhaps render my assistance that much faster."

Dalton regarded him steadily for some time. John looked steadily back. It wouldn't do to be too obsequious. He was here as a guest, after all, and even if he wasn't really a gentleman, he wasn't a servant either.

"What do you know of pearls, Blake?"

What on earth?

"A little," John said, in the tone of voice that means 'quite a lot'.

Dalton harrumphed again, eyes narrowing suspiciously. Then he snapped, "Are you married? Children? Eh?"

What the hell did that have to do with anything? Or was this Dalton's idea of small talk?

"No, my lord," John said.

"Devonshire's not the marrying type. Perhaps you aren't either."

"Perhaps not." John didn't like where this conversation seemed to be leading. Not that he'd had the slightest whiff of anything of that type from the Duke. He decided to be more direct. "I mention doctors, my lord, because perhaps you have some old trouble."

"What the devil are you talking about?"

"Trouble that started when—forgive me—when the first Lady Dalton passed away."

Dalton jerked to his feet. "What do you know of that?"

John got to his feet, too. "Nothing, my lord. If you would confide in me, perhaps I could find someone who could—"

"Could what, damn you? What do you mean by coming in here with your hints and suggestions?"

"Perhaps I could find someone who could help you."

"You, I suppose?"

"Not necessarily me. I would help you if I could, sir." He tried to sound sincere, in case there was a part of Dalton, somewhere deep inside, that wanted help. "If you could give me any information. Anything that might help me, or a colleague, to understand the situation."

"And how do I know I can trust you, eh?"

"You could ask Mr Paxton, perhaps? I believe I have given satisfaction at the Crystal Palace."

"Hmph. Haven't seen it. No wish to see it. All right, Blake. I'll think on your suggestions. It's true, I need a new angle. Good day to you."

And he walked out, slow and stately as usual. John stared after him, wondering what had just happened, and whether it had gone well, and whether he'd got any kind of clue that could help him unravel the curse.

Chapter Eight

When Thornby got back to the house, Prout and Abbott half-dragged him upstairs to his room and sent one of the maids up to bandage his ankle. They sent a new girl, who did the job with shaking hands, showing the whites of her eyes when he cursed under his breath at the pain. So, he dug his nails into his palms and didn't curse again. She'd brought food and hot water, so he ate, washed and shaved. Once, having to shave himself had felt like the pinnacle of humiliation and inconvenience; these days he did it without thinking. He put on clean clothes and tossed the muddy rags that were his old ones outside the door.

Father had squinted suspiciously at his healed face, but in the end had shrugged and ridden away. He hadn't said anything, but then, he didn't have to. He'd said it already: "Miss Grey and Miss Lazenby. You'll make yourself pleasant."

Thornby lay on his bed, but straight away got up. It hurt to walk, but walking was one of the ways he stayed sane, so he limped about the room anyway. How like Father to have made Thornby inflict the pain on himself. If he'd been able to stop himself from fighting the chain, he wouldn't have been hurt. But when it came to leaving the estate, he'd never been able to think rationally or control himself.

John's revelation about Mother seemed a lot less shocking today. Perhaps she hadn't been human, but she was still Mother—beautiful, spirited, and laughing. He didn't feel any different in himself, either. He recalled some cherished memories—reading Ruskin in a sunlit room at Oxford, a day's hunting in Dorset on that marvellous borrowed grey, fucking that handsome guardsman—but they all felt just the same. He was still himself. The only bad thing about it, as far as he could see, was that somehow it gave Father some hold over him.

But did it mean he also had latent magic in him? He'd never noticed any odd abilities. He'd never feared iron or had trouble going to church when necessary. He'd never had trouble crossing running water—or was that witches? The problem was, he knew so little about it all. Except, he had been able to answer the fairy queen's questions and that was encouraging.

Although his face was healed, he'd scratched it afresh in the hazel thicket and it stung. His ankle throbbed. He was trembling with a potent mix of fear, loathing for Father, and frustrated excitement for John. God, what a night! The sheer panic of being chained outside the estate. And then, John undressing him in the middle of a thicket, and the nightmare was transformed. That was truly magic; to be able to take such a terrible situation and turn it into something sweet.

More than anything, he wanted to see John again. John Blake, with his clever, serious eyes and reassuring hands. John, who had murmured some really quite surprising things last night, while still managing to look like a paragon of middle-class respectability. "I will make you beg," he'd said.

Thornby flexed his ankle. Agonising. Nevertheless, he limped along the passage to John's room. He knocked, but there was no reply. Damn. What now? Last time he'd gone in, that pathway had opened and they'd nearly been trapped. John's theory that you couldn't open the pathway by accident was comforting, but—

He was still dithering at the door when Lady Dalton appeared at the top of the stairs. She wore a morning dress of turquoise velvet trimmed with lemon-yellow ribbons. He remembered it from last autumn; perhaps her dressmaker had stopped extending credit.

"Oh!" she said, going white, then red. "Lord Thornby. Good morning. I was looking for Mr Blake. Your face—it—seems much improved."

"Ma'am." He bowed, coldly, and was about to walk away when he remembered John saying, "Leave her out of it," at dinner. Also, her cousin was John's friend. "He's not here," he added. "I'm looking for him, too."

She looked as if she would turn away, then stopped. "Lord Thornby, I owe you an apology. I thought you were doing things to frighten me. But Mr Blake says you're quite innocent. So, I beg your pardon. I hope you will forgive me."

A dozen memories of being rather cruel to her jostled in his head. At the beginning, she'd tried to be friends, and he'd pushed her away every time. He'd lumped her in with father and his lackeys.

"No, really," he said. "Easy mistake to make. Think nothing of it."

"There's something strange going on, though, isn't there? Mr Blake says there is."

"Yes, he thinks Father's cursed."

"Oh." She paled again.

"Forgive me. Perhaps I shouldn't have said that."

"No, no. I want to know. Lord Thornby, I'm so glad your face is better, but you do look pale. And you're quite scratched. Should you not sit down?"

As she spoke he felt the world spin around him. "I probably should."

He started to move away from John's door. When she saw how he was hobbling, she took his arm.

"Did you overdo it in the park?"

"It's my ankle. Father chained me to a tree."

"Oh, I *wish* you wouldn't say such things! I know he has his faults, but he is your father!"

Thornby sighed. "It's the truth. But if you prefer, I can say I got it stuck in a gin trap. The poachers are terrible, aren't they? What we need is a decent gamekeeper."

"Why do you make up these stories? I can never tell whether you're telling the truth."

"I always used to tell the truth, but no one ever listened. Or they didn't believe me. So now I just say whatever I like."

"No one believes what I say, either."

They looked at each other, both recognising something in the other. Then she added, "Mr Blake listens." And blushed.

So, she fancied John, did she? He didn't blame her. *But he's mine*, he thought, so fiercely it surprised him. *Or I wish he was.* He remembered John putting a careful, deliberate hand on the wall of Father's room; the intent look on his face as he listened to whatever he was learning from it. She was right. Now he thought of it, he'd never met a man who listened quite as well as John.

"He believes me, too," she said. "He says I'm not imaging anything. And he says there's a curse? On Lord Dalton?"

"I'm afraid so. I'm sorry you're caught up in this, my lady."

"Well, Dalton is my husband, I suppose."

"How on earth do you stand it? Being married to him?"

"Oh, I—"

"Sorry, you needn't answer that."

They got along in silence for a bit. Eventually she said. "I'm not really married to him, am I? We stay in the same house in winter. That's all."

Thornby had never really noticed women in the past. They'd been vaguely decorative objects with which he'd danced at balls, while keeping a sharp eye out for which fellow might be keen on something more interesting afterwards. Or they were servants, or models that posed a challenge of form and technique. He'd never been unkind to them, but he'd never really thought of them at all, until he'd been forced into the proximity of his Aunt

Amelia. He'd been so lonely and she'd been so surprising. As surprising as John in her way. She'd smashed all his preconceptions about what women liked and wanted, and she'd made him see that her thoughts and wishes were as valid as his own. And yet, despite these realisations, he'd still been treating his young step-mother as a pantomime cut-out; the gauche social-climber who'd married for position, and damn everything else.

"I'm sorry, my lady," he said. She gave him a bleak smile. "You should've kept that parrot," he added.

"The parrot? The one you brought to the wedding? But I did keep it! It lives in Hertfordshire with friends of mine."

"You know it's trained to say 'hello, dear'?"

"Of course! It says it all the time."

"So now you see why I gave you it."

"Er..."

"Well, it's a better conversationalist than Father. I thought you might need someone sensible to talk to."

She gaped at him for a moment, then began to laugh. He hadn't thought it that funny, but the more she laughed, the more impossible it was not to join in. She put one hand to her side, weeping with laughter. They'd almost stopped when she said 'Hello, dear!" in a croaky voice, not at all like a parrot, and with a frown that resembled Lord Dalton's habitual expression.

They were still standing there, helplessly clutching at each other, when John arrived. He gave them a sharp look and raised an eyebrow.

"Lady Dalton. Lord Thornby. Are you all right?"

Lady Dalton, already bright red, gave a small shriek. "Oh! I must—that is—good day, Lord Thornby. Mr Blake." She patted Thornby's arm in a familiar way, and fled back along the passage.

"Ah, Mr Blake," Thornby said, grinning at him.

***

John had left his interview with Lord Dalton and made his way upstairs thoughtfully. He wasn't sure if he'd learned anything or not. Why *did* Dalton persist in this failing seaweed venture that was churning through money he didn't have? Was the seaweed business really a cover for some scheme regarding pearls? What did being married, or not, have to do with anything?

At least he'd discovered that Dalton knew enough about magic to have tried theurgists and found them useless. But what had he tried them *for*? Did he know he was cursed? Had he tried to have the curse removed? No wonder it hadn't worked if the magicians had been using ordinary magical methods. Or was there something else? Lord Dalton was a man with secrets. Was it the natural caution about business in a man facing ruin, or something more sinister?

He decided he'd look in on Thornby. Probably, Thornby was asleep; but possibly he was upset from his awful ordeal. Either way, it wouldn't hurt to check, and anyway the temptation to see him again was too strong to ignore.

The last thing John expected was to find Thornby neatly dressed, standing in the passage in fits of laughter with Lady Dalton. An unworthy stab of jealousy went through him to see them so plainly enjoying each others' company. It seemed magical that Thornby could find anything to laugh *at*. In his place, John felt sure he'd have become gloomy and grumpy and beaten-down. You'd never guess Thornby had been in torment half the night. He looked paler than usual and a bit scratched, but that was all.

"Well! You look all right," John said. "Did the soil from the estate help? What on earth were you saying to her?"

Now he looked more closely, John could see that, in fact, all was not well. Thornby might be able to laugh, but there was a nervous glitter in his eyes, and tension in his jaw and shoulders. He was wound tighter than a steel cable on a suspension bridge. He hid it well, but at any moment, he might snap.

"Just being silly," Thornby said. "And the earth did help. Quite a bit, I think. Being closer helped too. What about you? You look thoughtful."

"I've been speaking to your father. I thought he might tell me something useful about the curse."

"Did he?"

"I don't know. I don't know what I'm looking for, you see, and he plays his cards damned close. So, I'm going to come up with as many obsolete charms as I can, in the hope that one of them has some effect on fairy magic. If I find anything that seems useful, I'll go and see him again, and see if I can unpick anything."

"Will that work? It sounds a bit hit or miss."

"My materials suggest things, sometimes. I think they know things I don't. That's how I got to that other place. I hope they'll help me now."

"Would it help if you tried things out on me? I mean, if something affects me, then presumably it'll affect the curse."

"Experimenting with magic? On you?"

His horror must have been obvious, because Thornby said quickly, "Bad idea?"

John opened his mouth, then closed it. The idea was appalling. And yet—would it be better than trying things on a cursed man? No, it was too dangerous. The whole point was to get Thornby away unharmed, not to ruin his life more. John opened his mouth a second time to refuse, then closed it again. How else would he know if he'd found something that worked? Experiment on a hedgehog and get trapped again? He might not get out a second time, even with Thornby's help.

"Why don't you come in while you think about it?" Thornby opened the door to his room.

The moment John went through it, Thornby closed the door and put his arms around him. "So, in five minutes, can I kiss you?"

John couldn't help smiling, even as all the blood in his body was rushing to his cock. "Maybe not five. Wait a minute."

He did the calculation he always had to do; time passed minus power expended. The rowan light, drying the clothes and dead leaves, stopping the wind, the wards, the work with the chain. Now it was about nine o'clock. This time he came up with a negative answer. Not worth the risk. He disentangled himself from Thornby, dug out a couple of iron pins and spent power into them.

Thornby was watching closely, lips parted, pupils dilated. Well, he'd said he liked being made to wait. John put the pins on the floor by the door, where they balanced like two little grey guardsmen. But the magic was impotent, contained harmlessly.

He took Thornby in his arms.

This time it was Thornby who said, "Wait."

"Are you being funny?" If Thornby was teasing him at a time like this, he'd make him sorry. Oh, how he'd make him pay.

Thornby rolled his eyes. "The door. There's no key. Can you do that thing again? Not that I'm expecting anyone, but—"

"The chimera key? It takes an age. I'm not waiting that long. Hang on." There was a chair in the study. John got it, on legs of aspic, and jammed it under the door handle.

"That's not very impressive, Mr Blake." Thornby's smile belied his snooty tone. "I was hoping for magic."

"I'll see what I can do."

Thornby leaned in, eyes closing. John kissed him—gently, just lips. Thornby angled his head and John felt the flicker of his tongue; it turned his knees to water. But after a moment, John pushed him away. Last time, he had been too overcome for any finesse. This time would be slower; more to his liking.

"First, some clothes," John said. He began to undress Thornby. He did it methodically, one button at a time, feeling Thornby tremble at his touch, eyes pleading. Thornby was biting his bottom lip, that beautiful red mouth getting redder from his own teeth. When Thornby tried to touch him, John knocked his hands away.

"John, can't I—"

Thornby was no innocent to need kind words and encouragement; their first encounter had shown that. John held up an admonishing finger. "No. You can wait."

Thornby balled his hands into fists, shifting uncomfortably. John finished unbuttoning his old-fashioned black shirt and let it fall to the ground. Shirtless, Thornby was even more desirable: thin, but strong-looking, arms well-knit with sinew and muscle. His chest was nearly hairless, nipples dark against the pallor of his skin, stomach taut. The front of his tight breeches did not leave much to the imagination. A spot of moisture was growing there, darker black on black silk. Not allowed to touch John, it was clear he wasn't quite sure where to put his hands. Ah, the triumph of seeing that elegance confounded; a little awkward, a little unsure.

"God, you're beautiful," John said. "Come on, take off the rest."

Thornby obeyed, finally standing naked in the cold morning light. Thornby's cock, pink at the tip, and jutting out in front of him, was already leaking clear fluid. John looked him up and down, trying to steady himself. The white bandage around Thornby's ankle drew his attention. Thornby's foot, below the bandage, was mottled, pink and white. An old burn? That must be why he sometimes limped. But it looked a little—odd. John hadn't noticed it last night in the rowan twig's unnatural blue light.

"John?" Half question, half plea. The pulse in Thornby's throat was beating as fast as a bird's wings.

"All right," John said. "My turn. You can do it."

He enjoyed making the better-born ones turn valet. Some of them hated it. But Thornby stepped forward readily enough and removed John's jacket, unbuttoned his waistcoat, untied his cravat. John let him struggle with his cufflinks, take off his shirt, unbutton his fly—but when Thornby reached into his drawers and trailed light fingertips up his cock, John grabbed his wrist.

"You have to wait. Remember?"

"I'm not sure I can."

John sat on the edge of the bed and took off his boots and socks. Slowly. He stood, removed his trousers, and finally, his drawers. Then he stood there for a moment, letting Thornby look, enjoying the expression on his face. Then John sat again and held out his arms in invitation.

Thornby came, putting his hands on John's shoulders. John put his hands on Thornby's hips and pulled him until Thornby's cock bobbed close to his mouth. It was a pretty cock; slender, like Thornby, with a graceful curve. John licked his lips and felt Thornby quiver. John looked up. Thornby's brows were furrowed. He was breathing through his mouth, his eyes huge and black.

It would be very fine to take Thornby in his mouth and give him what he wanted. But not yet. Ignoring Thornby's cock, John rested his head against that lovely narrow chest. He used his tongue on a nipple, stroked Thornby's round buttocks, fondled his balls, and finally ran a wet knuckle down the cleft of his arse, smiling to himself as Thornby made a sound like a sob. He did it several times, finally grinding his knuckle against Thornby's puckered arsehole. Thornby whimpered, and pushed his hips forward so the tip of his cock grazed John's chin.

"Oh, Christ! John—"

John stood and pushed Thornby down on the bed. Then he lay down himself with his mouth on Thornby's cock, his own cock pushing at Thornby's lips. Thornby opened his mouth and took him inside. His mouth was hot and eager. But the twin sensations of sucking and being sucked made it almost impossible to concentrate on either one. Thornby was moaning, his mouth losing suction.

Thornby pulled away and pushed John onto his back. John considered retaliating, but Thornby gave him a wicked sideways grin, pushed John's legs apart, knelt between them, and closed his lips over John's stand. He was tonguing the slit, cupping John's balls in one hand, then taking the whole thing in his mouth, finding a rhythm—

John looked down, and the heir to Raskelf glanced up, lips swollen red and stretched. The beautiful, untouchable Lord Thornby, with his mouth full of cock. It was too much. John gave warning with a fervent groan, thrust with his hips, and spent, pleasure thrumming along his nerves like magic down the threads of a brocade hanging. Only when the last shiver had run through him did Thornby take his mouth away. He gave John that same wicked smile and licked his lips. Thornby's hair had fallen around his face, patches of colour had spread across his cheeks, and his cock was red against his pale belly. He looked at once a peer of the realm and a tuppenny whore.

"Say something," John said.

Thornby raised an eyebrow, half smiling, a little puzzled too. "Well, how about, 'From now on, I shall never see the obelisk in the park without thinking of you'?"

John smiled. Next time, if there was a next time, perhaps he'd get Thornby talking while he fucked him. He'd like to hear that well-educated voice growing ragged and turning into an animal howl.

He sat up and pushed Thornby down on his back. To suck him off would be fair, and a pleasure, but he hadn't forgotten what he'd said in that thicket.

John lay next to him, licked his own hand until it was slick, and wrapped it around Thornby's cock. He didn't move it much at first. Just held it there and started kissing him. Thornby was rock hard—he wouldn't last much longer. Already he was moaning into John's mouth. John sped his strokes for a while, then slowed down again. Thornby made a noise of protest.

"Didn't I say I'd make you beg?" John said into his ear.

"Fuck." Thornby said, between gritted teeth.

"Manners, my lord! Try 'please'." He gave Thornby's balls a squeeze, making him gasp, then kissed him again.

Thornby muttered something.

"I beg your pardon?" John was moving his hand again. Slowly, then a little faster.

Thornby was writhing, he couldn't kiss any more—he'd lost control of himself.

"Shall I stop?" John murmured into his ear. "Or will you say 'please'?"

"No, no. Please, *please*!"

With that, John slid down the bed and took Thornby's swollen, leaking cock into his mouth. Thornby convulsed under him, hips bucking, breath sobbing. John waited until

Thornby had gone limp beneath him, then gave his cock one last kiss and lay down beside him. Thornby had his eyes shut and his mouth open; his breath was steaming in the air.

"All right?" John said.

"My God. Quite dictatorial, aren't you?"

"I don't think you minded."

"*Minded*? I think you turned my balls inside out."

John pulled the covers over them. The fire was burning low. He should get dressed and go and make it up, but Thornby had flung an arm across his chest and was holding onto him. John wouldn't have dislodged that gentle grip for anything.

Thornby took a few more deep breaths, then said, "So, making me wait in the spare room, and those big iron nails of yours this time, it's to do with magic?"

"Yes. If I haven't used much magic, I need to get rid of some before I have sex. Otherwise, when I spend, I lose control, and magic comes out. It's involuntary. So, I have to work it out beforehand. And if there's too much magic, I get rid of some, into those pins. I'm sorry for yesterday. All I could think of was doing the calculation as quickly as possible and grabbing you."

"But what happens if the magic does come out?"

"Oh, melted windows, nails popping out of walls, that kind of thing. Very messy. Inconvenient too."

"You melted a window? By spending?"

"Twenty windows, actually, all down the north side of the Institute. I was sixteen." John smiled ruefully. "I got such a beating, and lines for weeks. Wasn't all bad, though. No glass, you see, so at least he got away nice and easy."

He looked for traces of alarm or fear in Thornby's face, but on the contrary, Thornby was gazing at him with such an expression of fascination that John felt his cheeks grow warm.

"Who was he? Another magician?" Thornby asked.

"No, an actor. He did a routine as a drunken lord at the local inn, and I used to sneak out to watch him. I never usually broke the rules, but I did for him. And he stank of gin and had filthy nails, but he sounded a lot like quality when he put on the voice. Good diction."

"You fucked him for his diction?" Thornby was laughing into his shoulder.

John grinned. "I hadn't realised there was plenty of the real thing to be had if I just went a bit further west."

"The real thing?" Thornby gave him a sharp look. "You mean, like me?"

"Like you," John agreed lightly, but the conversation was getting onto what felt like dangerous ground. He cast around for something to change the subject and remembered Thornby's suspicious-looking scarred foot. "Now I want to know something; what happened to your foot? Not your ankle, but that old burn—may I look at it?"

"What? No, you may not!" Thornby stiffened in his arms.

"But what happened? Did you step in a bonfire?"

"Will you forget it? It's hideous, and I'd rather not think about it."

"It isn't hideous at all," John said mildly. "Come, tell me."

"I was nine. It was a case of spontaneous combustion. Luckily some quick-thinking nursemaid got my boot off and threw a jug of milk over it."

"Spontaneous combustion?" John frowned. "Are you sure?"

"How else could it have happened? I was minding my own business, looking for conkers, I think, and suddenly this terrible pain, and smoke and flames, and—well, you've seen it. Horrible."

"Were you at Raskelf?"

"No, it was—I don't know. Some other house. I don't remember."

To John's horror, Thornby got out of bed and began dressing.

"Soren."

It was the first time John had dared to use his Christian name. He'd imagined saying it a number of times, but not quite managed it. Now he heard his own voice and could hardly believe he'd said it. The syllables in his mouth felt more intimate than a kiss. He'd called an earl by his first name, and despite everything, he half-expected Thornby to throw him out for presuming to address him thus. In the hazel thicket Thornby had said 'I don't think you should call me Soren.' Of course, he'd been joking, but perhaps, deep-down, he'd meant it.

Thornby stopped, breeches on, bare-chested. He gave John a long look, and something flitted across his face. It was that recognition that sometimes passed between men engaged in difficult and mutual toil; a look that said, *So you will not let me down.* It was almost respect. Then Thornby folded his arms and looked away.

"I don't like talking about it. A friend at school used to say it made me like Byron, to make me feel better about it. But I've always hated it. I hate how it happened. I used to think it was a punishment from God for being wicked. Mysterious things are always happening to me, aren't they—oh!" He stared at John. "You think it's related, don't you?"

"I've seen a lot of burns in the foundries. They don't look quite like that. Please may I look?" He reached for Thornby's hand and pulled gently. "How about this? You let me look, and I'll kiss you anywhere you like."

Thornby gave him a flustered smile, but he allowed John to push him onto his back on the bed. John kissed his mouth, chest, stomach, thigh, knee and shin. Only then did he take Thornby's scarred foot in his hands.

The fire had left both the usual signs—the shiny patches, the mottled pink and white colouring, the two smallest toes fused together—and something unusual. There was a hatched pattern, as though someone had drawn a multitude of fine lines across Thornby's foot. That was a clue too obvious to miss. John glanced up to see Thornby watching him anxiously, almost wincing.

"Isn't it hideous?" Thornby said. "It makes me feel like a gargoyle. Is it any sort of clue?"

"It's not hideous. Can you remember any more about how it happened?" John kissed the instep, where the skin was pink and shiny. Thornby jerked away.

"John, please stop. At least let me hide it under the covers. I'll tell you if you let me hide it."

"All right, then I'll give you that kiss. If you can't decide where you want it, I have some ideas."

Thornby smiled, almost shyly. John put an arm around him. Thornby could be so prickly, and then so sweet. If only John could keep him in bed forever.

"All right—well—it was the school holidays. We went to the seaside. North of here. It might have been Scotland. Father took me. Mother had died, of course, and he—do we have to talk about this?"

John stroked his hair. "Shall I tell you why I want to know? I think someone tried to burn something belonging to you. Not an ordinary thing, but a token. Something that is you, in a way. And when they burned that, they burned you as well. It's witchcraft; it's not uncommon. People do it with mommets usually, little dolls made in a person's likeness. That's why I want to talk about it."

"Oh," Thornby said faintly. "On the whole, I prefer the spontaneous combustion theory. Not always the most reassuring of companions, are you?"

"It might be important. What I don't understand is why someone would do it to a child. Unless they were blackmailing your father."

"Huh! Father didn't care. He told me not to be such a sissy. He made me dip it in the sea to harden it." Thornby shivered. "God, I hated it. Every night we'd go down to the shore and he'd make me put my foot in the water. It hurt like hell and it was bloody terrifying. It was pitch black and I kept thinking something would grab my foot and pull me under. We never did go to the sands in the daytime; I suppose it was because of my foot being so horrible. And Father—God, I was excited when I heard he was taking me to the seaside. I thought he was going to be decent to me again, like he was when Mother was alive. He used to be, you know—I'd be brought down to see them and he'd show me his watch and let me pet his dogs. It's hard to imagine isn't it? But when Mother died, he changed. At the seaside he scared me so much I started wetting the bed. So, I got thrashed for that too."

Thornby put a hand up to his face. John could see it trembling.

"Soren, I'm sorry." He pulled Thornby closer.

"It's Father who's the bastard, not you. You're—well, I like you very much, Mr Blake."

"Even though I bullied you onto Howarth's moorland and went through your things?"

"I find I can forgive you. I can't think why." Thornby closed his eyes. "I suppose we should go and look for this token, but let's have five more minutes. Yes?"

"I should get to my salt. See if it has any ideas."

"All right, I'll come." But he yawned, and sighed, settling closer, and in another minute, he was asleep.

John admired the curve of his cheekbone, the feathery darkness of his lashes, and that mouth—just looking at it made his cock twitch. He was in over his head, he knew it. Not only did he feel as if Thornby had clouted him hard in some tender part he'd never known he had—but professionally speaking too.

He hadn't said so, but finding a token he couldn't trace with magic would be nearly impossible. When he'd thought they were looking for a spell, he'd been confident he'd recognise it if they found it. But a token could be anything. They were often crudely-made dolls, but it could be a ring or a seal, a pen or a button. Raskelf stretched around them—miles of passageways, hundreds of rooms, a million hiding places. And then there was the estate. They could search for a lifetime and never find it.

John knew where he was with iron, or salt, or a sulky furnace. He knew where he was with his sigils and herbs. But he was trained for industry, for the painstaking preparations and day-to-day drudgery of factory magic. And now he was caught in a morass of mystery and magic and lust, and he was out of his depth.

He should go back to London, tell Catterall what was going on. John had never asked for help with magic before, but this was different. Perhaps Catterall would pay for back-up. But who? He considered the other materials men, but no-one seemed quite right for a job as unusual as this. Perhaps a theurgist? Not Rokeby, Catterall wouldn't stomach him. And, frankly, John wasn't eager to see the effect of Rokeby's best smile on Thornby. Or Lady Dalton. Or anyone. Rokeby was, sort of, a friend, and could generally be relied upon in an emergency, but he had also fucked half of London, and swindled the other half. No, not Rokeby.

Perhaps Armstrong, though he was busy at the Home Office just now, and unlikely to obey Catterall's say-so. Maybe Christie would help, if he could be pried away from the Palace. John found himself scowling at the mere thought of Christie's supercilious nose poking around Raskelf. "Spot of bother, Blake? All a little too much, eh? Why don't you run along and play with your pins and needles? What we need here is some real magic."

But did it matter, if it meant Thornby could get away? If the curse on Lord Dalton could be lifted and Lady Dalton's happiness restored?

Only, would Armstrong or Christie let Thornby free once they knew what he was? They both dealt in demons; would they see Thornby as one? Although he'd never conjured up a demon himself, John knew they came from somewhere. Somewhere different again from the place he and Thornby had gone. But would Armstrong or Christie see it as different? They would probably hate Thornby on principle, with added revulsion thrown in if they realised he preferred men.

And in any case, something kept revolting in him. Something fierce and proud he thought he'd left behind at thirteen, when it had become clear to everyone that he was no theurgist and never would be. When he'd been accepted at the Institute at ten years old, he'd thought he'd be like Prospero one day, only younger. Magic would sing in his blood, and storms rage if he snapped his fingers. Caliban would do his bidding. And Ariel be his friend.

And then it had all turned to dust. He worked with materials. With common clay. He must support industry. It was fitting, really. His father was a shop-keeper. Armstrong's father was a gentleman farmer. Christie's was a barrister, with some connection to the Palace. Rokeby's origins were discreetly veiled, but rumour had it he was a by-blow of royalty.

And so John's magic had become a tool, a chore, a skill he could peddle like any tradesman. True, he'd gained the respect of the industrialists he worked for, and they'd paid him handsomely, too. He tried to be grateful. But since when was magic so mundane? Since when did it mean he had to spend his days strengthening bridges or testing ore samples? The only joy he ever felt in it was on those rare occasions when his materials spoke back to him— and that was a dangerous indulgence, a mere side-effect.

He allowed himself another long look at Thornby. He could gaze at him all day if he let himself, but that would help no-one. Instead, he kissed Thornby's cheek where it was criss-crossed with a dozen small scratches from the hazel thicket, then slid carefully out of bed.

As he did so, his bare foot crunched something small and fragile. He lifted his heel to find a white shell, like a tiny wing, now lying broken on the threadbare carpet. He frowned and pushed the two halves back together with his toe. It must belong to Thornby; perhaps he'd been sketching it.

He pulled on his drawers and trousers, and was putting on his shirt when he noticed another shell, so white it glowed in the grey morning light. Then he saw another, and another. Maybe six or seven, leading in a trail to one of the iron pins that stood quivering by the door. He froze, casting about with all his senses, then glanced at Thornby, still asleep. Should John wake him? And say what?

He touched the nearest shell. Nothing. Just a shell.

He crept to the pin and found a growth of barnacles clustering upon it, as if the pin had spent weeks underwater. And when he picked it up, there was emanating from it not merely his own pent-up magic, but an undercurrent of something rich and strange that made his heart leap and his skin prickle. Then the barnacles began to crumble to nothing under his fingers. The shells winked out, one by one, like tiny gas-lights, and the room was once again as ordinary as it could be with a man as beautiful as Thornby asleep in it.

John picked up the other pin, finished dressing, moved the chair, and very nearly ran down the passage to his room to begin his experiments. Once there, he laid out the materials he used most often—the salt, the pins, the spancel, the eye, the sand, the ward stone, and the rowan twig. He tried to explain the situation to them—with magic, with words. He asked for help. And then he waited.

What he got was silence.

And yet, as he sat on the dusty floorboards with the materials spread in front of him, he felt strangely hopeful. Because it was not a dead, uninterested silence; instead, there was a quality of surprise to it. It was the kind of gobsmacked silence he might get if he went to a workhouse, found the least considered, lowliest resident, and asked her what she thought of the New Poor Law and how things could be improved.

It was the silence of someone who has never thought to be asked; the silence of someone frantically and inexpertly gathering their thoughts because they are hardly ever invited to articulate them. At least, that was what he imagined. He listened, and listened, and occasionally tried to explain what he wanted in a slightly different way, and then he listened some more.

When he finally looked up, it was to discover he was stiff from sitting on the cold floor, that it was past midnight and the entire household was in bed. He dimly remembered turning the maid away at the door when she'd come to draw the curtains and light the fire, saying he'd do it himself, and then forgetting. He went to bed, still listening, still with that deep, considering, surprised silence emanating from his materials.

Chapter Nine

The following afternoon, the Greys arrived; Mr Grey, Mrs Grey, Miss Harriet Grey, and two younger girls who looked just out of the schoolroom. John understood that the family had no noble connections, but that Mr Grey had made a fortune in textiles. Mr Grey's plump, red, untroubled countenance was vaguely familiar; surely John had seen him at some Manchester mill? Mr Grey gave no sign of recognising him, but all the same, he mentally rehearsed a few remarks about Lord Dalton's business interests, in case Mr Grey should suddenly remember him and think to quiz him on his place in the world.

Mrs Grey was a worried-looking lady with fluttering hands and a nervous laugh. She was obviously ill at ease taking tea in such exalted company, but Lady Dalton was doing her best to be charming, and her best was considerable. Mrs Grey was soon smiling more naturally and talking with less forced animation. There were curd tarts and tiny sandwiches; very decent ones, for Raskelf. John gathered that Dalton had borrowed the Howarths' cook.

The Lazenbys would not arrive until the following day, and Miss Grey had obviously been told to press her advantage. Her light-brown hair was elaborately arranged and she wore a showy dress of primrose satin that suited her creamy complexion very well. She displayed none of her mother's nerves, and accepted Lord Dalton's antique courtesies with grace. Probably she was pretty enough to be used to all manner of attentions being paid to her.

Then Thornby made his entrance. He was late, of course. John gathered he made a habit of it to antagonise his father. But, for the majority of this party at any rate, the wait had clearly been worth it. All the female members of the Grey family froze and widened their eyes. Even Mrs Grey blushed prettily.

Perhaps in honour of the occasion, Thornby had abandoned his usual black, and indeed, the century. He was a vision of Georgian style in a cream silk court suit: tail coat and breeches, cream silk stockings, and a waistcoat of pale green and cream stripes sprigged with pink flowers. He wanted only a sword and powdered peruke and he would have made a suitable escort for Marie Antionette.

John found his own eyes had narrowed, partly with amusement and partly with speculation. It was impossible—for him, anyway—to look at Thornby dressed in such a way and not imagine undressing him. Mr Grey looked puzzled, and slightly suspicious, as if he was trying to work out whether Thornby's costume was a subtle insult. Miss Grey almost dropped her shawl when Thornby was introduced to her; her first sign of nerves. Thornby bowed, very properly, and took her for a halting stroll in the long picture gallery, it being too wet outside to walk along the terrace.

As Thornby limped past, John could hear him saying, "Yes, a gin trap, Miss Grey. Such a cruel device! But let us find something more pleasant to discuss. Are you interested in art?"

Lord Dalton, watching his son, seemed to veer from barely concealed rage to satisfaction that the Greys were here, and that Thornby was, at least for now, being civil.

About half-way through the afternoon, Miss Grey went to talk to Lady Dalton. Lord Dalton had taken Mr and Mrs Grey into the long gallery and was impressing some family history upon them with the aid of the paintings. The two younger girls were looking through a cabinet of curiosities with Mr Derwent. John found Thornby standing next to him.

"Well, this is torture, isn't it?" said Thornby.

"Miss Grey seems nice enough."

"She saw Ophelia six times. You've no idea what a wretch I feel, lying to a lady who admires Millais. What a way to spend an afternoon!"

Thornby pulled fretfully at the cuffs of his tight coat. No one was watching, and John allowed himself one sideways glance. But it was not the pleasure he'd expected, because he could see that, for Thornby, the afternoon really was torture, almost as bad, in its way, as being chained outside the estate. One saw the Georgian confection he was wearing and expected frivolity, but there was nothing light-hearted about him. His eyes were defeated.

Of course, John had known for days that Thornby was desperate to leave Raskelf. It was so easy to forget, because Thornby hid his desperation behind that careless and teasing facade, but it was just that—a facade—and if it crumbled, as it appeared to be crumbling now—

What Thornby needed was to be held. To be gentled with hands and voice like a frightened horse, and then given a damned hard ride until he forgot everything except his own need. And then—release, even if it was not the more fundamental release he craved, but only the momentary sweet release of the body. For now, in the drawing room, John couldn't give him that. But he could give him a few more bricks for his facade—a chance to tease, and maybe smile, and feel human once again.

He cast about for a topic that might do, and asked, "Why do you wear those old-fashioned clothes? I've been wondering since I arrived."

Thornby looked at him blankly for a moment, then managed a tiny, intimate smile. "You don't like them?"

"I wasn't complaining, just wondering why."

"I made a vow to my grandfather on his deathbed that I would always dress as he believed a gentleman should—which is thus." Thornby made an elegant gesture. A spark of mischief had appeared in his eyes.

"A deathbed vow? Is that what you tell the ladies?"

"The ladies, Mr Blake, are too polite to ask. But it's what I tell those persons who think it acceptable to ask me personal questions."

"I beg your pardon, Lord Thornby. No personal questions? A pity. Then I'd better not ask how you'd like me to fuck you later."

Thornby's eyes widened and his lips parted. He made a noise in his throat, part gasp, part horrified laughter, and glanced over his shoulder.

"No one can hear," John said.

"Christ, I hope not." Thornby closed his eyes for a moment. "If you give me a cockstand in public I'll never forgive you. These breeches are awfully tight."

"Yes, thank you, I noticed. So perhaps now you'll tell me why you wear them?"

Thornby smiled—a genuine smile that lit up his eyes. "You're a very determined fellow, aren't you?"

"I'm patient too. You know, I enjoyed hearing you say 'please' yesterday. Perhaps I might give you another lesson in manners, by being very, very patient with you, later on tonight."

Thornby stared at him, a faint flush colouring his face. "Play fair, John. Miss Grey could step over any moment. Come then, I'll give you the truth. It's all down to my doctor."

"Your doctor?"

"Yes. We have very singular miasmas here in the north. Trousers allow more bad air to circulate upon the limbs, and to well-bred gentlemen this can be very detrimental. Of course, common persons, such as yourself, aren't affected, but my blood is more puissant, and is therefore more sensitive to such things."

John regarded him as sternly as he could, trying not to laugh. "Later, you will genuinely regret this."

"I won't."

"What if there is no 'later', until you tell me?"

"I don't believe you'd do that."

"Let me remind you how patient I am."

Thornby smiled again. "I look forward, Mr Blake, to testing the limits of your patience. But for now, I think I'd better just tell you that I wear these clothes because I haven't any others."

"That's true?"

"Gospel. Well, mostly."

John frowned. "Why not visit the tailor?"

"Because I can't."

"Ask him to visit you."

"Father told him not to."

"Yes, but—"

"Really, it's true. When I got here, I had the clothes I was wearing when Father hustled me away from London. One pair of trousers and a silk smoking jacket. Nothing else. Not even a hat. When I complained, Father said he'd be happy to buy me a suit to get married in, or I could find plenty of old clothes in the attics. Obviously, he thought I'd fold when I saw what was there, but I called his bluff and put them on. It annoys him no end that I walk about as though I like them. I must say I felt a little eccentric the first time I went out, but it's not as though I go anywhere, so it hardly matters."

"So, your father makes you dress like that?" John said, still struggling with the idea.

"Not as such, today. In fact, he provides a very decent range of contemporary tailoring when there are ladies present who may want to marry me, but I stick to my breeches just to show him."

"That's the most bloody-minded thing I ever heard."

"Who? Father? Or me?"

"Both of you."

"I can tell you, it was actually a damned nasty surprise to find my trunk was practically empty when I got here. I didn't believe Father's valet when he told me there were only a few under-things and a couple of pairs of shoes. I suppose that was all my man had time to pack before they took the trunk. I even went to the box room to check, but it was true."

"Your trunk came with you from London? But it was empty?"

"Yes, I've just told you."

"So, why bring it?"

"I've no idea. I suppose it was the look of the thing."

"Rubbish. Your father dragged you out of London without a hat or coat? He'd rather you walked around in ancient hand-me-downs than some decent clothes? He fights with you at the dinner table. He doesn't give a damn how things look, does he? No more than you do, really."

"I hope you're not comparing us and finding similarities."

"But listen; he brought the trunk. So, it's important."

"A trunk? A battered old thing I've had since I went away to school?"

"You've had it since the first time you left home?"

"Yes, he gave it to me himself, along with a lecture about taking care of my belongings— Oh my God, there's something in it, isn't there? Or there was. This—whatever it is—this token. Come quick, before someone stops us."

They made their escape through the faded glories of the Venetian saloon, Thornby opening one of those doors that resembled a panelled wall, with the handle cleverly concealed in the wainscoting. He led the way, taking a confusing route through both narrow servants' passageways, and wide public corridors.

In the gloomy box room, the trunk squatted in a corner. Thornby had called it a battered old thing, but for an item of luggage nearly twenty years old, John was struck by the quality. It was made of the strongest materials, and the Dezombrey arms looked freshly painted.

John sank to his knees, opened the trunk, and ran his hands around the inside. "Right, we're looking for something that dates back to your childhood. You got that burn when you were nine, so it's at least that old. Maybe older."

"You don't think the trunk itself could be the thing?"

"Does it feel important to you?"

Thornby shrugged. "Not especially. But it is mine."

"Your father is keeping you here with something damned powerful. I think you'll know it the moment—wait! I felt something. That other feeling."

Thornby, examining the side of the trunk closest to the window, said, "There are marks here."

Along one bottom edge, lines were scored in the heavy leather. Thornby prodded these and a flap in the leather came loose. Thornby wiggled something, then pulled out a shallow drawer, a couple of inches deep and a foot square. He put his fingers in the empty drawer, then snatched them back as though something had bitten him.

"There was something here, all right. I feel—peculiar," Thornby said.

"May I look?"

John touched a cautious fingertip to the inside of the wooden drawer. There was no ordinary magic to be sensed, and nothing else came clear. But that seemed the way of this other kind of magic; if he looked directly for it, it slid away from him. He carried the drawer to the box-room window.

"What's that?" John pressed a finger into one corner of the drawer. Stuck to the end of his finger was a hair. It was an inch long, brown, but gold where the light struck it.

Thornby peered at it. "It's not mine. Wrong colour."

"Were you fair as a child?"

"I suppose I was, now you mention it." Thornby looked again. "But that's not a child's hair, is it? It's not fine enough. It's a bit bristly. It's more like—" He went spectacularly white, and backed away to sit on the nearest trunk. "It's from an animal, isn't it? Is that bad? What does that mean?"

"I'm not sure."

"The token's supposed to be part of me, isn't it? What if it's—oh, God—what if I'm a werewolf?"

"This isn't wolf hair." John angled his finger to the light again.

"Isn't it? How do you know?"

"Because I use wolf hair in one of my charms, and this isn't it."

"Oh." Thornby ran a shaky hand across his face. "Christ, you're useful to have around, aren't you? I don't suppose there's another man in Yorkshire who could have told me that."

"But I do think it's from an animal. Sorry, Thornby. Still, you seem to have got on all right as a man for—how old are you? Twenty-seven years—so whatever it is, I think you just need it in your possession."

"I could put it in a safe and never think of it again?"

"Exactly. So long as it's yours, you can go where you like, I suspect. Which is why you were able to go off to school and Oxford and London and so on. Because it's your trunk and so its contents were yours, too. Until your father took it. Anyway, we've another clue, thanks to me asking you rude personal questions."

Thornby managed a watery smile. "I'm beginning to appreciate your impertinence, Mr Blake."

"Good. You've no idea how impertinent I plan to be, once everyone's gone to bed. And don't lose your nerve about this hunt because we found a hair. It doesn't mean you're half beast. Maybe it's a lucky rabbit's foot. Your mother might have charmed it for you."

He looked at the hair again, trying to place it. Could it be from a rabbit? It was an odd colour for a rabbit, but perhaps. Or if colour was no clue, maybe some kind of golden fox? Or a deer?

Thornby sighed, head bowed as if contemplating his silk-clad knees. "You've no idea how discomforting it is, learning you're not fully human. It's not that I mind Mother being different; it's because it gives Father this awful hold over me. I'm bloody frightened. I've been going slowly mad this last eighteen months, and now I— Look, you don't think it would be better to marry Miss Grey or whoever, and then—well, I know he'll take the money, but at least I could get away. I'd have my name. I could borrow, or get some position with an income to support her. Couldn't I?"

"You trust him to give it to you?"

"But if I've done as he wants? I can't get married more than once, can I? So, if I'm no further use to him, why *not* let me go?"

"Of course, it's up to you."

"But you wouldn't, would you?" Thornby said.

"No, and for the same reason you haven't; because you won't put an innocent girl into the middle of all this. Because you're a gentleman. When you're not sucking my cock, that is."

Thornby gave a helpless snort of laughter. "You're right. I just—I think I shall go mad if I have to stay here another minute. John, you will get me out, won't you?"

"Of course I will. Come, you go back to the Greys and I'll tidy up here." John took his pocketbook out and carefully put the hair between two blank pages. "I've shown my face downstairs. I'll go back to my materials now."

"I wish we could stay up here. How's it going, your research?"

"Fine. I'm onto something. And this hair will help tremendously. It's part of what we're looking for. If I can find the right sigil, this'll lead us straight to the token. So, chin up, and I'll see you at dinner."

Thornby left him, and John tidied up and went back to his room. He'd told Thornby things were fine, but in fact he was far from sure. His materials had still not offered up much in the way of suggestions, but the quality of their silence was less stunned, more pensive.

So, he hadn't lied to Thornby. It *was* going well.

Wasn't it?

Chapter Ten

The following morning, Thornby went to breakfast early, hoping to catch John alone before the rest of the household came down. He'd been to John's room late last night, and John, as promised, had been very impertinent indeed.

He had used his tongue. Everywhere. He'd made Thornby writhe and whimper and plead. And then John had fished a small vial of oil from one of the many pockets of his discarded jacket. He had applied the oil liberally, and fucked Thornby so expertly that he'd begged some more. And afterwards, John had held him, and kissed him, and smiled his rare unguarded smile. Thornby had had plenty of lovers, but never one as intent as John. Perhaps all the listening to walls and tables the man had done had given him some sort of magical intuition, because he seemed to know instinctively what felt good and what felt so-so, and what felt so incandescent one forgot to breathe.

John had talked of this and that—of his childhood, talking to the nails and tools in his father's shop; of training at the Dee Institute; and of his last job, helping to build the Crystal Palace and then protecting it from magical attack. Apparently, there were a number of men from the professions who didn't think a jumped-up gardener's design should have been chosen for such a great edifice. So, among other things, there had been freak storms and flurries of ensorcelled bats flinging themselves at the glass at night. Some people had wanted very much to make Joseph Paxton look bad. They had gone so far as to hire magicians to try to make it happen. John had stopped them.

He hadn't been boasting. In fact, Thornby felt, it was rather the opposite; John was giving him the facts about his life, letting him know who he was. He was an ironmonger's son made good. And if he spoke like a gentleman, it was because he'd had it beaten into him at the Institute, because they prided themselves on turning out magicians who could serve at the highest levels. In the same way one wouldn't tolerate a valet who wiped his nose on his sleeve, one preferred one's magicians with manners.

Thornby gathered that magic, as a profession, was on something of a cusp. The Dee Institute that John was so proud of having attended had been founded in 1578 as an Academy by Queen Bess' court magician, Dr Dee. Alchemy had been worth investing in, back then; even the Queen had had stakes. But over the centuries the Academy had degraded. It had become a dark place, of superstition, charlatans, and poppycock. Magic had become bastardised and ineffectual.

John was a new kind of man. He'd come, as a boy, to an Institute revitalised during the Regency by recent discoveries in the fields of both theurgy and materials. Now, John and his colleagues sought recognition; respect, even. Because although magic was once again becoming a force to be reckoned with, it was not yet respectable. Indeed, to hear John tell it, much of society saw magicians as akin to the prostitutes who served London; they were regrettable, a necessary evil. One barely acknowledged their existence, yet sometimes nothing else would do. John was determined to change this attitude. He considered that magic should be at least as well-regarded as horticulture, medicine, or law.

Whatever John had intended by telling him all this, the end result was that Thornby felt a little overwhelmed. Not only was it the most fascinating pillow-talk he had heard, but it was becoming clear to him that John wasn't just *any* magician, but a very remarkable one. John didn't say so, but Thornby felt sure Paxton could have had almost any magician in England—and it turned out there were quite a few of them—and he had chosen John. Because when it came to iron and glass and other inanimate things, John was the best in the land.

John had said he planned to rise early and get out of the way of the party so he could work on finding the token. Thornby had gone back to his own room, expecting to sleep like a man who's just been fucked into oblivion. But he'd woken almost hourly. When he woke for the fifth time at five o'clock, he finally realised it was because he was hoping to see John again before the day started.

As he entered the breakfast room, he saw that Lady Dalton had beaten him to it. She was sitting next to John, but neither of them seemed to be eating. Lady Dalton looked rather red in the face, and shot to her feet like a startled rabbit when she saw him. She nodded to him, gave John a look of plain entreaty, and fled the room.

Thornby looked after her. "Is she all right?"

John gave him a hunted, distracted look. "I suppose she's as right as anyone could be with a cursed husband and a troupe of fairies moving their things around. Anyway, I told her to start putting walnuts out; that will probably help."

"But what was she saying?"

"I'm sorry, Thornby, I'm not sure I should say. It was a private matter."

"I hope you trust me." It came out more stiffly than he'd intended.

He could not help looking at John, so neatly buttoned and tied, and thinking about what they'd done last night. He was fairly sure John was remembering too, because he looked

Thornby up and down and a fleeting look of satisfaction crossed his face, to be followed by a covetous one. Then his harassed expression returned and he picked up his fork.

"Of course I trust you," he said, then muttered, almost to himself, "I'll never complain about factory work again." He put his fork down again and put his fingertips to his temples.

"John, what on earth did she say? Please tell me. Who would I tell anyway?"

"I shouldn't."

"Did she tell you not to?"

"No, but I..."

"Well, maybe I can help?"

John gave him an odd look, almost as if he was trying not to smile. "I doubt it. But I suppose it is sort of family business. She wants a baby. She wants me to—see to it."

"A *baby*? She wants you—you to—" He couldn't go on.

John looked up at him, frowned, and then, to his surprise, gave a splutter of horrified laughter. "What do you *think* I mean? She wants me to make a charm for her. To make your father—you know—*visit* her. Christ!"

"Oh. I thought..."

"Thornby, she's married. She's a *lady*. With morals. Why would you even think that?"

"She fancies you."

"What? Of course she doesn't. But the point is; should I do it? I said no, at first, but then I agreed to think about it."

"A baby, eh? Can you do that?"

Thornby helped himself to ham and eggs and sat opposite. It looked as though John had eaten about half a plate of kedgeree before being distracted by Lady Dalton. Now he picked up his knife and fork again. He had nice hands, well-proportioned and capable-looking.

"I never have. I don't do magic on people, usually, except for wards. I sometimes use the Voice on factory owners, but if anyone found out, I'd never work again, so I don't do it very often. Ethical and family matters are for church mages, or political theurgists, not someone like me."

"But, you could?" Thornby realised he was starving and hove to. Everything was done properly for once, thanks to the cook borrowed from the Howarths.

"I don't know. I can't make him love her. I told her so. Love charms never work. Not that that stops people like Rokeby charging through the nose for them. But it is possible to incite lust. And, perhaps, if I give her an extra strong fertility charm at the same time..." He put his knife and fork down without having eaten anything and sipped from what looked like a cold cup of coffee. "Then there's the curse to consider. What if the magics react with each other? Mind you, the curse didn't stop him having relations with her in the past—so I suppose that's safe enough. I wouldn't be charming him to do something completely against the grain."

"Well, why not? She hasn't had much else out of him, has she?"

"He could hurt her. He could hurt other people. You can't focus lust—you have to put the right person in the right place, and hope it all goes to plan. Even most theurgists won't touch this sort of thing. Let alone with a fairy curse complicating matters."

"But you're better than them."

John laughed, mirthlessly. "Where did you get that idea? I'm really not. There's a reason theurgy's called the Royal Road. It's far more powerful to raise a demon to do what you want. Once you've trapped it, there's no more messing about with materials. It has to obey. And a demon can do almost anything—they can travel fantastically fast, create instant illusions, affect the weather—all kinds of things I can't do."

"Well, I don't see it that way."

"Forgive me, Thornby, but you don't know anything about it."

"But demons are demons, aren't they? It's not just a name? They're evil. Aren't they?"

"They're vile. Hideous. They'll trick you if they can. That's why it takes so much power to call them up and make them serve."

"There you are, then. You're better than that. Your materials help you. They're not out to get you. Are they?"

"No, but—" John frowned. "You're missing the point."

"I don't think so. Would you rather have a friend who wanted to help or a powerful slave who'd kill you the first chance he got? I know which I'd prefer."

John glared at him for a moment, and then blurted out, "But how can anyone be *friends* with a glass eye or a bag of salt? I mean, really? How can I trust some random side effect? Sometimes I think I must be fooling myself! Magicians don't *take advice* from their materials. In fact, we're told not to, because we're meant to be in control. But for most men, it never comes up because they discard their basic materials. I'm a freak, Thornby, for always sweeping up my salt like a thrifty housewife. And my results are unexpected. I can't replicate them. I mean, at the Crystal Palace, when those damned bats started hurling themselves at the glass—I used a shield charm at first, but I had the salt out and it— You know, I can't believe I'm bothering you with all this. You don't know the first thing about magic."

His tone had run from annoyance through self-loathing to defeat. Thornby put down his knife and fork, a cold slither of despair running down his back. The food he'd just eaten sat in a lump in his stomach. If John was defeated, then he was stuck.

Then a spark of hope lit in him, because there was something he'd noticed about the way John talked about his abilities, and about the abilities of the demon-masters he called theurgists. In spite of all the marvellous things he could do, John needed confidence, and it was up to Thornby to provide it. Hadn't most of Thornby's upbringing been based on the premise that one day he'd lead men? To command, yes, but also to boost morale and do whatever else was necessary. He'd never bothered about it all before, but if there was one man in the world he cared about inspiring, it was John Blake, magician.

And at any minute someone could walk in and disturb them. The sun was well up now.

"John, I might not know about magic, but I can smell snobbery a mile off, and that's what these theurgists are. Snobs." John opened his mouth to protest and Thornby held up a finger. "Don't interrupt. And the reason I know about snobs is because I used to be one, and I know they'll stop at nothing to belittle anyone who isn't like them."

John said nothing, just stared at him across the table.

Thornby went on, urgently, "And while you're at it, you can stop fussing about experiments and replication. It's magic, isn't it? It's not science."

"Yes, but—" John broke off, frowning. "Well, you're right, it's not science."

"No, even though they've taught you to use it in a methodical way. I'm not denying it's damned clever, all this stuff you've learned to do. But if you want to be friends with a bag of salt, I really don't see why you shouldn't."

John was still staring at him, shaking his head a little. Not disagreeing, exactly, just trying to assess what he'd said. Thornby could almost hear his mind whirling. Then John gave him a baffled smile, and when he spoke there was hope in his voice, and wonder too. "I think you may have just turned three hundred years of magical theory on its head. I never, ever thought of it like that."

A giddy lightness was beating in Thornby's chest—a marvellous feeling of having cheated something awful and at the same time given John something he valued.

"Well, no, because you were brought up to respect the experts. Whereas I was brought up to know I'm always right because I'm me. I think you should have a little more confidence in your observations, because *I* think you're onto something wonderful."

"And you're always right."

"These days, I have been known to make the *occasional* mistake. It's the low company I've been keeping. It's tarnishing my infallibility."

John smiled. "You can still sound like an arrogant little prick when you want to."

"Yes, can't I? Perhaps you should make me beg for it again. It might bring me down a peg or two."

"Ha, it hasn't yet. Perhaps next time I'll *leave* you begging for it, and read a book by the fireside for a bit."

"You wouldn't dare! If you did, you might get a surprise. Perhaps it would be a pleasant one? Do you ever let people fuck you, Mr Blake? Because I would. Like a shot. If you wanted me to."

John blinked. "I don't, usually."

"I didn't think so. But you have tried it?"

"I didn't like it."

Thornby opened his mouth to say; "Well, never mind", but John added, slowly, "Actually, perhaps it's more that I didn't much care for the fellows I tried it with."

"Then I hope I'm nothing like them."

"You're not like them."

To Thornby, the phrase seemed to ring in the air like the chime of a knife against crystal. John was just sitting there, fingers on the handle of his cold cup of coffee, not even looking him in the eye.

"John, did you just agree to try it again?"

"I don't know. It's been a long time."

"I'm *almost* as good at it as you. I'd make you come so hard the chandeliers would turn into swans and fly away—even if you did your trick with those pins."

John smiled. "We'll see."

His eyes, always dark, had gone black with arousal, and something else Thornby couldn't quite place. But he felt that, given the slightest encouragement, John would probably try anything. Some men just wouldn't, no matter how you tried to persuade them. Some men, he knew, took one look at him and saw: pretty, skinny, artistic, and made up their minds right there about what he liked and wanted. And it annoyed the hell out of him.

John might have a taste for being dictatorial in the bedroom, but there was something receptive about him, too. Of course, a man might be adventurous in some aspects of his life and conservative in others, but John, for all his wariness, seemed open to the idea of experimentation. Look at all this business about taking advice from a bag of salt! And God, he was handsome. Thornby had thought him good-looking enough when they had met, but he seemed to get more attractive the longer one knew him. It was the way he made the air crackle with possibilities, the way his hands seemed to listen when they were on one's skin.

Thornby cleared his throat. "Well, today's going to last forever, isn't it? The Lazenbys arrive this morning, and then there'll be shooting, followed by tea, and dinner with about twenty courses. And then music, probably, until I scream."

John, who had been staring at him, said, "Yes," as if he hadn't heard, then sat back in his chair, visibly changing tack. "You know, if I vary the wards when I give her the fertility charm—it'll be bulky, but she could manage—I could—"

"I think I'll leave you to it. You should eat, too."

"Sorry. Talking shop at you again."

"No, it's more—if I keep looking at you, I shall die of swollen balls. Did you know, when you're thinking, you have a ferocious scowl that I really find quite devastating."

"Thornby. Soren. Wait; before you go." John reached into his pocket and brought out what looked like an ordinary grey river pebble. "I want to give you this."

Thornby took it on the palm of his hand and looked closer. It was swirling internally with what seemed to be pearlescent smoke.

"It's a tracker stone," John said. "If you put it in your pocket, I'll be able to find you. I can't find you using the ordinary methods, but if your father tries that trick with the chain again, I can set up a sigil and it'll lead me straight to the stone."

"What a clever thing!" He held it to the light; the grey swirls shifted and sparkled. "Thank you, John. You're marvellous."

It was only once he was walking along the passage towards the gun room that he realised what he'd said.

He'd meant to say '*it's* marvellous'. But that wasn't what he'd said at all.

Would John have noticed? Of course he would; he noticed everything. Thornby felt strangely exposed—as he had the morning John had held his scarred foot in his hands. Did it matter, to feel that way? Thornby liked flirting with people, and giving those light, overblown compliments that perhaps one didn't really mean. But he hadn't spoken like that at all. It had sounded quite sincere; almost a little breathy. Like a girl swooning over a flower.

He realised he'd frozen with his hand on the balustrade of the main staircase. He could hear voices coming along the first floor passage—Mr and Mrs Grey coming down to breakfast with at least one of their daughters.

Swooning? He didn't do that. He had enough to worry about.

John wanted him. And John could get him out of Raskelf. Wasn't that what all this was about? A fair exchange? And if he enjoyed it himself then so much the better.

But *you're marvellous*? Not sleeping for wanting to see the man at breakfast? But the thing was; John *was* marvellous. Stunningly marvellous. A bloody magician. With those dark eyes and that smile, and in bed—

It was as if another woodland path had opened up in the middle of a threadbare spare room, and Thornby was being invited to walk down it.

The voices were getting closer. If he didn't go now, the Greys would find him standing in the hallway, gawping at nothing with a cockstand like a flagpole. He adjusted his breeches as best he could, and hurried on down the passage to make sure Stewart wasn't too soused to see that they got the guns ready properly.

***

That night, when the last shooting story had been told, the last piano piece applauded, and everyone had gone to bed, Thornby took his candle and crept along to John's room. He hadn't managed to speak to him in private since this morning at breakfast. He was desperate to know whether John had discovered anything. And just as desperate to see him. But the room was empty.

Eventually he found John loitering in the passage near Lord Dalton's door. A candle was guttering in a tarnished ormolu sconce, sending shadows flickering up the walls.

"John?" he said softly.

John's face lit up for a moment, then went solemn. "Look, I can't see you tonight. You'd better go."

"You've done it, haven't you? You've charmed Father."

"Yes."

Thornby couldn't help shivering a little. Although, in theory, he agreed that Lady Dalton deserved to have things her way for once, in practice it was a bit horrible to think of John doing something so intimate, so controlling to anyone. Surely no-one should have that much power over another person? Thornby put his candle down in an empty marble niche that had once held a Sèvres vase. It had probably been sold, like so much else.

"Is she in with him?" he said.

"No."

"Oh. So, it hasn't worked?" He almost felt relieved.

"I don't know," John snapped, then added, "Sorry. I thought, better it doesn't work at all than something goes wrong. But I may have been too subtle. He may not seek anyone out. He may just—" He made a slight, but unmistakable, movement with his hand.

Thornby shuddered. "This whole thing's rather horrible, isn't it?"

"Worse for you, probably. He's just a man to me. And not a very nice one either."

"Where's my lady?"

"Waiting inside the door of her room. The moment she hears him come out, she'll open the door. Or I'll go and knock on her door. He'll see her. He'll go to her. That's the theory anyway."

"Wouldn't it be safer if she waited here?"

"She's in her nightgown. Mind you, everyone else has gone to bed now. He's still awake though, I think. I heard a noise not long ago."

"He won't—I mean—if he sees you. He won't have a go at you, will he?"

John gave him an unreadable look. "He's not that way, is he?"

"I doubt it. How would I know? No." He realised he had never thought about his father's predilections, and certainly did not want to think about them now.

The sound of a door opening made them both jump. But it was down the corridor. A moment later Lady Dalton came out. She wore a white nightgown with a lace shawl wrapped around her shoulders, and carried a candle. When she saw Thornby she paused, then raised her chin and came towards them.

"My lady," John said.

"Mr Blake. Good evening, Lord Thornby."

Thornby bowed. "Ma'am. I was just leaving. I'll wish you a good night."

"You know, don't you?" she said to him.

John went crimson. "My lady, I—I—"

"It's not his fault. He wasn't going to tell me. I wheedled it out of him," Thornby said quickly.

"Actually, he persuaded me to go ahead with it," John managed.

"Then I thank you, Lord Thornby. It's all right, Mr Blake. I would rather you hadn't mentioned it, but since you have—well. It doesn't matter. In any case, I intend to knock on the door."

"Oh, are you sure?" John said.

"I'm not waiting in my room another minute. You've done your part. Now I'm doing mine. It may not be ladylike, but I shall do it anyway."

"Brava," Thornby murmured.

Lady Dalton raised her chin a little higher. "You may both leave now."

"My lady, I would rather stay," John said.

"And I would rather you leave, Mr Blake."

"Just in case something goes wrong."

"It will not. I'm done being scared, Mr Blake. I've asked you to do this and I'm taking responsibility for it. And I would prefer—"

Lord Dalton's door opened abruptly, startling them all. His lordship stood swaying in the doorway for a moment, backlit by the fire that was warming his room. Brandy fumes came off him and his clothes were dishevelled. Before anyone could speak he stepped forward and grabbed Thornby by the jaw.

"What the hell are you doing here?"

Thornby tried to pull away. "Just saying good night, sir."

"Damn my eyes, you look like her."

Thornby stared at him in horror. His father turned his face slightly from one side to the other, examining him. Thornby tried to twist out of his grip, but Lord Dalton held tight.

Lady Dalton said loudly, "My lord!"

"Eh?" Dalton turned to her. He didn't let Thornby go, but his grip loosened and Thornby managed to break free. He staggered a few steps backwards, away from his father.

"My lord," Lady Dalton said again, a little quieter, but a challenge rang in her voice.

Lord Dalton made a harrumphing sound in his throat, but he was looking at her. Thornby realised John had taken his arm and was trying to make him retreat silently down the passage. They backed away until Lord Dalton's door closed, with both lord and lady inside.

"Bloody hell. All right?" John said to him.

"Fine." His jaw felt burned by Lord Dalton's grip as if by some kind of acid that would not wash away. He shuddered. It was a filthy feeling, having his own father look at him as if he was a whore for the taking. He wrapped his arms around himself. "Will she be all right, do you think?"

"I hope so. He is her husband. She's been with him before."

"Had we better wait?"

"You should go. I'll wait. There's a spare room opposite. I'll leave the door ajar. If she screams—"

"Can I wait with you?"

"Better not."

"If she screams, aren't two better than one?"

"Damn it, Soren, do I have to say it? It nearly went wrong because you were here. Because you look like your mother."

"But he wouldn't have. Not really. Would he?"

"I hope not." John glanced at him, and added, "No, of course not. But I still think it'd be better if you weren't around."

"What an absolutely ghastly business."

"Yes, well, that's magic, I suppose. Why don't you go to bed? I'll look in on you first thing. Yes?"

"All right." He couldn't stop shivering. Going to his cold bed alone was the last thing he wanted. Not that he wanted sex just now, either. But he wanted John's arms around him. Wanted some evidence of kindness or tenderness in the world, not just manipulation and horror.

John was already walking silently back down the passage to the spare room opposite Father's. Thornby turned and began to walk slowly in the opposite direction to his own bedchamber, wondering suddenly if John had ever tried to incite lust in him. Then he remembered that, of course, John's magic didn't work on him. So, everything he'd felt with John was quite natural—or at least divinely unnatural.

He'd almost managed to make himself smile, when he remembered that he was doing everything he could to encourage John to discover certain old sigils that might work on him.

To free him, of course.

But what if, when it came to it, John didn't choose to free him?

Only, he would, of course.

All the same, Raskelf felt lonelier and colder than usual, and when he got to his room he was almost relieved John wouldn't be coming tonight. He got into bed, and lay awake for a long, long time.

***

John sat on the floor in the dark just inside the door of the spare room and waited for Lady Dalton to scream. Or not.

When Dalton had grabbed Soren like that—

He breathed out hard, trying to get rid of the tension. So easily it could have gone wrong. He wished he could have gone with Soren. Perhaps not for sex; the knowledge that Lord Dalton was in with Lady Dalton was somehow the biggest passion-killer imaginable— but just to be with him. Just to hold him and feel his warmth. How good it would be to look into those beautiful grey eyes and see them smile.

He had waited several hours, and almost dozed off, when he heard the door open, and Lady Dalton whisper, "Mr Blake? Lord Thornby?"

He scrambled up and pulled the door open.

She stood in the doorway of Lord Dalton's room, a candle in her hand. He was so relieved to see her without bruises or tears that, at first, he couldn't speak.

"I knew you'd wait," she whispered. "You must read this."

She was pushing a piece of paper at him.

"What is it? Are you all right?" He took it but didn't look at it.

"Yes, *yes*, I'm quite well." She sounded impatient. "Read it. It was in his pocket."

"Is he—?"

"Asleep."

He listened and could indeed hear faint snores. "The charm lasts until daybreak," he reminded her.

"For goodness sake, Mr Blake," she hissed. "Will you read the letter!"

She lowered her candle to make it easier for him.

> *Lord Dalton,*
>
> *I am relieved to hear Lord Thornby's periods of mania appear to be less frequent and severe in nature as his marriage prospects improve. As your lordship has so rightly pointed out, behaving kindly and morally in these cases is always for the best, and the loving guidance of a father may be the only*

treatment required in this case. Many young men of a sensitive temperament may be nervous before this great step in life, and all may resolve itself once he is happily settled.

Regarding the periods of listlessness you mention, I do suggest that some therapeutic employment suitable to a young man of Lord Thornby's station would be advisable, as long as it is not too taxing or exciting.

Your last letter has set my mind much at ease and I believe there are true grounds for optimism. However, should you require my services in the future, please do not hesitate. Reversals can occur quite suddenly and quick action may be better than delaying overly long.

Should you find yourself in this position I can assure you that the interior of Clifton House is most commodious and well adapted, having been built for the purpose.

Your servant, sir

Gilbert Holmes, MD,

Superintendent, Clifton House, York

John stared at her, blood running cold.

"Clifton House," she said. "It's a lunatic asylum near York."

He nodded, finding no words.

"You must get him out, Mr Blake."

"I'm trying."

"He must delay marrying as long as he can. I never believed him. All those things he says at dinner. But it's true. His instinct has been right all along! Dalton will marry him off, wait until he has the girl's money and then discredit him and take the money himself."

"Yes."

"Dalton's a—a monster, isn't he?" Her voice suddenly broke. She gave one sob, and clapped her hand over her mouth to silence herself.

"My lady, it may not be in his nature. He's cursed. It may be driving him to do these things."

"To put his son in an asylum, even though he's sane? What could be so important that he would do that?"

"The money, I suppose."

"But he will simply spend it on some useless bits of rock in the middle of the sea! What is the point, Mr Blake? What is his purpose?"

"I don't know. I am trying to discover it. If I could understand—"

There was a sound in the room behind her, of a man snorting and turning over in bed, then snoring again at a slightly different timbre.

She at once had control of herself again. She plucked the letter out of John's hand. "You may go now, Mr Blake. I am quite capable of managing for the rest of the night."

"I see that, my lady. Thank you."

She gave him a nod, and was gone. He stood in the dark, staring at nothing for a long moment, then pulled the rowan twig and sulphur from his pocket, made a light, and set off through the dark passages to Soren.

Chapter Eleven

Thornby woke to find his room bathed in unnatural blue-white light, and John standing by his bed looking as pale and ghastly as a corpse. He shrank away instinctively and reached for the matches.

"What's happened?" By the warm glow of candlelight, John looked more alive, but still haunted. "Is she all right?"

"She's damned brave. Your father doesn't deserve her."

"Yes, but is she all right? You look terrible."

"She's fine. I think it may have worked. Everything felt—right."

"But isn't that good? Then what's the matter?"

"I'm afraid I've something to tell you."

Thornby listened in silence to the tale about the letter and all it implied. He'd thought he had no illusions left about Father, but the words 'lunatic asylum' sent a bolt of terror through him that, for a moment, seared rational thought away. Perhaps there had still been a part of him that wanted to believe the whole thing some awful misunderstanding; that Father wanted him to marry for benevolent reasons. Now that part of him died.

"May I sit down?" John said, making him jump.

Thornby nodded, not trusting his voice, and moved over to make room. John sat on the edge of the bed and put a hand over his. His usually tidy hair was rumpled, his cravat loose, dark smudges were under his eyes. He was glaring at nothing, as if he'd eat one alive if one so much as cleared one's throat.

Yes, he looked daunting. Yes, he'd just magicked Father. And, yes, he could probably do a thousand alarming things with merely the contents of his pockets. But he was a decent man trying to do the right thing. No, it was more than that. He was the kind of man who gave walnuts to hedgehogs, who listened to frightened young ladies, and who tried to make you smile when it felt as if the world was caving in. And then he might fuck you until you forgot your own name. Thornby was suddenly ashamed for having been afraid of him earlier. It was Father who cast horror across everything. If John found a way to let him go, of course he would use it.

Thornby turned his hand over and laced their fingers together. John looked at him and tried to smile. He couldn't quite manage it, but the fact that he was trying filled the empty place inside Thornby with something warm. Perhaps it was hope?

"Did you look at that hair?" Thornby asked. "You said it might be useful."

"It is useful. I just have to find the right sigil."

"I expect you scarcely had time today."

"I did get a sigil from the spancel. It felt partly right." John shook his head, eyes distant, probably remembering occult lines and curves of salt. "But something was missing. Some extra material, maybe? I don't know. And I daren't experiment until I'm sure; it might destroy the hair."

"I see."

John stroked his thumb over Thornby's wrist, soothing, encouraging. "It was promising, but the spancel gets distressed if I press it too hard. And then it's difficult to make out what it means. I'll ask it again tomorrow."

"It gets distressed? What on earth is it?"

"It's a tether for magic. It's very old. Much older than anything else I use. That's partly why I'm so hopeful. It's seen centuries of magic."

"But what's it made from?"

John gave him a long, thoughtful look. "Trade secret."

In spite of everything, Thornby almost smiled. "Go on, tell me."

"You don't want to know," John said, primly.

Deliberately aggravating, Thornby was sure. "I hope you realise I shall hound you until you tell me," he said. "Can I see it?"

"What for?" John sounded suspicious.

"If it's distressing itself trying to help me, then I should like to thank it."

"Oh."

The stunned look on John's face actually made him smile. "One must always be a gentleman, John, no matter the circumstances."

John closed his eyes for a moment, shaking his head in disbelief. When he opened them again, they were smiling, and the furrow between his brows was not so deep.

"Here then," he said, and pulled the thing from his pocket. It was coiled tight; pale brown, fine-grained leather with those ancient-looking runes written upon it. Thornby wondered that it did not come unravelled in John's pocket, but perhaps it did not care to.

He touched it with the tip of his finger. "Well, Mr Spancel, you have my thanks." He felt rather a fool, now it had come to it, but at least John was smiling again. "Did it understand?"

John gave a noncommittal shrug.

"Can't you tell what it's thinking?" Thornby said.

"To tell the truth, it's rather afraid. Don't take that personally, though. It's had a hard life. It's afraid of everyone but me."

"I hope it knows I wouldn't hurt it." Thornby gave it a wary stroke, wondering again what it was made from. "Are any of your materials afraid of you?"

"Of course not." John frowned, perhaps trying to imagine such a peculiar state of affairs. "They like magic. Without it, they wouldn't—well, they're not exactly alive, but they wouldn't feel anything."

"But people are afraid of you. Sometimes. I nearly was, earlier. Knowing what you'd done to Father."

John, who had been putting the spancel back in his pocket, looked up, the pain on his face so naked that Thornby put out a hand to wipe it away. He stroked John's jawline with a finger, and ran his thumb over his mouth.

"Mr Blake, you may be one of the most alarming men I have met, but I think you're the kindest as well. I am *not* afraid of you. And to prove it, I shall take some liberties with you. Possibly some no one has dared take before. If you aren't too tired." He pulled John down onto the bed and began to take his clothes off. "Hmm, here's a part of you that's waking up. The rest of you can go to sleep, if you like."

"Soren, the pins. I've done no magic for hours, apart from the light."

"All right then, get on."

Thornby sat back, fretful at the delay, while John pulled pins out of his pocket and did what he had to do. John didn't get up. He handed each charged pin to Thornby, who leaned over the side of the bed and stood them on the carpet. They felt perfectly ordinary, cold and lifeless, but they balanced on their points in that impossible, gravity-defying way.

Ah, but John was good to kiss. He kissed with utter conviction, with nothing held back. He kissed as if he would, through sheer force of will, somehow transcend corporeality and kiss Thornby's very soul—and he had not yet even removed his cravat. Thornby pulled his own nightshirt off with one quick movement, knelt astride him, and began to take Mr Blake apart, starting with his clothes.

Matters proceeded until Thornby was kneeling between John's legs, mouth tight around his cock. After a while, John tried to sit up, to pull him down on top of him. Thornby shook his head.

"No, Mr Blake. Tonight, I'm in charge. I am an earl, you know. I have all kinds of rights over you. So, lie back and shut up. Yes?"

John obeyed. Probably not something that happened very often. Thornby smiled a little around his cock. Better make the most of it.

He was, as he had told John, quite experienced in fucking men. Certainly, he was experienced enough to know that if John had tried it and not enjoyed it, it would not do to go too far, too fast. So, he would be gentle; he would tease, and lick, and caress and press. He would take his lead from John, but there would likely be no fucking—not tonight, anyway. But perhaps he would get a finger up that very tempting arsehole.

So, he sucked John's cock until he could taste sweet liquid, and John was groaning, head thrown back, the cords of his neck standing out. Then, still sucking, Thornby began to caress John's thighs, balls, and the area between balls and arse. He wet his fingers and began to trail them around John's arsehole.

"Can I touch you here?"

"I thought you were in charge?"

Thornby rubbed a fingertip down the dark pucker, quite gently, but firmly enough not to tickle. He repeated the action. John's breathing stuttered. His cock was very hard. Thornby made sure everything was really wet and slipped his index finger inside, up to the first joint.

John shifted a little on the bed; almost a flinch, and his cock softened slightly. Thornby withdrew his finger.

"Too much?"

"I don't usually allow that."

"Sorry."

"No. You can. I'll say if I want you to stop."

Thornby grinned, and slipped his finger in, this time going a little deeper, letting John get used to the idea of being touched inside. Then he withdrew his finger most of the way and began to concentrate on John's cock again—licking and sucking, sliding the foreskin up and down, occasionally bringing his other hand into play, stroking the shaft, squeezing gently.

John was hard as a rock, the head of his cock almost purple. Thornby let another finger join the first, and pushed a little harder. He was feeling for that spot that makes men quiver and sob and spread themselves wide to let you in. The moment he found it, John tensed and clutched the sheet with both hands and gasped, "Ah, Jesus! Fuck!"

Thornby made an encouraging noise, and began to suck a little faster, and at the same time to move his fingers faster too, and more firmly.

"Ohhh, fuck," John said. It was an anguished groan, like a man praying for his life. He was moving his hips, pushing against Thornby's hand, and a moment later he was spending into Thornby's mouth, arse clenching tight around Thornby's fingers, crying out into the cold room in a way that was most unwise.

Thornby waited until the last shudder had gone through him, then slipped his fingers out and looked up. John was staring at him, slightly dazed. "Bloody 'ell," he said. He sounded, for a second, not the gentleman he had learned to be, but an ironmonger's son who has surprised himself.

Thornby racked his brains for something light-hearted to say. If John was feeling vulnerable, as men sometimes did, a joke would let him laugh and feel better. And in any case, he liked to see John smile. But he could not for the life of him think of anything. He felt as if something had happened that wasn't just sex. John had given him something precious. And he hadn't even come himself, though his cock was throbbing as if a single touch would undo him.

Then he remembered that cry. It had really been quite loud. Flattering, of course, but how delightful if Mr Grey or Mr Lazenby had heard it and decided to investigate. He got up, put the chair under the door handle again, and washed his hands in the dribble of cold water from the bottom of the ewer.

He was about to get back into bed when he noticed something white undulating gently next to the iron pins by the bed. He'd nearly stepped on it. He peered closer and nearly gave a yelp of surprise.

It was an octopus. And it must belong to John, because it had one tentacle wrapped around a pin like a gentleman holding a malacca cane. It gave Thornby such a look of affronted dignity that he muttered 'beg pardon' at it.

"You realise there's an octopus under the bed?" he said, getting under the covers.

John, who had been slipping an arm around him, went still for a moment. "Is there? Yes, all right. I'm not surprised."

"Yours, is it?"

"No." John began kissing Thornby's neck, biting it a little; the shivers made Thornby's toes curl and his cock twitch.

"It's not?"

"Near the pin, wasn't it?" John said.

"Yes."

"Mmm. There's been something every time now, when we have sex. Always things from the sea: shells, barnacles, starfish. Now an octopus. It's us, I think, manifesting them."

"But I thought the pins put a stop to all that. Isn't that what they're for?"

John had been trailing kisses down his chest, curling his tongue around a nipple. He glanced up. "Yes. But then I've never been with anyone like you before. And I've never felt—" He broke off, and instead planted a kiss near Thornby's navel. "What about you? Ever had a magician before?"

"I don't think so." The idea that he might have, unknowingly, was faintly alarming.

"No? And the sea? Fond of it, are you?"

"I can't abide it, apart from Turner's maritime pieces. It reminds me of that awful time at the seaside with Father. And my foot."

"Well, don't worry about the octopus. It'll go away soon." John was tugging at his hips, moving him into a more convenient position.

Thornby frowned. "Yes, but—"

But he got no further, because John suddenly pinned him to the bed with firm hands, and began sucking him unmercifully, presently sliding a couple of fingers up *his* arse. And soon there could have been a kraken under the bed and he wouldn't have cared about it if John didn't. There was only John's mouth and hand, and the sensation pulsing through him. He came, urgently and sweetly, biting his own fist to stop himself yelling. He wasn't usually a screamer, but there was something about the way John did it that almost made him forget himself entirely.

"I should go," John murmured afterwards. His voice dragged with tiredness.

"Go to sleep. I'll see the maid off when she comes." But he yawned himself.

"You should sleep, too. I'm going."

John got up, put on just enough clothes for decency, gathered his pins, and was gone. It was much colder without him. Thornby pulled his nightshirt back on and glanced over the edge of the bed. The octopus was nowhere to be seen, yet he did not feel relieved. Instead, he was a little crestfallen, as if a friend had left without saying good-bye. He settled into the spot where John had been lying. It still smelled of him, faintly, and there was some residual warmth. Thornby pulled the eiderdown over his head and was asleep.

***

Thornby woke to a sharp pain in his chest, as if something was biting him. He gasped and convulsed, curling his knees up, trying to grab the source of the pain. His waking brain threw him some confused ideas about adders or rats. But his hands met nothing. His eyes flew open. The fire had been lit and the curtains opened, and in the grey light of morning, the red bloom of blood was soaking the front of his nightshirt.

Then the agony returned double-fold. He jack-knifed in the bed, clutching at his chest, trying to get away from whatever was hurting him. He pushed himself up on one elbow. Nothing sharp was there—just the laces of the nightshirt. Yet the pain seared through him again. He struggled out of bed, half falling, and ripped the front of the nightshirt open. There were two long slashes across his chest, nearly from nipple to nipple, both bleeding freely. And as he watched, another began to open up. He grabbed at it, trying to hold his skin together with his hands, twisting in agony, trying to escape.

An attack. From nowhere.

His foot catching fire all those years ago.

This was the same. It was magic. Father was cutting the token.

He must get to John, because John could find people. Father would lead them straight to it.

He staggered to the door, chest burning and throbbing. The front of the nightshirt stuck to him, glistening red, as if he'd had his heart cut out. He put blood-sticky fingers to the door handle, and froze as footsteps hurried past. But he had to get to John *now*. He opened the door to see the vanishing form of one of the housemaids. Apart from that, the passage was empty. For now. He ran, hunched over, expecting more pain at any moment. He got to John's door and burst through it.

John sat bolt upright, hair tousled, eyes already alert. "Soren? *Christ*! What the fuck!" He leapt out of bed, wearing nothing but his drawers and shirt.

Thornby clutched the bedpost. "The token. He—he—"

Words were far too difficult. He let the torn nightshirt fall open. There were three long cuts, the bottom two masked with blood, as if he'd been sliced open with a razor. Blood had dripped down to his stomach, and beyond.

John was pulling things out of the pockets of his jacket, which lay over the stand. "Don't be afraid. This is a good thing. If it's your father doing it, he'll lead us straight to it, the bastard."

136

Thornby bunched the ragged edges of the blood-soaked nightshirt and tried to stem the bleeding. Don't be afraid? He was shivering with fear. Father could hurt him any time, without warning. At least, with a blow, one could usually see it coming. And what if Father decided to do worse than cut him? What about fire? He'd used it before. What if—?

John was kneeling on the carpet, making an intricate pattern of salt. He put a cigar cutter in the centre of it, shook a small vial and poured something that looked like blood onto the salt nearby. He took the glass eye in one hand. Then he touched the salt in that purposeful, deliberate way, and the cigar cutter glowed red and melted into a yellow puddle, scorching a hole in the carpet.

"He's in the park. To the west of the house," John said.

"In the park?" The edges of Thornby's vision were darkening. He sank to his knees. "Where?"

"Don't know." John was pulling his clothes on. "He's on the move."

"I...don't..." Thornby closed his eyes for a moment, trying to concentrate. "Where, exactly, in the park?"

"Don't know. I'm going to look." John paused in front of him to grip his shoulder, then ran out of the room.

The sigil John had made was still on the floor, the melted cigar cutter a black ash-encrusted blob. He'd gone in such a hurry he'd left his salt behind. That was unlike him. Thornby touched the closest line of salt with one bloodied finger. It made him feel a little better, as if he was touching John's hand. John had acted fast. Look how he'd had that cigar cutter, which must have belonged to Father, as if he'd been expecting this very eventuality. But it had still taken time to get here, make the sigil and locate Lord Dalton.

Would Father still be there, with it? Or would he have hidden it again and left?

Thornby should go himself, out into the park to help John look.

He staggered back to his room and kicked the bloody nightshirt under the bed like a guilty secret. There was warm water in the jug, so he cleaned himself up and started to get dressed. But his hands were shaking so he could barely do his buttons. His chest burned, and his head kept spinning. Worst was the hideous anticipation: expecting, all the time, that the pain could come again, and he would never know when. He fumbled with the buckles at his knees, but they defeated him entirely. What did it matter? He was only wearing these ridiculous clothes to annoy Father. And Father didn't care, not really.

He started down the passage. It seemed darker than usual, and narrower. Strange smells kept assailing him: old perfume and dusty stone overlaying some sickly carrion stench. The air seemed to be pressing down on him so he could barely draw breath.

He'd reached the bottom of the stairs when darkness descended as if it were pitch black night. He clung to the banister. There was a peculiar rushing in his ears. Was it his own blood surging around? His knees were giving. He was sure he had not let go of the banister, but could no longer feel it under his hand. He was lying on some cold, uneven surface that was not the stairs or the hall floor. It was so cold, so dark. And, somehow, it had *always* been cold and dark. He twisted his head, trying to find a whisper of fresh air, or a glimmer of light. But there was none, and there never had been. He tried to rally—of *course* there was sunlight and fresh autumn air. But these things didn't seem real. All his life, he had been stuck here in this terrible cold, this terrible dark. Always confined. Always.

***

John got outside to see Lord Dalton arriving back at the house at a gallop on his big chestnut thoroughbred. He tried to follow the horse's trail, but it led towards the village, and the way was so muddy it was difficult to make it out. How long had it taken Soren to get to him? How long to cast the sigil, get dressed and get outside? Ten minutes? To be safe, he must suppose the token could be anywhere within a fifteen-minute radius. How fast could Dalton's horse gallop? Pretty fast—it was a fine creature.

He'd set the sigil to find Lord Dalton. But what if his lordship had sent someone else to do the dirty work? What if Lord Dalton had simply been enjoying an innocent early morning ride? John examined the idea. It smelled like horse-shit, so it probably was. Chances were that Dalton had done it himself. John felt a pang of guilt; he couldn't help but wonder if this was somehow revenge. For a moment, last night, Lord Dalton had seen his dead wife in his son. Perhaps he realised his appetites had been manipulated. Was this vicious act some kind of retribution?

But at least they now knew that the token was in the park, somewhere within a fifteen-minute gallop. They were closing in. Where would Dalton hide it out of doors? It could be buried, or tucked into a niche in a stone wall, or perhaps in a hollow tree. John looked up from the muddy track, considering the old oaks and elms and the gentle green curves of the park.

He wanted to keep searching, but there'd been something wrong with Soren beyond those nasty-looking cuts. When he'd touched Soren's shoulder, a jolt of that uncanny otherness had pulsed through him, and it had been screaming—the mad, magical scream of something pushed beyond its limits. Something was breaking. Would Soren break with it?

John turned and ran back to the house. He came in Raskelf's wide front door to a cluster of people, all with their backs to him, all looking down at something on the Great Stair. The Greys were there, all five of them. A flustered-looking housemaid with a dust-pan ran away from the group.

John pushed to the front to find Soren lying on the stairs. He was dressed in his usual black Regency breeches and coat, but he was dishevelled, and ashen-pale with a bloody handprint on his face. His eyes were open, but unfocused. He was gasping for breath. Mr Grey was trying to help him to his feet.

"Oh, Mr Blake, Lord Thornby is ill!" He wasn't sure which of the ladies had spoken. One of the girls was crying.

"Ah, Mr Blake! Your assistance, please," said Mr Grey, and then, to his wife, "My dear, make sure that girl fetches a doctor. Good lord! The staff here!"

They got Soren up and began to carry him to his room. He wasn't walking; his feet trailed behind him, and his head lolled.

"What happened?" John said. The magical screaming had stopped, but he could still sense that terrible wrongness. Had Dalton done too much? What if Soren never came back to himself?

"We saw him on the stairs. Looked like he was seeing a ghost! I've never seen a fellow look so. Then he collapsed. I think he's bleeding from the chest. I don't understand it." Mr Grey's round face was red with effort and alarm.

Soren's arm was limp around John's shoulders, his hand like ice. They got him to his room and put him on the bed, which was in disarray with blood on the sheets. John took his hand. "Soren? *Soren!*"

"Mr Blake, does Lord Thornby have some trouble I should know about? Consumption, maybe?" said Mr Grey.

Soren's fingers suddenly tightened on his own, but his eyes didn't focus. "John?"

Relief flooded him. "Yes, I'm here. And Mr Grey."

"You didn't find it, did you?" Soren said.

John glanced at Mr Grey. "I can manage, Mr Grey. Thank you for your help."

"I'll stay till the doctor comes, eh?" Mr Grey said.

"We'll never find it, will we? John, I—I don't think I can bear it—" Soren began to cry.

"Soren! Of course we'll find it!" Watching him weep had been bad enough that night in the hazel thicket. Now John felt as if his heart was caught in a vice.

"Why does he hate me so much? It was him, wasn't it, who burnt my foot? And now—"

"What's he on about?" Mr Grey said. "Feverish, I think."

"Mr Grey, perhaps you could make sure someone brings brandy? And smelling salts? And bandages and water and towels and so on?" He made the list as long as he could, hoping to give Soren time to recover. "The bells don't always seem to work here. It might be best to go down to the kitchen yourself."

"Yes, all right. I must say I don't think much of the staff here. Lord Dalton must be a saint; *I* wouldn't tolerate it." Mr Grey left the room.

"Soren, what happened?"

"I thought I'd died. It was so cold. And dark. I couldn't remember the light. I couldn't remember the sun."

"Can you see me, now?"

"Nearly." He touched John's cheek. His fingers were so cold they almost burned. "John. I wish I'd met you in London."

"Soren—"

"Actually, no. You'd have hated me."

"Of course I wouldn't."

"You would. I was horrible. A stuck-up little snob. You might've fucked me though."

"You can't talk like that. Mr Grey could come back any moment. And they've sent for a doctor."

"A doctor!" He lurched up, nearly knocking their heads together. "I'm not seeing any doctors! I don't *need* a damned doctor! *You're* the one I need. You have to get me out! I don't care how. Do whatever you like. Use that sigil the spancel told you. You wouldn't experiment before. But it's going to get worse and worse."

"Don't ask me to do that."

"But I am. I'm begging. John, can't you see I can't take it any more? It's not the cuts, it's afterwards. That—that choking dark. I can't take that again. If I stay any longer I shall go mad."

They stared at each other.

"Please," Soren whispered, voice trembling.

Finally, John said, "You do as I tell you. If I say we're stopping, we stop. And if I tell you to run, you run."

"Yes, of course." His voice was still a whisper.

"All right. We can't stay here. Someone could be back any minute. Can you walk?"

For answer, Soren stood up and tried to limp across the room. His knees nearly gave way. John took his arm and put it over his own shoulders. He led Soren to his own room, instinctively heading to his materials. But once there, he realised that when the doctor came, this was one of the first places they might look.

John sat Soren on the edge of the bed while he recovered his salt, then put an arm around him again. He considered the things in the trunk. What might he need? There'd been something missing from the sigil the spancel had given him. It was something potent. But what? He could hardly take the whole trunk. He had the basics in his pockets—he never went anywhere without them. He sat there, his arm around Soren's shoulders, Soren's cold hand in his. He could feel the salt pulsing in his pocket. The spancel seemed to be slithering around in there too, like a live snake. Impossible. It was imagination. Nerves.

Or was it?

He could feel something emanating from the materials in his pockets, some kind of message. A warm tension was growing the pit of his stomach, almost a sexual thing, as if Soren might kiss him at any moment. He wouldn't of course; he was white as a sheet, with his eyes closed, and was clearly concentrating on staying upright. But the feeling gave John heart; there was potential here somewhere. The materials knew it. Best to go somewhere close by, but deserted; the west wing.

"Come then," John said, and they left his room, left his trunk, and made their way along the passage to one of the many empty rooms.

***

Thornby half-lay in a dust-sheeted easy chair, watching John, who was kneeling on the floor a few feet away, his materials arrayed in front of him. A long, listening silence filled the spare room. It was so profound, Thornby could almost see it thickening the air, swirling like turpentine; he could almost feel it, soft against his skin. John began to arrange things; the spancel in a large circle, the glass eye there. He began to lay the salt in one of those odd patterns of lines and circles, then half-way through he stopped, and there was another long pause.

In the past, when John had done magic, Thornby had watched him interestedly enough. It wasn't every day one saw a magician at work, but he'd felt nothing more than a natural curiosity. This time was different. This time there was a strange smell in the air. It wasn't exactly unpleasant, but it was pungent, sharp and sweet at the same time, like vinegar shot with vanilla. There was something bracing about it. His head began to clear. He leaned forward in the chair, feeling more alert.

It wasn't just the smell; John looked different too. Shadows seemed to be gathering around him, as though he was sucking the light out of the air and putting it into his salt pattern. But the strangest thing was how everything in the room seemed to be aware of John. Somehow the door, the walls, the window, the rolled-back carpet, the bed and all the holland-sheeted furniture seemed to be listening to John the way a crowd listens to a fire and brimstone preacher.

John was adding more loops and lines to his pattern. Then he took out his pocketbook and removed from its pages the single gold-brown hair they'd found in the secret compartment in the trunk. He put the hair in the middle of one of the circles of salt. Thornby remembered what had happened to the cigar cutter. They had one chance. If John got it wrong they'd lose their single clue.

Thornby found he'd risen unconsciously from the chair and backed away. Of course, he'd asked John to do this. Of course, he trusted John. What choice did he have? Anything would be better than staying trapped here at Father's mercy. Or being sent to a lunatic asylum. But he could not stop his teeth chattering, nor his legs trembling, nor his breath stuttering in his throat.

John looked up, eyes unfocused, mouth grim, the way it went when he was concentrating. "Something's missing," he said. "What? What is it?"

Thornby knew the question wasn't being asked of him. But it was unnerving to know there was a silent conversation going on, right in front of him. John was staring at nothing, fingertips touching the spancel and the salt, that intent, listening look on his face. After what felt like forever, John blinked. Then he looked at Thornby with a strange, speculative expression, as if he'd been told some shocking rumour about him, and couldn't quite believe it.

"I see," John said. Then he smiled and held out his hand. "Come here."

142

His voice had the tone he used during sex—brooking no refusal, but intimate, subtly acknowledging the game.

Thornby stepped carefully inside the spancel and knelt in front of him. John put his arms around him, and Thornby almost sobbed with relief, because although everything else was terrifyingly different, John felt just the same. He had the same warm solidity, he gave the same sense of reassurance. And underlying that vinegar and vanilla pungency, he smelled the same as well.

All the same, when John began to kiss him, undoing Thornby's breeches as he did so, Thornby was so surprised he froze. *Now?* At a time like this? John undid his own fly, took Thornby's hand, limp but unresisting, and put it on his cock, which was already hard. Thornby did not take his hand away, but neither did he wrap it around John's stand. His own cock was entirely soft, balls shrivelled with fear and pain. He wanted to say, "Are you *serious?*" but his voice seemed to have deserted him.

John was murmuring in his ear, "Come on, now. This is part of it. This is what was missing: you and me."

Soren found his voice. "John, I don't think I can."

"The magic's calling for it. Can't you feel it? It's some sort of hybrid; human magic, with that hair, and you and me mixed in. It's bloody strong. It's affecting me."

"Yes, I feel that, thank you."

"Mmm. So? Can you feel it?"

"I can feel the walls watching us, if that's what you mean. And the bed and that horrible old carpet. All gawking like boys at a dog fight. Is it like this for you all the time? How do you stand it?"

"Don't think about them. They don't judge; it's the magic that draws them. In every way that matters, we're alone. I promise."

"All right, well, give me a moment, will you? It's not often one's called upon to perform under such circumstances. This morning has hardly been conducive. My chest stings." *And my own father did it to me.*

"I know. I'd see to it, but there's hardly been time. I've got an anodyne necklace but that'd put you to sleep. I'm sorry."

"It's all right." Soren let his forehead rest on John's shoulder. He could still sense the room and everything in it, now hushed like a crowd before the opera begins. "God, I wish we were anywhere but here."

Into his ear, John said, "Ah, Soren. My dear. I wish the same."

Soren's breath caught. John was physically affectionate in bed; he liked to kiss and caress and embrace. And he knew how to give a compliment, and of course how to tease in that delightful, playful, candid way. But this was the first time he had said anything so intimate. In London, men in Soren's set had called him "my dear" all the time, but it had been nothing but a kind of flippant, friendly punctuation. From John, it was profoundly moving. One could tell that he meant it, that he did not say things like it often, or lightly. Soren was used to people wanting him. John actually *liked* him.

John was stroking his back, hands occasionally venturing lower to his arse. Soren could feel John's breath, warm in his hair. If one did not allow oneself to think beyond this moment, it was, actually, very nice. The fear had not gone, but it was lurking further and further away. He felt John's lips at his jaw and turned his head.

John kissed him, slow and soft, then pulled away, looking at him, considering. He smiled—not a reassuring smile, more the private, devilish smile of someone trying *not* to smile—and reached, very slowly, for one of the inside pockets of his jacket. What was he reaching for? What did that smile mean? Thornby watched him the way a mouse watches a cat, but suddenly his heart was pounding for a different reason, and his cock was beginning to stir.

John brought out a small vial of pale gold oil. Thornby recognised it; John had used it before. Now John undid the cap with his teeth, and poured some oil onto his right hand. He let it spread, rolling his wrist to allow it to trickle around. Then he held his hand up, fingers and thumb moving, glistening in the light.

"Hmm?" John said, raising an eyebrow.

Thornby made a noise in his throat. His chest still hurt, but that seemed not to matter now. All he could think about was that golden, glistening hand. In fact, he was trembling with anticipation.

John gave him another of those secret smiles. "Stand up."

He obeyed, breathlessly waiting for John to reach up and take his cock in that slick hand. The oil would be warm. It would feel—

But, still watching him, John reached deliberately down and began to stroke his own cock, covering it in shining oil. John groaned as he touched himself, and closed his eyes.

Thornby watched him, mouth open.

John opened one eye, smiled at the expression on his face, then closed the eye again, letting his head fall back. "Ah, God, that's good. Sorry, did you think it was for you? *Fuck*—no, this would be wasted on you. It's almond oil, but I've—*Christ*—charmed it—*my God*—so it remembers my touch, so it's like having about five hands—*fucking hell*—down there."

Thornby made a noise of protest. He couldn't quite believe it was happening. Part of him was genuinely outraged that John should tease him so. Although, John was clearly putting on a show for him, and watching John pleasure himself was almost as good as having that warm, golden, oily hand on his own cock.

Almost.

John opened his eyes again and looked up, grinning, still frigging himself with long slow strokes. "Well, my lord, how about something to think about while you watch?"

He closed his mouth over Thornby's cock.

Just before he came, Thornby realised, with a tail end of awareness, that something else was different. His gaze had happened to trail away from John's hand and cock and mouth, and across John's iron pins—which were not standing up on their points as usual, but lying prone and dead-looking on the floor outside the spancel.

If he'd been a little less close to the crisis, he might have said something, but John was sucking him now as if his life depended on it, cheeks hollowed. And a moment later Thornby was grabbing John's hair, thrusting helplessly into his mouth, crying out, and John was making stifled, desperate noises too, somewhat muffled by Thornby's cock. There was one of those pure, silent moments that comes after sex, and then—

—there was an explosion of power so strong, it knocked Thornby off his feet. He was flung sideways across the shrouded bed. John was thrown onto the floor, landing with his shoulder against the door. Thornby staggered to his feet. He'd intended to help John up, but instead stood staring, hands at his sides, mouth and breeches hanging open.

Something had smashed a tunnel through Raskelf, right through guest rooms and ante-rooms, passageways and all. It was as though a cannon-ball as big as a carriage had ripped through the west wing and out the other side. Through the settling dust and hanging planks and ruined pictures, he could see daylight at the other end. And the tunnel seemed to be *moving* at the margins—long strands of what looked like seaweed were waving in the air. White crabs scuttled up broken beams. He thought he saw an octopus—could it be the same one?—clinging to a broken chandelier. And for a brief, impossible moment, a school of silver fish seemed to glint across the tunnel, only to be lost a moment later in the gloom of some ruined spare bedroom.

Not using the pins was deliberate. John had done it on purpose.

He was aware of John at his side, looking down the tunnel. Then John was kneeling, coiling the spancel, pocketing the pins and eye, sweeping the salt up with careful fingers. He got to his feet and gave Thornby one of those turned-down smiles, mouth severe, eyes alight.

"Come on," John said.

"But what—?"

"That's our heading. That way." John pointed down the tunnel. "West. Your token's at the end of it."

"I—I—"

"We'd better run. It's quite a big hole. Your father's bound to notice. You might want to do your breeches up, though."

"John, I—"

"Don't you want to get there first?"

Thornby did his breeches up, and they ran.

Chapter Twelve

Once out of the house, the heading remained clear. Big holes were ripped in trees, huge branches scattered like twigs. They ran west for perhaps twenty minutes, following the trail of destruction. Thornby wished for a horse with part of his mind, but he could hardly feel his chest and ankle now.

They came upon the post and rail fence that marked the estate boundary at this point. On the other side was a narrow field. Beyond that, a screen of yew trees, with a stone pumphouse behind them, its steep slate roof like a dunce's cap. The yew hedge had a huge hole in it, and the pumphouse wall now sported a crater, the broken stone pale yellow against weathered grey.

Thornby hurled himself over the fence, but turned back immediately. He gripped the fence rail, wanting to scream with frustration. "The boundary. I can't."

"Isn't that an estate building?"

"He owns the building, not the land. I can't go there."

There was no need to ask John to go for him; he was already climbing the fence. But then he paused for an agonisingly long moment. "What if he comes?" John was looking back the way they'd come, towards the Hall.

"I don't know. Don't care." He grabbed the front of John's shirt and gave him one quick, hard kiss. Then he pushed him away. "Quickly, go on! Go!"

***

John ran towards the round stone building. He'd heard it had something to do with the draining of the lake that had drowned Soren's mother. It had never occurred to him that Dalton might own the building but not the land. It was the ideal place to hide something from Soren—completely out of his reach, safer than Dalton's own pocket.

Once past the yews, he could see a tiny hole in the centre of the crater in the stone wall. He put his finger to it, feeling a draught of chill air from the inside. The stone gave back an echo of the sex-charm; he could almost taste Soren in it, could almost hear him moaning. No wonder inanimate objects sometimes confused magic with sex; sometimes they were the same thing. If they ever got out of this mess, it was a concept that required extra thought. And further experimentation.

But despite the crater and the hole, the wall was still solid. It was three feet thick.

He ran around the building. There were no windows, but he found a door on the western side; black iron, bound with iron. He'd renewed the chimera key last night, thinking he might need to get into Lord Dalton's room in an emergency. The charm would be faded, but it might work. He was getting the key out of his pocket when he put a hand to the door, and felt a faint cold thread, running like veins of ice through both door and threshold. A ward. Demon-wrought. About twenty years old, laid by some other magician when the place was built. He'd have to unpick it before he could use the key. Lucky he'd realised, or the ward would have broken the key.

He pulled out the salt and made a sketchy Petit Clé sigil on the threshold. He was about to start tidying it with his fingertips, when the power surged through it, blazing bright. They would have said it was impossible at the Institute, yet the more he worked in accord with the materials, the less the details seemed to matter. The salt understood his intentions. It was helping. The ward threads in the door began to frizzle and wither. He tore them away as easily as spider-webs. The chimera key spun in the lock almost of its own accord. That shouldn't have been possible either, but it was helping, too. He pushed open the door. Inside was a round room, but it was no pumphouse.

It was a mausoleum. There was a raised dais in the middle, on top of which lay an ornate coffin in ebony and gilt. Decorative pillars ringed the walls, festooned with stone garlands of flowers and fruit. Muddy footprints, quite recent, went from the door to the coffin. And beneath the sourness of cold stone and dust, he could smell blood. He glanced over his shoulder. He could see across the graveyard to the village church, but no one was in sight. He approached the coffin. There was nothing on top of it, nor behind the dais. There were no other obvious hiding places. He hesitated only for a moment.

The coffin lid was not nailed down. He lifted it and stood staring in horror and pity, holding the lid in front of him like a shield. The body looked as if it had been entombed yesterday, not twenty years ago. The first Lady Dalton was white as alabaster, her unearthly beauty a little bloated. She wore a dried-up rose in her dusty hair, and a yellowed dress of fine lace that could have been her wedding gown. A bunch of fresh violets, still wet with dew, lay on her breast.

And across her dainty ankles lay the small, crumpled pelt of an animal. It was the same golden-brown as the hair they'd found in the trunk, and it smelled of blood, though there was no blood on it.

He set the coffin lid down and picked up the pelt.

The moment he did so, the door slammed shut and he was surrounded by utter darkness.

He backed away from the coffin, feeling for the door handle. The after-image of that pale, unearthly face was seared into his eyes.

But there was no handle. The door would not open. He took several deep breaths trying to calm his racing heart. It didn't matter. Perhaps he hadn't fully disabled the ward. He'd use the salt again. The Petit Clé outside would help too. He thrust the pelt under his arm. But he couldn't work blind. He grabbed the rowan twig, which sputtered into weak blue light before he could dip it in the sulphur.

The corpse was standing at his elbow.

He leapt away from it, away from the door, dropping the pelt as he did so, a cry of horror escaping him. Yet even as he moved, the corpse flickered like a candle flame and appeared on his other side. Her eyes opened; black all over. A malevolent snarl marred her beautiful lips.

"No! I'm here for Soren! *Soren!* Your son!"

But with another strange flicker she was upon him, reaching with hands like claws. He ducked again, knocking the coffin with a flailing arm. It made a hollow sound, but, said the rational part of his mind, not *that* hollow. He scrabbled backwards, and as his bare hand hit the floor he sensed something familiar: a musky animal stink overlain with the cloying sweetness of privet.

Demon reek. But not from Lady Dalton. From the floor.

He scrambled to his feet and lifted the rowan twig high. The real corpse still lay in the coffin. The flickering thing that was approaching him again was merely an illusion. All the same, he threw salt at it, and watched as holes burned in it, and it vanished. He grabbed the pelt from the floor and tucked it inside his shirt. It was immediately warm against his skin. What was it from? Some kind of dog? He had no time to wonder.

He crouched, made another Petit Clé by the door, but a wind came up from nowhere and blew the salt away. The demon must be in the building; they sometimes bound one in the foundations as a watchman. For all his scornful dismissal of theurgists, Lord Dalton had employed one when he'd built his first wife's mausoleum.

John straightened and realised his feet had sunk into the stone flags as if the floor were a mire. He pulled free with difficulty, sinking again, even as he struggled out. Most of his scattered salt had caught like a small snowdrift against one of the decorative stone pillars.

He managed to get one foot onto it and found the ground firmer. He scraped as much as he could spare from under his feet and held it tight, trying to decide what to do. He had a demon trap in his pocket. The trap was a good one—Rokeby had made it—but it wouldn't work through several feet of stone and earth.

And what was happening to Soren? Dalton would see the enormous hole in his house, put two and two together, and be back any minute. John *must* get out. What to do? The salt seemed to be pulling at his hand, trying to rise. Perhaps it was a hint. He put the rowan twig between his teeth, checked the pelt was safe, pocketed as much of the salt as he could gather, and began to climb.

The stonework twitched under his hands, and when he fell, the floor sucked at him, but eventually he got to the cross beams that held up the roof, and began to smash his way out, brittle slates sliding down the roof. The demon seemed to have less power up here, but it was making the beams feel greased.

Soon he had a hole large enough to see through. His heart lurched in his chest. Five horsemen were approaching fast from the direction of the Hall. One was surely Lord Dalton, and two wore the blue livery of Raskelf; Prout and Abbott. John held tighter and kicked slates. He could hear Soren shouting, but couldn't make out the words.

But he could guess. As soon as the hole was bigger, he pulled out the pelt. In the light of day, it was a pathetic thing, barely as long as a new-born babe, stiffened and shrivelled by its long banishment in the dark. Nevertheless, this was it; the source of so much trouble to Soren, and so much power to his father.

He'd thought to throw it to Soren, but it was too light—it would fall short. To be sure of Soren getting it, John would have to climb down and give it to him. He stuffed it back in his shirt. He'd kicked out as many slates as he could reach. Could he crawl through? Not quite. He bashed away more with forearm and elbow. Now the hole was large enough, but when he tried to climb through, his left foot would not budge. He tugged at it, disbelieving, before realising the demon had bound it to the beam. The delay could cost them everything. His heart sank, but he fumbled in his pocket for a handful of salt.

In a thunder of hooves, the horsemen reached the fence, reining their horses in so fiercely, the creatures slipped. Lord Dalton's face was red with rage. Soren climbed over the railing, putting it between him and his father. John began to grind salt into the spell on his foot, his hand shaking so much he dropped half of it. The spell came plain, but did not dissolve. *Shit!*

"Well, well, Mr Blake." Dalton's voice was tight with fury, but pitched to carry up to where John perched on the roof. Dalton's horse danced under him, snorting. Soren was backing away from him, clinging to the fenceline.

"I see my son is with you," Dalton continued. "His cat's-paw now, are you? I hope you don't believe whatever he's told you. He's got nothing. Whatever he's offered, I'll double it. Now give me that—thing."

Soren started forward across the field, but only managed a couple of steps before staggering back to the railing. "John!" His voice was frantic, pleading.

"John?" Dalton repeated. "You are on familiar terms for men who met a week ago. How familiar, I wonder? Well, Mr Blake, you're a clever man. You understand business. Give me the skin for now, and once I'm done with it, you can have it. Keep it in a safe place; you'll have him forever. Do whatever you like with him. What do you say?"

Dalton was guessing. It was best not to respond. John tried to concentrate on unpicking the binding spell. He had the trick of it; it was simply a matter of time. But the skin would be no good to Soren if he was trapped, and Prout and Abbott had dismounted and were advancing on him.

"Come, Mr Blake," Dalton was saying. "We're above the law, aren't we, men like us? I'm a man of the world. If you want him, we'll say no more about it. Just give me that skin!"

John pulled an iron pin from his pocket and threw it, hard. It hit Abbott in the arm and stuck like an arrow in a target. Abbott screamed and grabbed at it, but it burnt his hand with an audible sizzle. He yelled again and began twisting out of his coat, trying to remove it that way. Prout backed away from his flailing figure, but the other two men—Warren, the valet, and Farrell the butler—were also dismounting.

"Stop your men, Dalton, or I'll stop them for you," John called. "I can help you. But you will leave Lord Thornby alone."

"Fool. You can't help me. You're all the same, you bloody magicians. So damn sure of yourselves."

"You're wrong. I know what's on you."

But Dalton wasn't listening. "Warren, if Mr Blake throws any more of those darts— shoot him. Prout, Farrell, we'll take my son back to the Hall."

"John! Throw it!" Soren shouted. Prout and Farrell were closing on him.

John could feel the pelt thrumming with urgency. Perhaps, once it hit the ground, Soren would find the strength to get it, even if it fell short. And then what would happen?

Would it confer power, or simply allow Soren to leave the estate? Perhaps Soren sensed something John didn't—it was Soren's pelt after all. John wasn't especially afraid of Warren's fowling piece—the ward stone would protect him, once he'd found a moment to charge it. He grabbed another pin, wrapped the pelt around it as best he could, and threw it hard towards Soren.

"There! Get that!" Dalton shouted.

Pin and pelt fell ten paces short of the boundary. Soren and Warren both went for it at a run, but Soren hunched, as if in pain, and stopped, swaying. Prout and Farrell caught up with him and grabbed him from behind. John pulled out another pin. He'd have thrown it at Prout or Farrell, but they were now grappling with Soren, twisting and turning. He'd have to get down and stick it in Prout like a dagger. Fine.

Instead, he threw it at Warren, who'd nearly reached the pelt. It hit Warren's right hand—a neat crucifixion. He yelped and dropped the gun. But Abbott, coatless, blood reddening his arm, had staggered over to help. Abbott snatched the gun in his burnt hand, flinched, and fired.

The shot cracked a slate next to John's head, and slivers of stone flew up, cutting his cheek. Shouts came from below—Dalton's voice booming out, "Get *that*, you damned fool! Forget your hand. Use the other. Get that bloody skin!"

John half-charged the ward stone. No time to do it properly. He must free his foot. The blood was pounding in his ears, everything imploring him to hurry, hurry, *hurry*. But that was not the way. He must simply keep going, unpicking the spell with all the methodical care of a lady at her tatting. He was nearly done. He glanced up.

Soren, Prout, and Farrell were still grappling on the mausoleum side of the fence. Soren had to be desperate to get back to the estate or to reach the pelt, and maybe that was feeding his fury, because John had never seen such a vicious fight. There were no gentlemen's rules here; Soren punched and rucked, gouged and bit and throttled. He was taller than Prout and using his long reach to good effect, but Prout was stronger, and Farrell was heavier, if a good deal slower. Soren had blood all over his face, and seemed not to be using his left hand. Soren landed a kick dead on Farrell's nose, and as the fellow reeled back, John threw another pin. It pierced Farrell's thigh and he dropped, shrieking.

The fowling piece cracked again and something hit John's chest, just below the throat. If not for the ward it would have done for him. As it was, it burnt like a branding iron and bounced off. Warren was up, the pelt in his uninjured hand. Abbott was reloading. John pulled out another pin. He had four left, and he wouldn't miss. First Prout—to stop him hurting Soren. Then Abbott, then Warren. He'd pick them off like flies. Farrell had crawled away; he was out of the fight. There'd be one pin left for nailing Lord Dalton right in the fucking face.

The unbinding was complete. He kicked his foot free and slid down the roof, rolling as he landed, reaching for another pin. Another shot rang out. Not even close. He began to run to where Prout and Soren struggled, a pin in his hand.

But he'd taken only a few steps when a blast of foul air and salty water hit him out of nowhere. It knocked him sideways onto the grass, blinded and choking. It stank of rotting fish and shit and blood, as if the curse that haunted Dalton had been magnified a thousand times and thrown at John with all the might of a hurricane. What the *fuck*? He struggled up, wiping his eyes. Magic, but who—?

He looked over his shoulder.

Dalton had a pelt draped over the pommel of his saddle. Another one. A larger one. It must have belonged to Soren's mother. Dalton had kept her here too; mother and son, both bound to him by their skins, for as long as he chose. Dalton had a pocket knife in his hand. He cut a small piece from the pelt and threw it at John.

It was only a bit of skin and hair. It had no weight, no heft. It left Dalton's hand and traced a gentle arc to the grass in front of his horse's hooves.

And yet, John was thrown to the ground again by a gust of foulness so strong it made him retch. Needles of salty water stung his face and hands. Then it slackened. The wind still blew, but the fury was gone from it. John shook his head, blinking brine out of his eyes. He'd dropped the pin. He groped for it and threw it at Warren, who had nearly reached Dalton with the pelt.

He had no idea if it found a mark, because another foul spell-wind hit him, blinding him. Soren screamed, a wordless cry of fury and pain. Something screamed back—a chilling echo. Not human. Dalton must have Soren's pelt, too.

The pins were no good against this wind. John fumbled out a handful of salt. He was on rough grass, no chance of making a sigil here, yet make one he must. He had a vague idea of getting his jacket off and making the sigil on that, when he felt the salt trickling out of his grasp, but not from the bottom of his fist, from the top. It was trying to make a line in the air.

He sketched the sigil that came into his mind. It was one he knew well; Amalthea's Mark, for increase. How could that help? But he made the lines anyway, running on instinct, trusting the salt. He had only to add the final trinity of dots when he ran out of salt.

His pocket was empty. Perhaps he could take a pinch or two from the lines he'd already made.

Prout had dragged Soren back to the estate. But even as John glanced up, Soren twisted out of Prout's grip and tried to jab him in the eye with a thumb. Warren was running to help Prout. Abbott was bent over, probably loading the fowling piece again.

Another of those blasts of foul wind and water hit John. He hunched over the floating sigil, protecting it with his body, but some of the salt was blown away anyway. The lines were now so thin they were only just visible. Would it still work? There could be no taking any for the three dots now. How could he get salt? The Petit Clé was too far away.

Salt.

Salt water; his clothes were drenched with it from the spell wind.

He'd never used his clothes for magic, but the suit he was wearing had been absorbing it for months. He'd noticed, without really noticing, that his older suits stayed cleaner than his newer ones. Was that magic? Perhaps.

He asked the suit to give him the salt and held out his hand, palm open. The suit trembled, rippled, vibrated. It was like wearing a swarm of bees. And a small grey drop of sludge dripped from his cuff and into his hand. Behind him, he could hear dull thuds as blows fell, the grunts and gasps of men in pain and mortal effort. Another shot hit him in the back. He hissed with pain, but didn't stop working. The first drop was joined by another. There wasn't much: a pinch, and not dry. He made the trinity—they were tiny grey smudges, hardly dots at all. Then someone grabbed the scruff of his jacket and jabbed the muzzle of a pistol into his neck.

"Stop that or I'll shoot you like a dog," Dalton snarled.

But it was too late. The sigil glowed red. There was a tremendous pulse of magic, like nothing he had ever felt before. It was accompanied by a roaring sound, as if a steam train was coming. Something hit John on the head and shoulders, knocking him down. And then there was silence.

The pistol was gone from his neck. And the world had turned sparkling white. He got to his feet; he was the only man standing. He turned, slowly, stunned. Lord Dalton lay behind him, barely visible beneath a thick glittering layer of salt. Other prone bodies lay about, outlines rounded, as if they lay beneath snow.

Then one of the bodies staggered to its feet. Soren, covered in salt dust, so he looked like a moving statue. He took slow steps, as if wading through glue, but he knew exactly where to go. John had thought Dalton had the pelt, but Soren went straight to Abbott, fell to his knees beside the prone body and started flinging great glittering handfuls of salt aside. Then he picked up the pelt. He knelt, unmoving, staring at it.

"Soren!" John called.

Soren's head jerked up. His face was a mask of blood, covered in white salt dust. His eyes were totally black, not a sliver of white or colour anywhere, and his lips were drawn back from his teeth. He looked like a demon about to attack. Then he blinked, and his eyes were their usual light grey, and his mouth took on a more natural shape. He glanced at the pelt, and said, almost conversationally, "I must go."

He might have been at his tailor, and remembered an appointment with his bootmaker. The lack of emotion in his voice sent a shiver up John's spine.

"Soren, wait—"

But Soren had already thrust the pelt inside his shirt and vaulted the fence. He was running back towards Raskelf. For a man with a cut chest, a raw ankle and a scarred foot who'd just been in a truly filthy fist-fight, he put on a fine turn of speed.

John followed him as far as the fence, and stopped.

Something was calling him, begging not to be left behind. The salt! Not the glittering blanket that had come from nowhere, but his salt. He'd lost most of it, but a good quarter was still in the Petit Clé. He glanced at Soren's disappearing figure. But he couldn't desert the salt. It had helped so much. And it was beseeching him to take it with him.

He could catch up with Soren. Though why the devil he was running back to Raskelf, and not *away*, John could not guess for the life of him.

He ran back around the mausoleum. The Petit Clé had escaped the avalanche from Amalthea's Mark, which was surely no coincidence, and lay startling white on the grey stone block, in exactly the shape he'd left it. It adhered to itself like magnetised iron filings, so that it came into his hand easily, all of a piece. He shoved it in his pocket and took the chimera key out of the lock. Then he heard a cry from one of his pins and went to retrieve that, then another, and another. He had to dig for them. One he had to pull bloody from Farrell's thigh. The salt creaked like snow as he walked on it. All about was a tremendous smell of ozone,

like the beach after a storm, warring with the rank smell of salt. He could hear one of
Dalton's men groaning, a feeble sound, but clearly they were not dead. Or not all of them.

He paused beside the motionless figure of the Marquess, buried under the salt. Should
he check if the man was alive? Find the other pelt? Take it? See if that would break the
curse? He knelt and shoved armfuls of salt aside, thrust back Dalton's coat and felt for the
pelt. Nothing. He glanced up. He could just see Soren in the distance, about to vanish behind
a huge rhododendron.

Damn Dalton. Damn the man. If Soren was free, John was going with him. If Soren
would have him. He climbed the fence and began to run. He was faster, but Soren had a good
lead now. Soren stumbled occasionally, once falling, but getting up and running again. He
didn't look back.

When he got to the house, Soren ignored the knot of people standing at the western
end, gaping and exclaiming at the hole. Lady Dalton was one of them, but she didn't call out,
as the others did, as first Soren and then John tore past. She stood, slightly apart from the
others and watched them go. John hoped she was all right; that Dalton had given her the child
she wanted.

Soren ran past the house and into the stables, and John realised, finally, what he was
doing. When John got to the stableyard himself, panting and dripping with sweat, Soren was
up on Lord Dalton's big chestnut thoroughbred. The creature must have fled home at some
point. Now Soren was taking it. An old stablehand was pleading with him, a hand on the
reins. Soren shook his head, and said, in a voice of command John had never heard from him,
"No, damn you. Out of my way." He sounded remarkably like his father.

He gave a wordless shout and dug his heels into the chestnut's sides. The horse leapt
forward, hooves striking sparks on the flags. As he clattered past, Soren glanced down at
John. John thought for a moment he would ride straight past, but once out of the stableyard
and onto the grass, the big chestnut suddenly wheeled. Soren made it turn two small circles,
all the while looking at John. The drying blood and salt dust on his face made it difficult to
read his expression. Was he waiting? Deciding whether to wait? Saying good-bye?

Part of John wanted to run and get another horse, but he couldn't look away. He found
himself shaking his head, as if to say, *No, no, no,* but what he was saying no to, he wasn't
sure.

Soren said again, "I must go."

There was a trace of regret in his voice, John was sure of it. Soren was trying to explain.

"I know. I'll come," he said, but Soren was already gone, sending the horse at a gallop across the parkland, leaning low, heading north-east.

Chapter Thirteen

John turned back to the stable yard. The rangy-looking bay Warren had been riding stood at the far end, still saddled and bridled, the old stable-hand holding its head. John ran up to them.

"Sir, what's going on? His lordship'll kill Lord Thornby. He don't let no one ride Pendragon. Where is Lord Dalton? All these horses—no riders—what's going on?"

"Give me that horse." John mounted. He'd had lessons at the Institute, but seldom ridden since.

"Watch her, sir. She drops her shoulder," the old man called.

She jinked left, shaking her head. John's heart was thundering in his chest. He knew no magic for horses. He'd have to do this the ordinary way. She shot out of the stable yard sideways, trying to drop her shoulder like the old man had said. He sent her at a gallop the way Soren had gone, and she went, grudgingly, shaking her head and trying all the time to veer left and circle back to the house. This part of the park was heavily wooded, and he cursed the trees and the gracefully curving paths that hid Soren from view. But here and there he saw a fresh hoof-print, carved deep into the wet grass, and sometimes a divot that had flung free.

In any case, he thought he could guess where Soren was going.

The moors.

There was something about the moors that sang of freedom—the great skies above, the distances stretching out, the gentle rises and endless horizons. John thought that if he'd been stuck at Raskelf for over a year, the moors would have called to him, too. Soon, he saw the pine spinney near the place he'd grabbed Soren's elbow—was it really only a week ago? He looked around, heart falling, realising he'd been half expecting Soren to wait for him here.

He found a sheep trail that led east and went along it at a brisk trot. It led over the brow of the hill, and a huge grey-green vista opened out, relieved here and there by a black and twisted thorn-bush. And there was Soren—heading north-east, apparently making for a cairn about a mile away. John adjusted his heading. Perhaps Soren would wait for him at the cairn.

But he did not.

Nor did he wait at the brow of the next hill, nor the next, nor any of the places where one man might reasonably wait for another. Yet he stayed within sight, and John began to feel he was doing so deliberately. At one point the hills folded in such a way that he lost sight of Soren for what felt like an age. He was beginning to think he would stop and make a sigil and look for the tracker stone, when he saw horse and rider silhouetted against the skyline ahead, not quarter of a mile away. But the moment he saw them, they disappeared again over the brow of the hill.

And so the day wore on. Soren set a spanking pace, and didn't wait for him again—if indeed he'd waited at all—but the moorland was truly open here, and John didn't lose sight of him for long. And John still didn't know for sure where Soren was going.

Though the further they went to the east, the more an idea was growing in his mind. All the clues the magic had given him—the shells, the barnacles, the octopus. And Dalton's obsession with coastal Scotland and Ireland. John was beginning to think the whole business with seaweed was just that—a bit of business to disguise what Dalton really wanted; to be near the sea. And to be near those things that come from it.

The more he thought about the pelt he'd taken from the mausoleum, the more he was sure it was not from any kind of dog, or cat, or from any animal that goes about on four legs. And, it seemed clear, it was not an ordinary token; it was more fundamental to Soren than that. He was, after all, not quite human.

Perhaps, despite everything, Soren did not trust that John would let him keep it. The idea gnawed at him. It was so unfair. And yet, he was so tired he began to wonder, after a while, if in fact he *was* chasing Soren. Not just to be with him, but indeed to take the pelt and keep him. Forever. *Mine.*

And have Soren hate him? What a hellish forever it would be. Just tired, he thought. Just so tired. Too much magic. The mind played tricks.

About the middle of the afternoon, they started to descend for the last time. In the distance was a leaden gleam, like a slab of pewter under the dove-grey sky. The sea. John reached a cairn marking the end of the way across the moors. And, hanging from a protruding stone, was a ripped black tailcoat, streaked with salt dust and spattered with blood. John reached up and took it down.

He could almost imagine it was still warm. He rode on. The sough of the sea was getting louder. Gulls were mewling like juvenile demons in the sky. It set his teeth on edge and he had to keep reminding himself they were harmless birds. Then the world seemed to open out and he was on the edge of it, with the sea close below and the sea-wind on his face.

His horse stopped abruptly, goggling at a black shirt flapping like a downed crow on the coarse grass. He dismounted and picked it up. The ground in front of him sloped so steeply he left the horse. He stumbled down the slope, half running, half sliding.

And there, just ahead of him, perhaps twenty yards further down, stood Soren, the pelt waving in his hand like a flag. He was standing at a place where the grass became rock and the rock fell away to the sea. His breeches, stockings, and shoes lay on the rock behind him. He stood naked, looking down into the tumult of the waves, sea spray flying around him, hair wild. He glanced back to where John had come to a halt on the slope. One quick glance. John thought he saw a white flash of teeth. A smile? A snarl?

Then Soren leapt from the rock, the pelt spreading up his arm and enveloping him, changing him in a fluid, impossible way. And a moment later a seal breached the surface, looked around, and then vanished beneath the waves.

John scrambled down and knelt at the edge, calling. The vast muscles of the sea heaved, rising and falling. Sea foam lay in lacy patterns on the surface, impeding his view of the depths. Icy spray got in his eyes, and he wiped his face frantically. He noticed a dark shape, sinuous, moving, and his heart leapt. But it moved again, in exactly the same way and in exactly the same place, and he realised it was his own reflection.

He'd shouted himself hoarse. He was wet with sea-water. His hands, clinging to the edge of the rock, stung from where he'd scraped them and the sea salt had got in. Then a larger wave came over the edge, wetting him to the elbows, taking his breath away with its cold, sucking at him as it withdrew. He lost his grip, grabbed at an outcrop to save himself from falling. He couldn't swim. If he fell, he would be dashed against the rocks and drowned. He found a different rock he could grip properly, but a few minutes later, that was underwater too. The tide was coming in.

He backed away from the edge. Another wave wet his feet. As it withdrew, it tumbled something black along with it. He darted forward and grabbed it; a pair of sodden black silk breeches. If Soren came back, he would want them.

If he came back.

If.

John scoured the rocky shelf and the grassy slope for Soren's clothes. He knelt and bowed his head to catch the scent of them. Once it was gone, no perfumier could bring it back; no musk could ignite the blood, no wood or ambergris delight in the same way.

Seal people; selkies. John had heard of them from the same Irish washerwoman who'd told him stories of Fionn MacCoull when he was a child. Selkies were from the same world as the hedgehog creature, but of the sea, not the land, though they could travel between both. One could trap them in their human form by taking their sealskins. A few images from a story came to him; a lonely fisherman, a stolen sealskin, and a weeping woman. But had the story ended happily or in tragedy? He couldn't remember. It was too long ago; more than twenty years since he'd listened to fairy tales.

And yet, here he was, living in one.

He held the cold clothes. He could feel the tracker stone, a little fizz of magic near the centre of the bundle. It was useless now. Soren had cast it aside without a thought.

Everything ached, as though Soren had unravelled John's heart and lungs and entrails, and dived into the sea with them, leaving him empty on the shore. He should take action, but he felt like a piece of limp seaweed cast up on the grassy slope. He couldn't leave. If Soren came back, he must be here. Waiting.

Eventually, he got to his feet. He folded the dry clothes in a neat pile and found a place to sit on a raised outcrop on the rocky shelf. He spread the wet breeches out to dry, weighing them down with rocks.

He got out the sand, the glass-eye and the spancel and set up the charm. Something seemed to complain as he set the magic through it—the spancel kept blowing in the sea-wind—probably that was the problem. What about the horses? If Soren came back, they might want them. Later. He sat cross-legged inside the spancel, Soren's clothes beside him.

After a while—it could have been minutes or it could have been hours—he heard a low thunder that wasn't the sea. Horses. He could hear shouts. The sun was nearly down and it was getting cold. He stood with difficulty, because he was so stiff, and turned his back on the sea.

It wasn't just Dalton and his men. They'd brought a portly, self-important looking fellow who was probably the local magistrate, half a dozen nervous-looking soldiers with muskets, and a rag-tag of villagers.

They could see him. Surely, they could. They were riding straight for him. They were stopping. He knelt to check his charm. It had been blown about, but the spancel was closed. The sand was set right. The eye—he turned it over to see a shatter-mark like a spider-web marring its blue stare. It had tried to tell him. If he'd paid more attention when he'd set the charm, if only he'd listened—

The magistrate brought his horse forward, peering down the hill. "John Blake, I am arresting you for the murder of Soren Dezombrey, Lord Thornby. You can come quietly, or my men can bring you in chains."

Murder? That, he had not expected. Though he should have.

"I'm innocent," he said.

"Then where is Lord Thornby?"

"He—" Instead of mooning around over Soren's clothes he should have been thinking, planning. But instead he'd managed to lead them straight to the spot where Soren had gone into the water. "He's escaped. And I charge Lord Thornby's father, Lord Dalton, with the kidnapping and unlawful imprisonment of Lord Thornby. I have helped right that wrong. I am Lord Thornby's friend."

"A friend who steals his clothes?" said the magistrate. "A friend who lets him go naked? Produce Lord Thornby now, if you have him. Or the charge stands."

"He's gone."

"Where? Into the sea? Then he's drowned?"

If they wanted another fight, he could give them one, though he had no heart for it. Dalton's men were bruised and bandaged already. One of Warren's eyes was swollen closed, and Prout looked as though he'd gone several rounds with the Tipton Slasher. John had very few materials left, but there were plenty of rocks, and he had his fists. He might even win. But at what cost? The soldiers and the villagers were innocent men. If he started slinging charmed rocks at them, it was hardly fair. He was no criminal; why resist?

To stay here? He glanced at the sea stretching to the horizon. If Soren had only said something, or given him some sign, John would have fought tooth and nail to stay. But Soren had simply escaped into the sea as quickly as he could. Soren had gone. And he wasn't coming back. Not ever.

He should go with the magistrate, let them put him wherever they liked for tonight. He would get Catterall on the case. Paxton would speak for him. And if things looked bad he'd manage somehow. Perhaps he could escape. If Soren wasn't coming back, there wouldn't be much point staying in England anyway. He remembered Lady Amelia saying "Anyone who stays in England must be mad." Maybe she was right. There was a whole world out there. Maybe he would go where the seals go. Maybe, one day, he would recognise one.

The soldiers were scrambling down the slope towards him. One picked up Soren's clothes. Another picked up the spancel, puzzlement on his face. A third took up the cracked eye and kicked the little pile of sand. It was Sahara sand; bright orange, the best, from near Siwa. John could hear it lamenting as it dispersed under the soldier's boot—it didn't like the cold and the wet. It wanted magic or the warmth of his pocket. If he could, he'd come back and collect it, grain by grain.

He went with them up the slope to where Lord Dalton sat on his second-best horse. Dalton beckoned him forward, and motioned the soldiers back.

"You've cost me seventy thousand pounds, you bloody fool," Dalton said. "Inchmorn Skerry. That's what you've cost me."

"Is that all he was to you? Money for a few rocks? You're the fool. I know what's on you. I would've helped."

"You *wouldn't.*" Dalton lowered his voice. "If I'd let you help and we'd got one— you'd have wanted her for yourself. Wouldn't you?"

And at last, John understood. All this time. All these years, all the money spent and useless coastal lands bought. All the lives ruined and lives interrupted. All because Dalton wanted another woman from the sea. Another seal-wife to replace the one he'd lost.

He couldn't help himself. He laughed. "You damned fool. You bloody fool. I don't want a woman." And then he wasn't laughing, but crying. He gritted his teeth to stop himself. Dalton's mouth was curling with revulsion.

"It's that way, is it? Yes, I wondered if it was. Then it's on your back now too." Dalton reached down from his horse, grabbed John's upper arm and hissed in his ear. "What did he say? Did you believe him? They say whatever will get them their way. You'll never get another. And once they're gone—" A look of unbearable pain crossed his face. "Anyone else will be ashes in your mouth."

Dalton's gaze drifted away from John and out to sea, but his hand was still locked around John's arm.

"Do you know where I met her? It was a coast like this, wild and lonely. And she came out of the sea to me. Naked, with pearls in her hair. And so *lovely.* You never saw her equal. Can you imagine? And she loved me. The moment she saw me. And I her. My God, we were happy. We fooled the whole ton, her and I. *Danish.* Pah! We laughed at the lot of them."

He stared past John, plainly seeing nothing but the past, the words flowing out of him like water out of a fishing net.

"But then, she wanted to go back to sea. To take the boy—to show him—"

Dalton's voice trailed away. His face relaxed into sadness—a lost, tender look. For a moment, John could see the handsome young man, in love with his beautiful wife to the point of madness.

"A man needs his wife at his side, doesn't he? She swore she'd come back, but how could I take the chance? They shoot them, you know, in Scotland. For the pelts. It would have been wrong to let her go." He looked at John, almost pleading. "Don't you see I *had* to keep her?"

John said, "You've a new wife—young and kind. She'd make you happy if you let her. You must give that old pelt back to the sea. Forget Soren. He's gone anyway. Do you think he'll come back? For me? Of course he won't come back."

Dalton looked at John for a long moment and John caught a flicker of something, maybe hope, maybe regret.

But then Dalton's expression hardened into revulsion. "You bloody sodomite. You're doomed." He let go of John's arm and kicked him viciously in the chest, sending him staggering back into the arms of the soldiers. Dalton raised his voice. "Right. I thank you for your assistance, Mr Howarth." He nodded to the magistrate, then looked back at John. "Actually, you're lucky. You'll hang."

"Give the pelt...back...to the sea," John gasped, still struggling to catch his breath from the kick. Then one of the soldiers pushed him, and they started the long walk along the cliffs to the prison cell.

Chapter Fourteen

As a seal, Thornby didn't think in the same way as a man. The past was a dream compared with the rush and boil of the sea, the black and purple depths, the light angling down golden when the sun came out. He was lost in the now of the swaying kelp, the flash and flicker of fish, and the shadows of the larger things that moved, half-seen, in the deep.

He'd been trapped—that much he knew—trapped for a lifetime. And now the sea was everywhere; limitless, ever-changing, eternal. He went like an arrow, sinuous, twirling, revelling in it, and the sea embraced him.

But after a while, through the joy came a dim sense that something was wrong. Or, if not exactly wrong, then—missing. Something was lacking.

John.

He stopped his headlong flight. The human part of his mind seemed to come to the fore. How long had he been swimming? It could have been minutes or it could have been hours. He'd caught fish and swallowed them whole, and nothing had ever tasted so good. He'd played in the waves and never thought of what he'd left behind, until now.

John. On the shore. How could Thornby have swum off without a word and left him? After everything.

How could he have forgotten him?

He turned in the sea, a perfect, graceful roll, and began swimming back. He knew the way; it was easy. After a while he began to play in the swell again. John would be all right. Thornby had never met anyone as capable as John. By now John had probably seen to the horses, made a fire, cleaned the salt and blood from their clothes, and asked the local stones to build themselves into a shelter in which to spend the night.

When Thornby got back to the beach, it was nearly dark. He removed his skin as easily as he'd put it on. It was as natural as breathing.

No one was waiting.

His clothes were gone.

Thornby bit his lip, hugging the pelt to his chest. As a seal, he'd not felt the cold; as a man, the sea wind was icy on his bare, wet skin. He'd been gone a couple of hours, to judge from the sun. But John was patient; he knew how to wait.

A nasty thought struck him. When he'd put the skin on, had he left this world and gone to the other? John had said time worked differently there. Thornby couldn't remember experiencing night-time as a seal, but perhaps that made no difference. What if he'd been gone for days? What if John thought he'd gone into the sea forever? But he wouldn't think that. Would he? He must know that Thornby would come back. But a cold trickle of doubt began to seep in. Why should John wait for an inconsiderate saphead who'd swum away without so much as a thank you?

He looked along the shore, but it was impossible to see far past the rocky outcrops. The light was going. Perhaps John had simply gone to find somewhere to spend the night away from the cold sea breeze? Thornby took a few steps across the rocky shelf. Walking felt like trying to dance without music; a little forced, a little pointless.

He should climb the slope and look.

But something kept stopping him. With the sea at his back, just a few paces away, he was safe. He could be gone in an instant. The moment he left the shore, he was a naked man with a sealskin in his hands. And the skin could be taken from him.

That thought was so alarming, he found himself backing away from the land. He crouched on the edge of the rock, watching, listening. The skin was much larger than when he'd gone in. Now it was the skin of an adult seal, and parts of it kept slipping from his hands. In the dying light it glowed like beaten copper.

He remembered the panic he'd felt at Raskelf. Riding across the moors, desperate to get to the coast. He'd half tried to wait for John, but it had been impossible—and, if he was honest, deep down he'd been afraid. Afraid that John would take the skin. The idea had seemed a little ridiculous even then, but in his panic to get to the sea he'd half-believed it. Now it seemed a madness had come over him. Or perhaps magic.

To John, it must have seemed a terrible betrayal. He'd spent days puzzling over how to free him, risked his own life experimenting with magic, and then fought for him, all to have Thornby ride away with barely a look. No wonder John wasn't waiting. He must be furious.

But, might John come back? Just to tell Thornby what a thoughtless, thankless little prick he was? If there was a slim chance that John would come back, then Thornby would wait. Hadn't he waited for months at Raskelf? Hadn't he learned patience?

It would be warmer to wait as a seal. He stood, thinking to put on the skin. He glanced down as he did so, and noticed for the first time that the cuts on his chest had vanished. So, for that matter, had the painful bruises, wrenched muscles and bloodied knuckles from the fight.

And so had the scars on his foot! He bent to touch it—the two smallest toes were separate again, as they'd not been since he was nine years old. The skin was as white and smooth as his other foot. He'd always hated those scars, and hated them more when John had explained what had caused them. Not that John had minded. He'd held that ugly scarred thing in his hands; he'd kissed it. No one had done that before. No one else had ever been permitted.

A pang of loss pierced him, sharp as broken glass. He had had something marvellous and he had dived into the sea and swum away as if it were nothing.

A final ray of sunshine broke out, low over the sea. And he noticed something—a handful of orange sand caught in a crevice. He crept forward. It was such a beautiful colour, one almost expected it to feel warm. But it was cold. And it didn't belong. And he remembered the last time he'd seen it; in a pile in the blue saloon, with John nestling that glass eye into it, and saying defensively, "It works with everyone else."

John didn't leave his materials behind. Unless he had to. Or was forced to. Something bad had happened to John, Thornby was suddenly certain. And 'something bad', around here, meant Father.

As if thinking about him had made him real, Father was there. Coming from *behind*, between Thornby and the sea. Thornby flung himself to one side, instinctively ducking and rolling. His shoulder struck rock, but he still had the skin in his arms and that was all that mattered. Father came after him, face twisted with fury. He managed to get a booted foot onto a trailing edge of the skin, and ground down. Thornby screamed. It was as if his hand was being crushed between Father's boot and the rock.

Thornby jerked at the skin with his good hand, trying to dislodge Father's foot, but with every tug, pain flared in his other hand. Now they each gripped a portion—Thornby naked, on his back on the rock, Lord Dalton on his feet, as if playing a tug of war that Thornby had lost but would not concede. The sealskin glowed golden-brown between them, taut where they pulled it. And a hideous tension ran through Thornby. He felt he would rip in two. But he didn't let go.

He glanced seaward. The edge of the rock was only a yard away. He must get to it; get to the sea. It was his only hope.

He pushed with feet and legs, half sliding, still clinging to the sealskin. Rocks gouged great welts in his back, and the side of his face stung as if sandpapered. But slowly, inch by inch, he gained ground. He turned his head again, and there was the sea, white foam surging only a hands-breadth below. Just a few more inches and he could tumble them both down into the maelstrom. He gave an extra hard tug and kicked Father's shin.

His bare foot had little effect, and kicking had made him lose purchase. He was dragged a few inches landward. The skin began to slip from his fingers. A shout came from down the shore. John? A surge of hope lent him strength.

But the figures hurrying into view wore the livery of Raskelf: Prout and Abbott were coming to help their master. Thornby shook his head and tugged with all his might, crying out with fury. He had seconds. Because the moment they arrived it was over. They would take the skin. Take him back to Raskelf—

It could not be. It could *not*. To have been in the sea. And now—

Tears of rage and despair trickled down his cheeks, mingled with his blood, and fell, to be lost in the surging vastness of the ocean.

And Father froze, staring out to sea, then let go of the skin as if it were no more than an old rag. Thornby, still pulling with all his might, fell back, winding himself, head snapping over the edge. Half dazed, he had just enough wit to hug the skin closer and turn onto his knees. He was about to fling himself into the sea, when he, too, stopped as if turned to stone. He knelt on the rocky edge, the skin in his arms.

About ten yards out, a woman was swimming in the icy water. Her bare white shoulders and wet hair were peachy-red in the setting sun. Her face was in shadow, but unearthly beauty shone out of it. Her eyes were large and luminous, grey as the sea.

Father stood with his hands at his sides, mouth open. Prout and Abbott stood next to him, battered and bandaged. Prout looked as if he might cry. Abbott was shaking his head in slow, uncomprehending disbelief. Father's expression was more difficult to read. Shock was giving way to reverence, but desire was there too, and greed. Something in his eyes said, *Mine*.

The woman swam closer. Thornby could see long strings of pearls woven into her hair and adorning her slender neck. Her breasts were white as sea foam against the black depths, and her arms stretched wide, as though she danced in the water. Beside her floated a dark, amorphous shape, which she clung to with one hand. It was a sealskin. She was like him. Like his mother must have been. He was dimly aware of more heads clearing the water further out—seals or people, he wasn't sure—but it was almost impossible to look away from the woman, she was so beautiful. She smiled at Father, who moaned in the back of his throat.

She came closer, reached for the edge of the rock and held on, rising and falling with the swell. The foam that had tumbled there was gone, as though she'd tamed the very waves for her convenience. Her sealskin floated behind her, up and down with the gentle rise and fall of the sea. She looked at Father out of the corners of her eyes and smiled again, coy, inviting. Her hair swirled around her in the sea like a pearl-embroidered wedding veil.

Father fell to his knees. He held a hand out to her. "Please." His voice was a croak. "My God, I've searched for you—so long."

Her smile deepened. Then, for the first time, she looked at Thornby. A long, lazy look. Her dreamy smile did not falter, but she glanced over her shoulder as if to remind him that the sea was there—his for the taking.

Then her gaze was back on Father.

"You," she said. Her voice was low, melodious, the voice of a woman recognising a lover. "Do you have something that belongs to the sea? Will you show it to me?"

A flash of uncertainty crossed Father's face.

"Come, show me, and we will be together." Her accent was charming, lilting and soft.

Father fumbled the other sealskin—Mother's sealskin—from a deep pocket of his great-coat. The cut edge fluttered in the breeze, but the woman's smile only grew more tender. She reached for it—or maybe she was reaching for Father. Father reached for her; their hands were nearly touching.

Thornby felt, rather than saw, the sea rising in a grey wall behind her. It was taller than the high roofs of Raskelf, and coming faster than a runaway carriage. He could see dark figures caught in it, and broken bits of seaweed. With a thrill of fear, he had just time to think that even a seal could be dashed to death on a rocky shore. Then he was in the sea, injuries forgotten, a seal, swimming as fast as he could.

The wave grabbed at him as it passed, dragging him backwards, then letting go. For a moment all was still, and then the tremendous back-surge tumbled him out to sea. Something pale caught his eye and he looked down to see the naked woman, her arms around his father. Her face was pressed into Father's neck as a woman might embrace her husband, and her sealskin covered them like a cloak. His arms had been around her too, but as Thornby watched they floated free. Mother's sealskin left Father's grip. Lord Dalton's eyes were closed as he and the woman sank together, down into the darkness and the cold.

Now there were other seals swimming alongside. He swam with them, keeping pace. They wanted to race, to play in the last dim light, and then find a place to haul out and rest for the night. They'd saved him. And he could join them, if he wanted, and be happy. He wasn't sure how he knew, but he knew.

But his heart wasn't in it. There was no need to choose. John's sand on the rock meant John needed help. He let the seals go. Two circled back, realised he wasn't coming, and vanished in a trail of silver bubbles, leaving him alone in the black water. He turned and swam back to land.

It was a damned uncomfortable thing to walk along a beach at night naked, especially in Yorkshire in October. He found the nearest town, probably Scarborough, by the lights, and decided the best thing would be to go ashore and ask around. At first, he draped the skin around his shoulders like a rude cloak, but the fear that someone would take it dogged every step. Eventually he found a large rock, well above the high tide line, and buried it underneath. Not ideal, but in a strange way he felt much safer walking naked towards the houses.

Damned cold though. His teeth were chattering, and he couldn't feel his toes. As he walked, he tried to come up with a story. Boating accident? Bathing disaster? What about John? What story might he have told someone?

And what about Father, who was now surely drowned along with Prout and Abbott? Might he have said anything to anyone before he died?

Father, drowned.

Thornby felt nothing beyond immediate relief. Perhaps he'd find the time to be really happy about it, once he'd found John and begged his forgiveness. And managed to get warm. Then a quick twist of memory showed him his father's hands, holding a golden pocket watch out to him—and he was six years old, and allowed to hold that wonderful, magical thing, because Father trusted him, and his parents were looking at each other, smiling.

Damn it, why did it have to be so bloody cold? His eyes were streaming and his nose was running. And he'd stubbed his toes again, because these small towns were so damned dark. Eventually he got up to the town from the sands. There were fishing nets spread out along a low wall and he wrapped one around his waist. Then he went up to the first door he came to and banged on it with his fist. If Father had taught him anything, it was that clothes could tell a powerful story, but were not nearly as important as people thought.

If one's a gentleman, one's a gentleman, no matter what one wears.

***

John sat in the cell, ate the stale bread they gave him, and drank the mug of sour beer. Then he lay on the bare plank that was both bench and bed. The barred window wasn't glazed and he asked the rowan twig to keep him warm. Tomorrow he'd demand lawyers and send for friends in high places. Paxton would speak for him, if necessary, and the Duke of Devonshire would probably take an interest if Paxton asked it of him. And Catterall, of course. For now, John was too heartsick to bother sending for anyone.

Lord Dalton's words kept ringing in his ears. *You're doomed. You bloody sodomite. You'll hang.* Damn the man, the fool. He was probably still out looking for another seal-wife, and with that stinking curse on him, so they all swam a mile the moment he went near the sea. So, Lord Dalton and his selkie wife had loved one another. John imagined them meeting on a wild shore: the handsome young lord, thunderstruck, already falling in love. And the beautiful naked woman with a sealskin in her hands. Had she been afraid, or had she smiled, desiring him too? Had Dalton taken her skin then, or had she followed him willingly? The latter, John felt.

But then, the years had passed and things had changed. She'd had a son, and she'd wanted to show him his birthright; the sea, where Dalton could never follow. So, Dalton had taken her skin to stop her from leaving. And there, right there, was the seed of Dalton's hatred for his son. If not for Soren, perhaps she'd never have wanted to go. And perhaps, too, if Soren had been a different kind of boy, Dalton might have loved him more. Instead, Dalton had found him a disappointment; a sissy, a bed-wetter, who had grown into an insolent and depraved young man.

Soren had told of arguments—his mother begging, his father implacable. No doubt, she'd begged for her skin. Then, with Soren gone to school, it had, perhaps, become too much for her to bear. Missing her son, desperate for the sea, she had gone to the lake at night. Had she meant to drown herself? Or in grief and desperation, perhaps, as the cold waters closed over her head, she had surrendered, because the dark lake was the closest she could come to the sea.

And even after her death, Dalton had not been able to give her up. He'd kept her body where he could visit. Kept her sealskin too. How had he learned that trick of cutting it? You'd have thought he'd let no harm come to it. But, perhaps, one day he had thought to end his obsession, to destroy the skin, had cut a piece and flung it away and realised it gave mastery of that foul spell wind.

Yet keeping the skin had also cursed him. Dalton had obviously hoped it would give him an advantage, and it had. The ability to raise a wind, even a foul one, would be no small thing for a man who spent his summers at sea, searching endlessly for another selkie wife.

That spell wind had nearly done for John and his salt; had nearly been the end of Soren's bid for freedom. Yet even if Dalton could not sense it himself, keeping the sealskin had done terrible things to him, and it had also ensured that no seal-woman between here and Greenland would ever come to him.

Soren. Oh, God, Soren. John had been trying not to think of him, but of course it was impossible. Where was he now? Did seals get cold at night? Were they prey to sharks? But Soren was no ordinary seal. Perhaps he had nothing to fear from the usual trials of life. Perhaps by now he was playing in a many-coloured sea with his own kind.

Or perhaps Soren was swimming back to London to reclaim his old life. Perhaps he'd put the skin in a bank vault and never touch it again; he had suggested as much at Raskelf. John had only the vaguest idea of the life Soren must have lived in London. But he supposed it was a glittering world of balls, clubs, private art shows, and rich lovers as handsome as Soren himself. In some ways, that world of privilege was even more removed; an ironmonger's son could never belong there.

Either way, Soren would never come back.

John gritted his teeth, curling up against the pain. He should never have allowed himself to hope for anything beyond a night or two at Raskelf. He had tried *not* to hope, but somehow had been unable to help himself. Soren had given him hope—the way he'd smiled, the way he'd kissed, the things he'd said, the tone of his voice—it had all seemed so genuine. As if he'd felt something too.

What had John expected? That a lord, a devastatingly handsome, *half-fairy* earl, would fall in love with him? The idea was so preposterous it helped to clear his head. Soren had needed help and had given all he had in return. And since all he'd had was himself, that was what he'd given. Soren had been lucky. If Armstrong or Christie had gone to Raskelf, they'd have flung his first attempt at payment back with a punch and a curse. So would most men. It was as simple as that.

John had been lucky himself to get a few nights with a man like Soren. Of course, Soren had made himself charming. He'd had no choice.

That idea of going where the seals go, hoping he might recognise one? Looking for clues, like Dalton must have done; spending his summers afloat; giving himself the gnarled hands of a sailor; and searching, endlessly searching, for pearls on a rock in the middle of the sea, for footprints on a deserted beach—

Ludicrous. That was the opposite of what John should do. Was he going to spend his life looking for someone who didn't want him? Stupid. He'd never expected to be lucky in love anyway. Men of his type never were. You were lucky if you never got caught.

But sod those bloody factories. He was never going back there. And sod the Institute. Everything they'd taught him was wrong. At least Soren had given him that realisation. In a way, he wasn't really alone and never had been. The salt, the pins, his other materials—they wanted him, wanted the magic. The soldiers had taken most of his things when they put him in the cell, but he could feel the salt in his pocket, a light, warm awareness, like having a cat on his lap.

Perhaps he'd leave England. Perhaps they had better ideas about magic in other countries. India, maybe? New Zealand? How did magicians there do things?

But he was thinking like a free man. He was assuming that justice would be done and his innocence proved. But Dalton wanted him to hang, not only for freeing Soren, but for loving him too. The glow of warmth from the rowan twig died, leaving him shaking in the cold. The word of a marquess carried more weight than that of an ironmonger's son from a not terribly respectable profession. John had never been on the wrong side of the law, but he knew well that the theory of things and the reality are often very different. In theory, English law was the best in the world and the truth would out. In practice, if Dalton lied on the stand, and got his men to lie, even direct intervention from the Duke would not save John. He wondered, bitterly, if he could make friends with the hangman's noose in the few seconds between meeting it and having it throttle him.

The iron bars of the cell door were murmuring at him and he put a hand to them. The cell was so small there was no need to get up. The bars had known all kinds of chimera keys, glamours and demons. The stone walls likewise wanted to tell what they'd seen. Spells to conceal, to disguise. Love charms. Love charms, in a lock-up? Yes, the walls kept telling him, *love, love, love*. He told them to shut up, and tried to put thoughts of the gallows out of his mind. He stroked the trembling rowan twig, igniting it once again, and tried to go to sleep curled around its feeble warmth.

He woke from a miserable half-doze to men shouting in the street, doors banging and the slap of feet on stone. Orange lantern light made wild shadows on the walls. And outside, directly under the barred window, a familiar voice said, with crystal diction and withering scorn, "Do I *look* like a drowned corpse, Mr Howarth? Well? I grant the costume is quite apropos. But I think you'll find my fist quite warm and dry. *If* you'd care to try it?"

Soren.

Something exploded inside John's chest. Joy, sheer delight, and a tide of relief. There was a mumbling response; that must be Howarth.

Then Soren again; "No, I damned well won't take a drink with you, sir. You'll open this door, and you'll do it now. I don't give a rat's arse what the Marquess told you. *I'm* telling you to *open it.*" The last two words were a feral snarl.

John got to his feet and nearly fell. The room was spinning. Whatever had exploded inside him had not abated. It was intensifying, now moving beyond the confines of his body and effervescing in the air around him. He clutched the bars of the door for support; they started to tell him about a glamour from twenty years ago. In his pocket, the salt was whining like a dog that hears its master. *Love, love, love* the walls started humming, despite the fact that he wasn't even touching them.

"Please," he said. "Quiet now." How on earth was he supposed to compose himself when everything was clamouring at him, and the entire world was fizzing like champagne? Was it magic?

Then Soren was there, grabbing John's hands through the bars and snapping at the man with the keys. At the same time, the salt was singing with joy, wriggling with ecstasy in John's pocket. The rowan twig kept flaring with heat, not quite in time with his heartbeat; it felt unnervingly as though he had two hearts, and both of them pounding. And the Och resin found it had a voice too, and began trilling like a canary.

Now Soren was standing directly in front of him, looking into his face and saying something that sounded urgent. Their hands were clasped together. John shook his head, trying to clear it.

"Please be quiet," John said. He was beginning to feel afraid. The magic was too strong. All he wanted to do was to gaze at Soren, but everything was too loud, too distracting. "Everyone. Please."

"John?" Soren's voice rang loud in the sudden silence.

John stared at him, taking deep breaths. Soren looked more handsome than before, if that was conceivable. Some subtle energy flowed from him; it lit his eyes, it was in the set of his shoulders and the tilt of his head. It was a fluid power that could not contain itself, even though Soren was frowning, looking at John in concern. Soren no longer had any marks on him. No scratches, no bruises. There were patches of colour in his cheeks. He looked as vital as if he'd just come from a morning walk. But he wasn't a dream. He was wearing a ghastly old canvas shirt and trousers, and a jacket that looked as though someone had once painted it with tar.

John tried to decide what to say. Should he explain that the world had just started talking at him? What about the murder charge? Lord Dalton and his hunt for another seal woman? The chase across the moors? The sealskin?

"I wouldn't have taken it." He realised only after hearing the words that he'd said them aloud.

"I know. John—I—*Christ*, I'm so sorry."

Soren threw his arms around him. John patted his shoulder, trying to pull away. He felt there were a hundred people crowding into the ante-room outside the cell and peering through the door. He had no idea who they were, but this was no place for displays of affection. Not of the kind he would display anyway.

"Can we—leave?" His voice dragged. The walls were whispering about love charms again. The air was beginning to bubble.

"Yes, come on," Soren said, leading the way. "Apparently, you murdered me, but since I'm walking around swearing at everybody, I think that charge is dropped. Are you all right?"

"Maybe. Are you?"

"I'm fine. It's you I'm worried about."

"Wait! What about your father? He'll come! Howarth'll fetch him! Where—"

"John, stop!" Soren lowered his voice. "Father's gone. Dead. The sea took him."

They'd made it into the street, but suddenly John had to sit down. There was nowhere to sit, so he put a hand on someone's house front so he could lean on it. It wanted to tell him about a spell for better grouting. He groaned and rested his back against it instead. The street was loud with chattering, people or things, he wasn't sure. The lantern kept swinging. Even the shadows seemed alive.

So, Dalton was dead. Without getting his heart's desire. Without seeing another seal-woman. John wished he could hate the man and be glad, but instead—To have someone like Soren's mother. To fuck it up. To never get over that person. What had Dalton said? *Anyone else will be ashes in your mouth.* John's own mouth felt like that. And Soren—back again. For how long? How long until he went into the sea again?

"John, what's the matter? Are you drunk? You don't *smell* drunk."

"When you came, everything started talking. The walls, the salt. Those cobbles—"

It was all too much. He bent over, head in his hands. He could see Soren's feet, in a pair of ancient boots that had probably never known polish. The boots were preening because Soren was wearing them. Soren put a hand on his arm.

"Come, John, we're staying with Mr Howarth." Soren's tone was carefully neutral.

"*What*? I'm not staying with him. He arrested me."

"Yes, but that was a mistake, and he has a spare room which he has kindly offered us. *A* spare room. Understand?" Soren kicked his ankle.

"No."

Then Soren was whispering in his ear again. His breath, warm on John's ear, made the rowan twig pulse faster and the wall chatter louder about grouting. "He has a tiny place on the front for seeing his mistress. *One* spare room. So, we'll have to share. Come on, I've already figured this out."

"Oh, God, I really don't care about grouting spells."

"No? I can't say I care about them myself. John, for goodness sake, come on. Don't you want to get to bed?"

"Why couldn't you trust me? I won't take it. I spent a week trying to help you *find* the damned thing! Where is it, anyway? I hope you've got it somewhere safe. I'm not bloody looking for it again."

"It's safe enough for now. You know, if this is what a few hours in a lock-up does to people, I think I'd better join a prison reform society."

"It's not that. It's you. I'll be all right soon. Things are calming down."

"Are they?"

"More or less." He put his head back in his hands for a moment. "I want my pins. And everything else. They took them."

"Did they, by God?"

John leant against the wall while Soren barked orders at someone. It was hard to tell which things were materials and which things were men. The men moved more, though. That was key. That was the way to tell. At least Soren was easy to tell apart. He glowed like sea foam in the dark. And he stood still, which was a relief, and he had stopped talking, which was also good. John let himself gaze at Soren, feeling the rush of the world around them slowing and quietening.

Someone brought John's effects, but dropped them with a cry before they could hand them over. The spancel slithered up his leg and into his pocket. Several of its runes had got scratched and it was shivering with fear. The eye, less terrifyingly for the bystanders, rolled to meet him, feeling its way with magic. It ranted incoherently at his feet until he took it in his hand. The pins stood up on the cobbles like flowers waiting to be picked. They seemed to be hissing. He realised they were saying, "Masssster, masssster, masssssster." They shouldn't be able to talk. Not really, not in English, not out loud. People would hear.

"That's enough," he said sharply, and everything went quiet again.

Soren gathered the pins, making some comment about scientific equipment as he did so. John thought it sounded thin, but couldn't bring himself to care.

It looked as though Mr Howarth's mistress had vacated her best room for them. It was at the front of the house, overlooking the sea. There was a huge bed, a small table and two chairs, an old sea chest, a crackling fire, and a fresh scent of lavender. Soren let people bring food and warm water, and then sent them packing, with orders that no one disturb them. Not for flood, fire or destruction. Not for *death*. Even Mr Howarth, who had arrived with a bottle of port, quailed at his tone.

Soren helped him wash, and put food in front of him. He ate slowly, letting the world go back to normal, though probably it would never be the same again. Then he sat stroking an empty wine-glass that had held remarkably fine port, thinking how restful it was that the glass knew nothing of magic. It was innocent as a daisy.

Soren was sitting at the table opposite him, talking softly, almost to himself. John began to pay attention, and to realise the import of what he was saying: Raskelf had a new master.

"—because Stewart needs to take a cure. All this land in Scotland and Ireland must be worth *something*, so we can get funds from selling that, and—" He realised John was watching him and smiled, that shy smile that surprised John anew every time he saw it. "Feeling better?"

"Are you sure he's dead?"

Soren's smile vanished. He looked at the tablecloth. "Yes."

There was so much in that single syllable: relief, hate, defiance, sorrow, resignation, regret. What did one say? *I'm sorry*? *I'm glad*? Eventually, John said, "This land in Scotland, these skerries, I think, if you go there, you'll find the locals have orders not to shoot seals."

"Of course they'll be under orders," Soren said bitterly. "He wanted one alive."

"He talked to me, on the shore. She chose him, you know. She came out of the sea to him. They hatched the idea of saying she was Danish together, from the sound of it. I know it went bad, but they were happy once. They loved each other."

"I should forgive him, should I? You know why he burnt me, all those years ago? Have you worked it out? I was bait. He was trying to make them come for me." Soren closed his eyes. "Do you have any idea what that burn did to me? He lamed me. At school I—" He put his face in his hands for a moment.

John sighed. "I'm not excusing him. It was unforgivable. But I thought you should know about him and her. Forget it, then."

John stroked the glass, trying to let it fill his consciousness. He felt, in a way, worse than he had in the lock-up, because now hope kept clutching at his belly, and he could see what he had to lose sitting opposite, even more beautiful than in his imagination, grey eyes defensive, mouth tense and unhappy, slender fingers knotted together, fingernails bitten short. The desire to hold him and never let go was so strong John closed his eyes. Perhaps he should leave. Now. Before things went any further. It could only end badly. He tried to imagine himself standing up, opening the door, walking away.

Soren said in a small voice; "John? Sorry. Thank you."

"Once you've sorted everything out at Raskelf, you could go to one of these skerries. It's probably the safest place."

Soren looked up quickly. "Oh, but—but, Scotland's a long way from London."

"You'll go back to London? Will you do what you said in the box room? Put the skin in a bank and never touch it again?"

"No! I shan't do that. That was before I knew." Soren got to his feet, face transforming with wonder, and began to pace back and forth. "Being at sea! It's the best thing in the world!" He smiled suddenly, glanced meaningfully at John, and added archly, "With a *few* exceptions. It's like those dreams where you can fly! My God, it's like being in a Turner painting! And I belong there!"

He shook his head a little, like a man who can't believe his good fortune.

"Yes. You belong there."

"Don't look like that. I belong on land too, surely? Father was human."

John schooled his face. It was difficult, because he wanted Soren so much, he felt it would choke him. He wanted to say something noble and understanding that would let him walk away with his self-respect intact. Because otherwise he'd end up begging Soren not to go to sea again.

"You swam away," he heard himself saying. And it wasn't dignified; it was raw with pain. At least he wasn't on his knees, pleading.

Soren crouched by his chair, holding onto the edge of the table with one hand, looking up into his face.

"John, I'm sorry. I didn't mean to desert you, but that skin had been waiting for the sea since the day I was born. I *had* to put it on. I know I shouldn't have ridden away, and I'll beg your pardon a hundred times for that if you like. But there was magic at work. It was telling me not to wait, not to risk it. It wasn't reasonable, I know, but then magic isn't always, is it? You know that. And then, when I was a seal—I wasn't just myself in a different shape. All this—" He gestured at his body. "I forgot it. It felt like a dream."

"All right." John had control of himself again. He managed a smile. "Tell me some more. Did you catch any fish? Did you eat them alive?"

Soren leaned in to kiss him. He did it tenderly, almost apologetically, as if John might refuse him.

He might as well refuse to breathe.

Soren removed his tarred jacket, shirt and boots. He sat astride John in the patched canvas trousers. John ran a hand over his chest. No cuts, not a trace. He could see, too, that Soren's once scarred foot was now a perfect graceful arch like its fellow. Wasn't that the way with toffs like Soren? They always managed to come out of things unscathed. John's own chest hurt like hell where the shot had hit him and Dalton had kicked him, and his face and shoulders were a mess of cuts and bruises from the slates. He touched the curve of Soren's brow, the line of his jaw. No marks there, either, not the shadow of a bruise.

"Where did you learn to fight like that?" John said.

"I went to Eton, silly. And I had a bad foot and couldn't run away." Soren began undoing the buttons of John's waistcoat. "Hadn't you better get the pins out?"

"In a minute."

He closed his eyes and let Soren do what he liked. Let him kiss his mouth and neck. Let him untie his cravat and unbutton his shirt and fly. Let him nibble the sensitive skin around his ear. Let him grind against him, breath quickening.

The chair creaked warningly. It was right. John opened his eyes. "Get off. And get those awful trousers off too. And wait for me by the fire. I'm going to fuck you in a minute, and I don't much care if Mr Howarth's windows melt, so I'm going to do exactly what I want, exactly how I want it. And you are going to take it. Understand?"

All the same, he took the pins and emptied himself of power. Who knew what would happen in the morning? But if he was going to have one more night with Soren, he was damn well going to be warm and comfortable, without a sea wind blowing through the bedroom. Raskelf had been an ice box. He wanted to see Soren sweat. Wanted him flushed and trembling, slippery and pliant. If Soren was going to vanish into the sea again tomorrow, then tonight would have to warm John for a long, long time.

Soren had stoked the fire, and was now waiting on the hearthrug, naked, as he'd been told. He stood hip-shot, smiling, cock plump, hands behind his back. "Have you considered, Mr Blake, that you're about to fuck the tenth Marquess of Dalton?" He raised an eyebrow. "What do you say to that?"

A week ago, the idea of having a marquess would have inflamed John beyond imagining. Now, he wanted only Soren. John glowered at him, deciding, and had the satisfaction of watching his smile fade, watching him swallow nervously. Soren needed wrong-footing, that was what he needed.

He stood in front of Soren a moment or two longer, just looking, and letting him look. Then he said, "Right. You undid my buttons. Now you can do them back up. And then you can tie my cravat."

Soren's eyebrows shot up in surprise, then down in puzzlement. "But—"

"Do it."

"But you—"

"Maybe I've changed my mind. Maybe I feel like going out. Do it."

Soren bit his lip, and began to do up the buttons of John's shirt, then his waistcoat. John glanced down and saw his cock had softened. Did Soren really think he was going to go out? Hm. Maybe he really did.

"Stand still." He knelt and took Soren's cock in his mouth. Soren gripped his hair, gasping. John sucked him until he was groaning and thrusting his hips forward, then stood up again. Soren's eyes were black, his mouth open, face flushed.

"All right. Now you can tie my cravat. Not too tight. You know how I like it." John made him do it twice. Soren's hands were trembling. His eyes had that pleading look. Desperate to come, not sure if it was going to happen. Perfect.

John checked his cuff-links, then unbuttoned the fly he'd just made Soren do up. He pulled aside the linen of his drawers and let his cock stand proud. It curved up, engorged, swelling with veins, shocking against the respectability of his good wool trousers and waistcoat.

Soren was already kneeling, already closing those impossibly red lips around the head of his cock. John let him suck it for a while, admiring the contrast between Soren's nakedness and his own nearly public appearance. But the sight and sensation were too much to bear for long, and anyway he wanted Soren sweating—wanted to lick his skin and taste salt. He pushed Soren onto his hands and knees on the hearthrug. Then John positioned his cock at that tight, puckered arsehole and pushed against it, just with the tip, nothing too much, not yet.

Soren moaned, and pushed back against him. John got the vial of oil from his pocket, sloshed some out and eased his way in, Soren writhing under him. Then he stopped for a moment, hands firm on Soren's hips to hold him still, trying to think of something dull. He was sweating now himself; the suit was slightly restrictive, a little annoying. Next time he'd make Soren wear the clothes; he'd have him in that ridiculously tight Regency coat, naked from the waist down.

Then he remembered there probably wouldn't be a next time, and that Soren's old clothes had been ripped to shreds in the fight and then lost somewhere. That helped him calm down anyway.

He began to move, gently at first, then harder. Soren tried, once, to frig himself, and John thrust really hard, making him grunt and whip his hand back down to the floor to stop himself falling. The firelight was shining now on Soren's naked back and his breath was coming in whimpers.

John grabbed a handful of Soren's hair and twisted his face towards the fire. That was better. Soren's mouth was open, eyes tight shut. His face was blood red in the firelight, sweat dripping onto the rug. His hair, in John's hand, was dark with sweat.

"Christ, John, *please*," he panted.

If he could still manage words, they weren't finished. He let go of Soren's hair and shoved him onto his forearms. Then he thrust harder and at a slightly different angle. Another "please" turned into a cry. Too loud? He didn't care. There was no trace of the elegant lord now; Soren was wailing into the hearthrug, hips bucking. John reached around and wrapped his hand around Soren's cock. Soren gave a strangled cry, then another, and another. John thrust extra hard, and was lost in a world of heat and pleasure so fierce, it was like fucking a man of fire.

At the very end, he ran his tongue up Soren's spine, feeling him shudder and gasp and clench tight around him, one last time. Soren's sweat was salt in his mouth, like the sea, like tears, like the stuff of magic.

***

Afterwards, Thornby undressed John with care and they got naked into bed. Thornby glanced down at the cluster of pins that stood by the bed. "No octopus," he said, unsure whether to be disappointed or relieved.

"The pelt's yours now. Maybe that's why. We don't need any more clues. You're free."

There was something final in John's voice, as if he was saying goodbye. Thornby turned to look at him. And he could see that, although John might have forgiven him, he did not trust him. And he did not understand. There was a wary look in his eyes.

"You know why I came back, don't you?" Thornby said.

John looked away, towards the fire. "Don't say anything rash, will you? You've got a whole new world at your feet. Who knows what you might find there?"

"But, John, I hoped, you know, that I could see you sometimes. I mean, not just sometimes. Whenever you like. If you have time. In London, or—or wherever."

There, he'd said it. Or at least, something approximating what he'd wanted to say. He couldn't help remembering all the men—and quite a few ladies too—who'd burbled and stammered at *him* over the years. Now, at last, he knew what it was like; his tongue was limber as a sea cucumber and he felt about as intelligent, too. He'd never had any trouble making his wishes known in the past, but then he'd never really cared before. Right now, he cared so much, he felt he might die of it.

"Is that what you want?" John said. "To see me in London?"

"Don't you want to?" Waiting for John's answer was like waiting for release from Raskelf all over again. The seconds stretched into years.

"You don't owe me anything," John said eventually. He put his hand over his eyes. "You know that, don't you? I know I got you out of Raskelf. But you got me out of that ghastly thorn-bush. And out of prison, come to think of it. So, we're quits. And Catterall will pay me."

"But it's not because I *owe* you something! John, I wish you'd look at me."

Thornby pulled at his hand and John let him take it. John's eyes were wet with tears; he rubbed them.

"Sorry, it's been a hell of a day. You've no idea how tiring it is, blasting holes in country houses and being arrested for murder. Of course, we can see each other in London, if you want to. Look at us, finally in a place where the walls don't keep whispering at me. That cell was as bad as Raskelf."

The subject was being changed in a way that was not entirely satisfactory. But John was clearly trying to pull himself together. And he had agreed they would see each other again, even if he seemed somewhat lukewarm about it. Perhaps John preferred other magicians, men with whom he could discuss the things that really mattered to him. Thornby's stomach lurched unpleasantly at the thought. But John *had* agreed they would see each other again. Thornby lay down against him, their legs tangled together.

"So, no-one's done magic here?" he said.

"That old chest's seen a bit."

"What does it say?"

"Smugglers used it once. If anyone opened it, they saw smoked fish." John's eyes grew unfocused for a moment. "It's never stored smoked fish. It thinks that's funny. Didn't know pieces of furniture could find things funny, did you? This bed does, you know. It thinks—"

"Don't tell me! I'll never be able to fuck on a bed again."

"Promises, eh? I'll have you over that chest in a bit. That'll give it something to think about."

Thornby smiled. "Well, I'm not dressing you again. When you made me button your shirt, I really thought you were going out. You absolute cad."

"That'll teach you to dive into the sea and forget about everything."

"I didn't say that. I forgot *I* was once human."

"Isn't it the same?"

"No. It's not." Thornby lifted himself up on one elbow. John's face was bruised and cut and there were lines of strain etched upon it. He needed to shave. "John, don't you realise? I forgot about myself. And Raskelf, and everything. I'd have stayed in the sea forever, probably. But I remembered one thing; I remembered *you*."

John's eyes widened, and, at last, the wariness in them melted away. "Me?"

"Just you." It came out in a whisper, and his breath hitched at the end. He wanted to say something else, to make it clear, to make John understand what it meant, but his voice seemed to have deserted him.

But perhaps John understood anyway, because he touched Thornby's cheek. With his thumb, he traced the swell of Thornby's lips and the line of his jaw. And he looked the way he did when he was working magic; serious, intent, possibly a little frightening. And to be touched like that, so tenderly, with those listening hands, was as precious and as heady as freedom.

Presently, John's eyes closed and he fell asleep, his face pressed against Thornby's chest. Thornby lay with his arms around him, and listened to him breathe. He was nearly asleep himself when he noticed that each slow breath John took was in perfect unison with the waves that broke outside on the shore. He'd have sworn the surf had been pounding faster not long ago, and thought it an odd coincidence.

Or perhaps it was not a coincidence at all.

If one has a selkie's affinity for the sea, and the man lying next to one is a magician with an affinity for salt—perhaps, when you are both at peace, even the ocean will sleep.

Chapter Fifteen

John half-woke. The bed was warm and comfortable, and sleep swept over him again in a gentle wave. But noises from outside kept bringing him to the surface; the rumble of a cart, footsteps, men's voices, the hum of London waking up. And yet, there was something not right. There was a high, shrill yelling, as though some careless theurgist had summoned something that was not yet under control. Perhaps he should go and—no, it wasn't a new-conjured imp; it was seagulls calling. And he wasn't in London, he was in Yorkshire, somewhere on the east coast.

Everything came flooding back. Soren. Raskelf. The whole world telling him its secrets.

Soren. He reached out, but his hand met cold sheets. He opened his eyes, taking in the bare expanse of pillow, the crumpled edge of the sheet, pale grey in the dimly-lit room. Perhaps Soren had gone out to relieve himself. Perhaps he'd be back any minute.

John could count on the fingers of one hand the times he'd slept in a bed all night with a lover. Generally, he didn't take the risk. After sex, it was safer to go home to sleep alone. But Soren had engineered last night's opportunity, and John had been too tired to protest. In any case, he had not wanted to protest. It had been bliss to fall asleep with Soren's arms around him. John had slept, feeling that if anything happened, Soren would deal with it. The sense of safety had been so profound it had been like something from childhood, when he'd still believed his parents invulnerable—his mother all-wise, his father all-strong.

He waited, trying to cling to last night's contentment, while the minutes lengthened. He could hear the sea. Half-asleep, he'd mistaken it for the distant sound of the city, but now its quiet, ceaseless rhythm was unmistakable, like the pulse of a lover when you laid your head on his chest.

He turned over. The fire was out, and the white light of dawn was peeping around the edges of the curtains. He glanced over to the spot where Soren had dropped his clothes last night—those awful old things borrowed from a fisherman. They were gone, of course. Even the tarred jacket.

So, Soren had gone out.

Would he be back? Or had the sea called him again?

Despite what Soren had said last night, despite the promise in his voice, John's skin began to prickle with disquiet. Whatever Soren might say, whatever might be growing between them—was it any match for the forces of magic? If a man's mother was a selkie, did he understand the instincts that might drive him? John lay under the warm covers, deep cold assailing him.

Then, through the turmoil of his thoughts, he began to sense something. He didn't recognise it at first, because the tone—delighted, almost smug—was not one he'd heard before from that particular material. But yes, it was the salt, trying to give him a message.

Soren had touched it. More than that; Soren had held it. Soren had let it trickle out of his hand. The salt was practically purring. John sat up. Last night the salt had been in its oilskin bag in the pocket of his jacket, which he'd hung over the back of a chair. But now—he got out of bed and went naked to the hearth. There, in big uneven letters of salt, was written one word:

WAIT.

Warmth and light flooded back, filling his chest with hope and his cock with blood. It was a tease, no more, no less. Wait, eh? When Soren got back, John would make him wait. Until he was begging for release. Until he was writhing and whimpering and pleading for it. Perhaps he'd make him wait all day. He'd given himself a fine cockstand, just thinking about it, which was probably what Soren had intended. To distract himself, he made up the fire, but it did not distract him very efficiently, because he was kneeling on the hearthrug they'd fucked on the night before, and it was impossible not to remember Soren's fists clutching the rug, the sweat dripping from him, the hot, tight pressure of his arse, and the taste of salt on his skin.

The flames caught on the new wood and began to fill the room with warmth. Feet came thumping up the stairs and John shot to his feet, hands covering his crotch. Soren burst in, a burlap sack in one hand. He closed the door, and took one look at John.

"I see you got my note," Soren said.

John took his hands away from his crotch; he wasn't fooling anyone anyway. Soren was wearing the old patched, tarred canvas trousers, shirt and jacket—and he looked utterly, devastatingly handsome. He was breathing hard, as if he'd been running.

John was about to say, "Wait, eh? No 'please'? And with my salt? Shall I remind you of your manners?" But something stopped him.

Soren had a strange look on his face, half defiant, half afraid. "May I show you something?" He spoke fast, as if to get the words out before he lost his nerve. He didn't wait for an answer. He reached into the sack, at the same time upending it, so that out poured something supple and golden-brown. It was so beautiful, flowing out of the rough sacking, that John caught his breath.

It was the sealskin; Soren's skin. But much bigger than the last time John had seen it, and a thousand times more beautiful. Before, it had been dormant, unused, dusty, half-dead. Now it was alive, as much a part of Soren as his heart or eyes.

The skin. Of course; he'd been to get it.

John stood staring, wondering what it had cost Soren to lie with him all night, when the skin was hidden somewhere else. Had Soren slept at all? Or had he lain there, on guard, letting John sleep, his mind bent the whole time on the skin?

Soren held it out, his eyes grave. John could see his hand trembling, the skin shivering and shining in the firelight. And well Soren might be nervous. What must it be like, to offer your skin to another person? Knowing that if they choose to take it, and keep it, you would be trapped. Bound to them. Forever.

Of course, John wouldn't take it. He knew what he was being offered; the chance to see, the chance to touch. He went closer—it was difficult not to—as the skin drew him. It was a hundred shades of gold and brown; it was honey and oil, Tokay and hot chocolate. It was shafts of sunlight in clear pond water. It was copper and gilt, topaz and brandy. And yet, it was more beautiful than all these things, because it was alive. Magic shimmered in it, ripe, ever-changing, eternal, like the sea.

He put out a hand to touch it, then let it fall back. Who was he, after all? An ironmonger's son. A magician, yes, but also a mere mortal. This was a fey thing, aglow with potentcy. The little dried-up pelt he'd thrust inside his shirt had been different; he hadn't minded touching that. This thing was perilous, as dangerous as love. A man shouldn't touch it lightly. He dragged his gaze from the glory of the skin to Soren's face. Soren was biting his lip; he looked as though he might cry.

"You don't have to let me touch it," John said, a little stiffly.

"Don't you want to?" Soren's voice wobbled.

John sank to his knees on instinct. He'd never been moved by the piety charms of the church mages—it was difficult when one could see right through them—but kneeling now seemed right and proper. And perhaps he was afraid, but Soren wanted him to touch it; so, touch it he would.

"It's the most beautiful thing I've ever seen. May I really?" He stroked that glowing, living fur.

Soren shivered, and gasped, and, to John's horror, snatched the skin away. They stared at each other. Soren was breathing in shallow gulps, holding the skin protectively against him.

"I—I'm sorry—I didn't mean—" John said, shaking his head, appalled. He didn't know what he'd done, only that Soren was looking at him as if he'd never seen him before.

"My God." Soren breathed out, almost a gasp, almost a laugh. He held the skin out. "Do that again?"

John did as he was bid, running his hand down the fur, so smooth, so warm—

"Christ! How—how—" Soren took a few steps backwards, pulling the skin away again. He fell to his knees as well, eyes huge and black. "How are you doing that?"

"Doing what?"

"It doesn't feel like that when I touch it. It certainly didn't when Father had it."

"How does it feel?"

"Are you using magic on it?"

"No." John looked at his own hand and frowned. "At least, I don't think so. You remember when you came to the cell last night and everything began talking at me?"

"I should hardly forget."

"No. Well, I think I, er, react to you. I can't help it. It's as though the magic breaks free when you're around."

"Oh." Suddenly Soren smiled. "That sounds most unfettered. Do you think it's safe?"

"I don't know. It's never happened to me before. You may find this hard to believe, but my usual social circles don't include that many handsome, half-fairy aristocrats. I don't think I'm using magic, but I wouldn't swear to it. I didn't think I was using it last night, but I still learned more about grouting spells than I wanted to."

"Good lord, Mr Blake. You never cease to surprise, do you?"

"How does it feel when I touch it?"

Soren began to laugh, a little weakly. "Give me a minute, and then stroke it again, and you'll see." He laid the skin carefully at his feet, and began to take off his fisherman's clothes. He kicked off the shapeless old boots, shrugged out of the jacket and shirt as one, and undid the single button that held the trousers up. He had no drawers to remove. His cock was so swollen it was almost purple. It was leaking at the tip. He raised an eyebrow.

"Getting the gist?" His voice was strained. "Stroke it again?"

John crawled across the carpet to him. It was an expensive Turkey carpet in scarlet and indigo silks, but the skin made it look drab and cheap. He pulled Soren by the hand, so he was lying half across the skin, naked, trembling.

John held out his hand, paused for a moment, letting Soren anticipate the touch. Then he stroked the skin for a third time. It was so smooth it was almost frictionless, so warm it was like putting your hand near a fire, so gorgeous the way the colours shifted and changed as your hand moved across it.

Soren's fingers were buried deep in the fur, body tensed, writhing. When John stroked the skin for a fourth and then a fifth time, Soren gave a strangled cry and spent onto his own heaving chest. John stared at him in wonder, and then at his own hand, which still looked perfectly ordinary.

"*That's* how it feels." Soren lay across the skin with his eyes closed, arms stretched out in abandon.

"Bloody hell."

"Quite." Soren opened one eye. "Would it be like that if any magician touched it, do you suppose? Or is it just you?"

"I've no idea. Will you let anyone else touch it?"

"No. Only you. Only *ever* you."

"You know, I was wrong before. It's not the most beautiful thing I've seen. It's not a patch on you when you're harder than a ramrod and spending all over yourself."

Soren gazed at him for a moment, open-mouthed. "Tut, John. You'll turn my head."

"I'm going to stroke it again in a moment. But just once, I think."

"Have a heart, you'll ruin my constitution. At least let me eat something first."

"You do look like you need something in your mouth."

"You're shameless, aren't you? I thought you were so respectable when we met. I thought you were a pillar of the community, probably with all kinds of awful strictures." As he spoke, Soren was pushing John back on the carpet, kissing his stomach, then working his way down the trail of hair that grew there, in a slow line of licks. And a moment later he was sucking John's cock, mouth hot and wet.

They ended up in a tangle of limbs and sealskin. It was as compromising a situation as John had ever been in—two naked men, kissing and thrusting against one another, hands on each other's cocks, a magical skin only partially covering them—and the door had no lock.

But somehow, he could not feel afraid.

Acknowledgements

There are a number of people who generously gave their time to help with this book.

Thank you a million times: KJ Charles, Amelia Faulkner, Clare London, Jordan Hawk, Jackie North, Amanda Whitehouse and the other authors from New Zealand Rainbow Romance Writers, the Write Wellington group, my readers (including Scott, Klaude, Carl, Heather, Dylan and Jane) and Rachel Maybury from Signal Boost Promotions.

And—for countless discussions about magic, words and Victoriana—thanks to Matt.

More by Lee Welch

Seducing the Sorcerer (m/m fantasy romance)
Mended with Gold (m/m contemporary romance)

www.leewelchwriter.com

www.ingramcontent.com/pod-product-compliance
Lightning Source LLC
Chambersburg PA
CBHW032006170626
46807CB00006B/2666